9/10

SPQR VI

NOBODY LOVES A CENTURION

Also by
JOHN MADDOX ROBERTS

SPQR VI

NOBODY LOVES A CENTURION

JOHN MADDOX ROBERTS

THOMAS DUNNE BOOKS
ST. MARTIN'S MINOTAUR
NEW YORK

THOMAS DUNNE BOOKS.

An imprint of St. Martin's Press.

SPQR VI: NOBODY LOVES A CENTURION. Copyright © 2001 by John Maddox Roberts.
All rights reserved. Printed in the United States of America. No part of this book
may be used or reproduced in any manner whatsoever without written permission
except in the case of brief quotations embodied in critical articles or reviews.
For information, address St. Martin's Press, 175 Fifth Avenue,
New York, N.Y. 10010.

www.minotaurbooks.com

Library of Congress Cataloging-in-Publication Data

Roberts, John Maddox.
    SPQR VI: Nobody loves a centurion/ John Maddox Roberts.—1st ed.
        p.   cm.
    ISBN 0-312-27257-X
    1. Metellus, Decius Caecilius (Fictitious character)—Fiction.   2. Rome—
History—Republic, 265-30 B.C.—Fiction.   3. Gaul—History—58 B.C.–511
A.D.—Fiction.   4. Private investigators—Rome—Fiction.   5. Caesar,
Julius—Fiction.   I. Title: SPQR 6.   II. Title: Nobody loves a centurion.
III. Title.
PS3568.O23874   S67   2001
813'.54—dc21

                                                                        2001034897

First Edition: September 2001

10 9 8 7 6 5 4 3 2 1

For

The Albuquerque Page One, Too

1st Friday Author's Group:

Shop-talkers par excellence

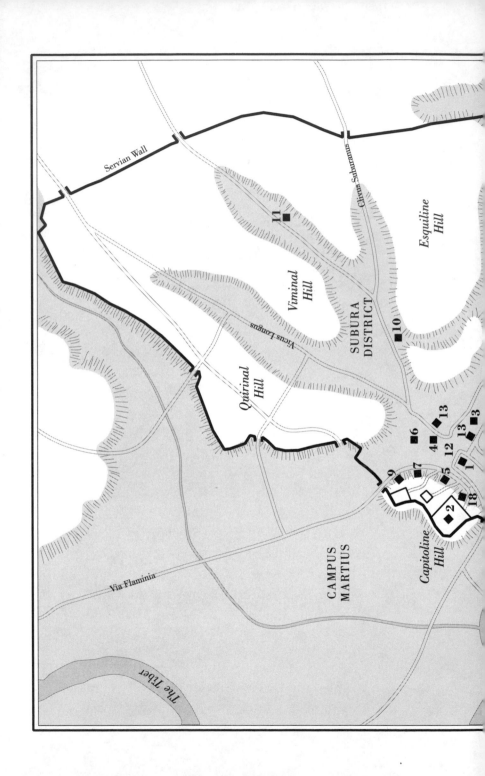

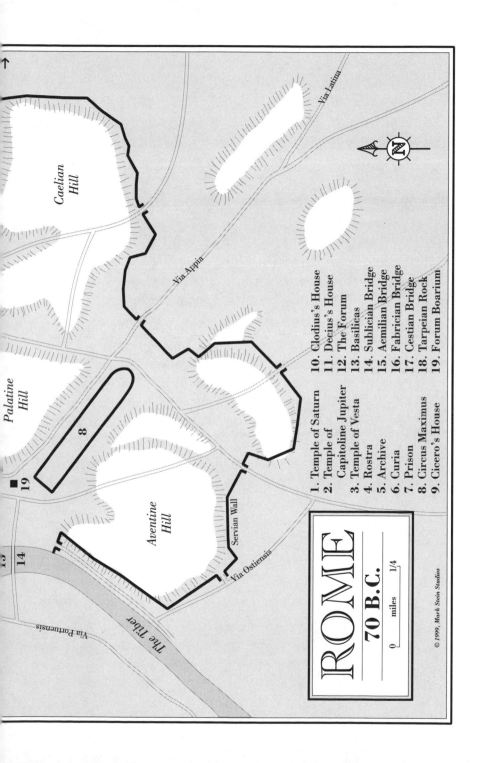

ROME
70 B.C.

0   miles   1/4

© 1999, Mark Stein Studios

1. Temple of Saturn
2. Temple of
   Capitoline Jupiter
3. Temple of Vesta
4. Rostra
5. Archive
6. Curia
7. Prison
8. Circus Maximus
9. Cicero's House
10. Clodius's House
11. Decius's House
12. The Forum
13. Basilicas
14. Sublician Bridge
15. Aemilian Bridge
16. Fabrician Bridge
17. Cestian Bridge
18. Tarpeian Rock
19. Forum Boarium

Caelian Hill

Palatine Hill

Aventine Hill

The Tiber

Via Latina

Via Appia

Via Ostiensis

Via Portuensis

Servian Wall

N

SPQR VI

NOBODY
LOVES A
CENTURION

SPQR

Senatus Populusque Romanus

The Senate and People of Rome

1

I BLAME IT ALL ON ALEXANDER THE Great. Ever since that little Macedonian twit decided that he had to conquer the whole world before he was old enough to shave, every fool with a sword and a decent pair of boots has sought to do the same. In the days of my youth there were a number of would-be Alexanders in Rome. Marius had a go at being Alexander. Sulla tried it. Lucullus tried it. There were others who never even managed to establish a reputation the equal of those men.

Pompey came close to succeeding. Since Rome was a Republic, he couldn't simply inherit an army as Alexander had, and he was too lazy to bother with holding the offices requisite for higher military command, so he just got his tame tribunes to ram legislation through the Assemblies, giving him the authority and claiming that a state of emergency forbade his return to Rome to stand for office. He usually manufactured the emergency himself. Most often, his tribunes gave him command after a better man had done most of the fighting, thus bestowing on Pompey the kill and the loot. But that just shows that Pompey was more intelligent than Alexander. Romans are usually more intelligent than foreigners.

Enemy leaders seldom checked the Romans. That was done by their political enemies at home. Political infighting was the bane of the Republic, but it probably saved us from monarchy for more than two hundred years.

And then again, Alexander was usually fighting Persians, which helped him no end. Rome never dealt with a Darius. Alexander faced him twice, and twice Darius ran like a flogged baboon at the first clash, deserting his army, camp, baggage train, and wives. All of the enemies of us Romans were hardfighting brutes, who bloodied us severely before agreeing to be reasonable and settle down and pay their taxes. Alexander never had to face Hannibal. If he had, he'd have gone straight back to Macedonia to count his sheep, which is all Macedonians are good for, anyway.

The unlikeliest contender of all was Caius Julius Caesar, and he came the closest to winning the imperial crown of Alexander. To my everlasting horror, I helped him almost get there.

IT WAS A LONG JOURNEY, AND a wretched time of year to be making it. Late winter brings the worst weather to the Italian peninsula, and it is no better in Gaul. Of course it would have been much faster to sail from Ostia to Massilia, but I hate sea travel as much as any other sane human being. So with my slave, Hermes, and two baggage mules, I set out from Rome, up the coast through Tuscia and Liguria to the Province.

I need hardly point out that I was not in search of military glory. I had to leave Rome because Clodius, my deadly enemy, had won a tribuneship for that year and was in a position to do incalculable harm, and there was nothing anyone could do about it for the duration of his year in office. Also, my family was grooming me for higher office and I needed a few more campaigns under my military belt before I could qualify to stand for the praetorship, and when the patriarchs of my family gave orders, they were to be obeyed by anyone bearing the name of Caecilius Metellus.

In those days, mine was by far the most important of the plebeian families. The *gens* Caecilia was ancient, incredibly numerous and distinguished beyond words, with a chain of consuls back to the founding of the Republic. My father had held every office on the *cursus honorum*, plus the non-*cursus* offices of military tribune, aedile, Tribune of the People, and Censor.

Of course, I stood every chance of being killed while acquiring my military qualifications. But, as I have said, my family was pestilentially numerous and doubtless a replacement would be found.

So, I made my way up the coast, taking my time about it; stopping to lodge with friends wherever possible, staying at inns where it was unavoidable; attending local games and festivals where opportunity presented. I was in no rush to get to Rome's latest war. Even in my youngest days I had never suffered from the callow recruit's anxiety that all the excitement would be over before I got there.

We passed from Liguria around the foot of the Maritime

Alps and into the Province, the earliest of our extra-Italian possessions, the greatest virtue of which is that it provides us with a way to get to Spain without drowning. The road passed through a string of Greek colonial towns, in time coming to Massilia. It was a lovely place, as colonies tend to be. When you plan a city from scratch, you can pay attention to things like order, proportion, and harmony. Cities like Rome, that just grow over a period of centuries, sprawl every which way with temples, tenements, and fish markets all jumbled together. Massilia was also about as far north as you could go and get a decent bath. In those days it was still an independent city and calling itself Massalia because Greeks can't spell.

Technically, this area was at war, so it was time to look military. I already wore my military tunic and boots. We dismounted while Hermes got my panoply from the pack mules. My slave was a well-grown youth, about eighteen at that time, with decided criminal proclivities. Every officer needs an accomplished thief while on campaign, to keep him supplied with the necessities and comforts.

First, I pulled on the lightly padded arming tunic, with its pendant skirt of decorated leather straps and matching straps hanging from the shoulders. Then Hermes buckled on my cuirass. There are two ways to acquire great muscles: one is through years of strenuous athletic exercise. The other is to buy them from an armorer. I had chosen the latter course. My cuirass was embossed with muscles that Hercules would have envied, complete with silver nipples and a meticulously sculpted navel. A Gorgon's head scowled frightfully from between the massive pectorals, warding off evil.

Hermes attached my red military cloak to the rings flanking the Gorgon and unpacked my helmet, carefully mounting its crest of flowing white horsehair. The helmet was of the Greek style, with a peak that jutted out above my eyes, the bronze polished to blinding brilliance and decorated all over with silver acanthus leaves. Or perhaps they were ivy. Or even oak or olive. I have forgotten with which god I was trying to curry favor when I bought the armor.

Hermes latched the cheekpieces beneath my chin and stepped back to admire the effect. "Master, you look just like Mars!"

"So I do," I agreed. "I may be an incorrigible civilian, but at least I can look like a soldier. Where is my sword?"

Hermes found my dress sword and I buckled it around my bronze-girt waist like one of Homer's heroes. My position was unclear, so I left off the sash of command. We remounted and rode into the town, where I was received with suitable awe, but the nearest Roman official had disturbing news. Caesar had marched north into the mountains to deal with some people called the Helvetii. They had a town called Genava near Lake Lemannus. All officers and reinforcements were to report to his camp with utmost haste.

This was an unexpected development. I had never heard of an army moving with such speed as Caesar's. He must have double-timed them all the way from central Italy to be at Lake Lemannus so soon. Knowing Caesar's lifelong reputation for indolence, I took it for an ominous sign.

So we rode on without even pausing for a bath or a good night's sleep. Our days of leisure were over, for Caesar had thoughtfully provided relay stations where his officers could acquire fresh mounts and have no excuse for tardiness. The punishment was unspecified but it was as certain as death, for only a Dictator has power like a Roman proconsul in his own province.

Our path took us north up the Rhone Valley, on the east bank of the river. The landscape had its attractions, but I was in no mood to appreciate them. Hermes, usually so insufferably cheerful, grew subdued. Massilia had been a civilized place, but now we were going into the Gallic heartland, where few but traveling merchants had penetrated before.

We passed a number of small, neat villages. Most of their houses were round, made of wattle and daub and roofed with thatch. The more pretentious buildings were framed in massive timber, the spaces between the timbers being filled with wattle, brick, or stone, all whitewashed to contrast pleasingly with the dark timber. The fields were well laid out, separated by low, drystone walls, but without the geometric rigor so familiar from Roman or Egyptian fields.

The people we passed watched us with curious interest but without hostility. The Gauls love color and their clothes are vividly patterned in contrasting stripes and checks. Both sexes wear massive jewelry, bronze among the poor, solid gold among the wealthy.

"The women are ugly," Hermes complained, noting the freckled complexions, snub noses, and round faces, so different from the long, heavy features admired by Romans.

"Believe me," I assured him, "the longer you are here, the better they'll look."

"These don't look so frightening," he said, trying to keep his spirits up. "The way people talk, I expected savage giants."

"These are mostly peasants and slaves," I told him. "The military class don't dirty their hands much with farming or other labor. Wait until you see the warriors. They'll live up to your worst expectations."

"If the Gauls are that bad," he said, "what are the Germans like?"

The question was like a dark cloud across the sun. "Them I don't even want to think about."

Caesar's camp wasn't hard to find. A Roman camp in barbarian territory is like a city dropped from the sky into the wilderness. It sat there, rectilinear as a brick, next to the handsome Lake Lemannus. Actually, the word "camp" fails to do justice to what a Roman legion erects every place it stops for the night. First the surveying team, marching an hour or so ahead of the legion, finds a suitable site, where they mark out the perimeter, the gates, the main streets, and the praetorium. With little, colored flags they mark out the squares where each cohort is to be situated.

When the legion arrives, the soldiers stack arms and get out their tools and their baskets for shifting earth. They dig a ditch around the whole perimeter and heap the earth into a wall just inside the ditch. The wall they palisade with the sharpened stakes they have been carrying on their backs all day. They post sentries and only then do they go into the now-fortified camp to erect their tents; one eight-man section to each tent, ten sections to the century, six centuries to the cohort, ten cohorts to the legion—all laid out in a grid so unvarying that, roused in the middle of the night by an alarm, every man knows exactly which direction to turn and how many streets he must pass to take his assigned place on the rampart. In a sense, a Roman legionary, no matter where he is, is always living in the same spot in the same city.

Just seeing a Roman military camp makes me proud to be

7

a Roman, as long as I don't have to live in one. It has been said that some barbarian armies have given up just watching a legion set up camp. Next to Caesar's legionary camp was the somewhat less rigorous but still disciplined and orderly camp of the auxilia, the troops levied on the allies or hired as mercenaries: the archers, slingers, cavalry, skirmishers, and so forth. Roman citizens fight only as heavy infantry, helmeted and armored, with the big, oval shield, the heavy *pilum* that can be hurled at close range clean through an enemy shield, and the short sword that is awesomely effective in the hand of an expert.

"Look at that!" Hermes said exultantly. "Those barbarians will never attack a place this strong!"

"This is what Roman might looks like," I told him, not wanting to dampen his spirits unnecessarily. Inwardly, I was less confident. A single legion and a roughly equal number of auxilia was not much of a force to pit against a whole barbarian nation. Perhaps, I thought, these Helvetii are not a numerous folk. That should have disqualified me for the office of augur then and there. It is with such comforting fictions that I frequently bemuse myself.

Beyond Caesar's camp, hazy in the distance, I could just make out a sprawling, disorderly town, doubtless Genava. The men were also at work on another project; an earthen rampart that stretched from the lake out of sight in the direction of the nearest mountains. It lay between the camp and the town, and I calculated its purpose to be to discourage the Gauls from trying to overrun the camp with their favored tactic of a headlong charge. I fully approved. The more barriers there were between myself and those savages, the better I liked it.

Our path took us to a spot perhaps a quarter of a mile from the legion camp, where a work party toiled atop the long rampart under the supervision of an officer. Their spears were propped in tripods with their shields leaning against them, helmets atop the spear points. The slender javelins and narrow, flat shields identified the men as skirmishers. Their officer grinned broadly when he saw us.

"Decius!" It was Gnaeus Quintilius Carbo, an old friend.

"Carbo! I can't tell you how happy I am to see you here! Now I know we'll win." I slid off my horse and took his hand, which was as hard as that of any legionary. Carbo was a long-service professional, from the rural gentry near Caere, and about as old-fashioned a Roman as you could ask for. Old frauds like my father and his friends put on a show of being traditional Romans, but Carbo was the genuine article, a man right out of the days of Camillus.

"I felt you'd show up, Decius. When I heard that Clodius was tribune and you were betrothed to Caesar's niece, I knew it was just a matter of time before you'd join us." Carbo, bless his iron-bound, martial heart, thought that I would be eager for action and renown.

"What are you doing out here?" I asked him. "Are you in charge of engineering?"

"No, I'm a commander of auxilia for this campaign." He nodded toward the party working atop the wall. "These are some of my men."

"You?" I said, astonished. "You've campaigned with Lucullus all over Asia and marched in his triumph! You should have a legionary command. Why would Caesar put a man of your experience and seniority in charge of skirmishers?" I felt it was an insult to him, but he shook his head.

"It's not that sort of army, Decius. Caesar doesn't do things like other commanders. He's put some of his most experienced men in charge of the auxilia. You've seen this terrain, these forests? Believe me, it gets worse as you march toward the Rhine. You can't march legionaries through that in any sort of fighting order. You have to take them through the valleys and to do that you have to have plenty of flankers out to clear the woods to either side of the line of march. Gauls like to fight at the run, too, so the advance skirmishers have to be the best, otherwise the barbarians will be on top of you before you see them coming. Auxilia are important in this war."

"I'd say that any sort of soldier is important if this is Caesar's whole force."

"That's right. I don't suppose you have any reinforcements following you?"

I jerked a thumb over my shoulder. "Just my body slave, Hermes. Do you have anything you want stolen?"

He made a sour face. "I suppose it was too much to hope. Pompey's supposed to be raising two more legions for us, but we've seen no sign of them."

Pompey and Crassus, Caesar's colleagues, had secured him his extraordinary five-year command of Gaul and had promised to support him. If he trusted those two, I thought, he might be waiting a long time for his reinforcements.

Carbo looked me over with an even more sour expression. "And Decius, do yourself, me, the army, and the immortal gods a favor and get out of that parade rig before you report to Caesar. This is not like the other armies of your experience."

"Really? I thought I was pretty well turned out." For the first time I noticed that Carbo wore a plain, Gallic mail shirt and a pot-shaped bronze helmet devoid of decoration, just like any legionary except that his sword hung on the left side instead of the right and he had a purple sash of command around his waist. Even as I noted this, we heard a series of trumpet notes from inside the camp.

"Too late," Carbo said. "There's commander's call. You'll have to report immediately. Prepare for a little ribbing."

We set out on foot for the camp, Hermes behind us leading the animals.

"How long is this rampart you're building?" I asked Carbo.

"It stretches from the lake to the mountains to contain the Helvetii, about nineteen miles."

"Nineteen miles?" I said, aghast. "Is this Caius Julius Caesar we're talking about here? The same Caesar I knew in Rome, who never walked where he could be carried and who never lifted a weapon heavier than his voice?"

"You're going to meet a different Caesar," he promised me. And so I did.

We entered the camp by the southern gate and walked up the Via Praetoria, which led straight as an arrow's path through the center of the camp to the praetorium, the inner compound containing the commander's staff tent, surrounded by its own low earthen rampart. The Via Principalis intersected the Via Praetoria at right angles; beyond it lay the quarter occupied by the higher officers and whatever troops they cared to keep separate from the regular legionaries, decurions, and centurions. Usually, these were *extraordinarii*, men with more than twenty years in the ranks who had no duties except for combat. I noticed an unusual number of tents ranked beyond the praetorium and asked Carbo about them.

"A special praetorian guard Caesar has organized. They're mostly auxilia, both foot and cavalry." Other generals used praetorian guards, usually as bodyguards on campaign, but often as a special reserve to employ at crucial moments in battle.

From the size of Caesar's guard, I assumed that their purpose was the latter.

Before the praetorium, along the length of the Via Principalis were ranked the individual tents of the prefects and tribunes. At the juncture of the two streets stood the legion's shrine: a tent containing the standards. Before it stood an honor guard, and since the weather was good the standards were uncovered on their wooden pedestal. The guards stood motionless with drawn swords, and from their short mail shirts and small, circular shields you might have taken them for auxiliary skirmishers; but their position and the lion skins covering their helmets and hanging down their backs proclaimed that these were *signifers* and the *aquilifer*, among the most important officers of the legion, raised from the ranks because they were the bravest of the brave.

We saluted the eagle as we passed, and I noted that the rectangular plaque below the eagle, with its dangling horsetail terminals, read: *LEGIO X*. That was comforting. The Tenth was rated by everyone as the best. By everyone except the other legions, that is. I knew a number of men who served with the Tenth, both officers and rankers. If I had to be out here with only a single legion around me, I couldn't have asked for better.

Two of the praetorian guards stood before the gap in the waist-high rampart that surrounded the praetorium; men armed with thrusting spears, bearing light armor and shields. The rampart was more a symbolic partition than a real defense. In the middle of its eastern wall was the high platform from which the general could address the forum, an open space where the legion could assemble, and where the traders did business with the legion and the local farmers could hold markets on specified days.

Naturally, we were the last to arrive. A large table had been set up before the big general's tent and all the senior officers were grouped around it. These were the tribunes and prefects, the officers of auxilia, and a single centurion. This last, I knew, would be the centurion of the First Century of the First Cohort, known in every legion as the *primus pilus*: First Spear. Alone among the officers he wore bronze greaves strapped to his shins, archaic armor abandoned centuries before by other foot soldiers but retained as a sign of rank for centurions. At the moment we entered, he was gesturing toward something on the table with his vinestaff, a three-foot stick the thickness of a man's thumb and another badge of the centurionate. As we walked in, he looked up, and his face froze.

Caesar was leaning on the table, looking at what I now saw was a map. Behind him stood his twelve proconsular lictors, leaning on their *fasces*. In Rome, the lictors wore togas, but here they were in field dress: red tunics with wide leather belts dyed black and studded with bronze nails, a custom dating to the time of the Etruscan kings. As the staff fell silent, Caesar looked up and straightened, then he took on his familiar, hieratic *pontifex maximus* demeanor. Slowly, solemnly, he drew a fold of his military cloak over his head.

"Gentlemen," he pronounced, "cover your heads. It is a visitation from Olympus. Victory must be ours, for the god Mars has descended to be among us."

The assembly broke up into raucous laughter so loud it probably alarmed the sentries. Even Carbo laughed so hard he got hiccups. I hoped my helmet hid the worst of my flaming face as I stood like an idiot with my arm still fully extended in salute.

"I don't suppose you brought any reinforcements, Decius?" Caesar said, mopping the tears from his face with his cloak.

"I am afraid not, Proconsul."

"I suppose it was too much to hope. Well, we were all in need of a good laugh, anyway. Join us, Decius. Titus Vinius was about to give us a report on the state of the fortifications and enemy action against it. Continue, First Spear."

Enemy action? I thought. There was no host massed out there in the usual Gallic prebattle fashion. A line crawled across the map from the mountains to the lake and it was toward the lake that the centurion pointed with his vinestaff.

"Weakest spot's here where we run into the lake. The ground is swampy there and they come around the end of the wall through the shallows, do what damage they can, and run back the same way. They can flank it just as easily from the mountain end, but they're too lazy to go that far. Plus, in the swamps we can't chase 'em with our cavalry."

Caesar looked up at Carbo. "Gnaeus, I want you to put together a small force of picked auxilia; good swimmers who aren't afraid of water. No armor, not even helmets. Just hand weapons and light shields. I want an end to these attacks by web-footed Gauls."

"They'll be on duty tonight, Commander," Carbo said. I cleared my throat.

"Mars wishes to speak," said Lucius Caecilius Metellus, a distant relative of mine, nicknamed "Lumpy" for a couple of prominent facial wens. He wore a tribune's sash over his plain armor.

"Good to see you here, Lumpy," I said, giving him a big smile. "Where are the hundred sesterces you owe me from the Cerealis races two years ago?" That shut him up.

"You have a question, Decius?" Caesar said.

"Please bear with me, Commander, since I have just arrived. There is no barbarian army outside the walls, so I presume the Helvetii are still treating with us. How can they do that while sending raiders to harass us?"

"These aren't coastal Gauls who know how to conduct themselves like civilized people," Caesar said. "Their envoys speak for the people as a whole, but they think it is to be understood that some of the young warriors will come out at night to send arrows and javelins into the camp. To them it's no more serious than a spirited horse vaulting a fence into another man's field."

"They like to catch sentries and roving patrols," said Titus Vinius, the First Spear. "They're head-hunters, you know. You'll find big heaps of skulls in the deep woods where their holy groves are."

He was a typical old soldier trying to scare the new recruit, but he was wasting his time. I had seen far worse than that in Spain.

"Decimus Varro," Caesar said, "the state of provisions, if you please." I noted that Caesar spoke in a brisk, clipped fashion, quite different from the languid style he affected in Rome.

"Stores of grain, preserved fruit, fish, and meat are sufficient for ten more days, twenty at half-ration. The supply train from Massilia is due at any time."

"Decius, did you pass a supply train on your way here?"

"No, Proconsul."

"Quaestor, increase purchases from the local farmers. I don't want to be caught short of provision when the Helvetii make up their mind to attack."

"They will demand exorbitant prices for inferior produce,

15

sir." The quaestor was a serious-looking young man who was vaguely familiar to me.

"Pay them with a minimum of haggling," Caesar said. "The state of the treasury means nothing to fighting men. The state of their bellies means everything."

"Yes, Caesar." The name of the quaestor came back to me: Sextus Didius Ahala. He had held the same office in Rome a year or two before and I did not envy him the position. Proconsul's quaestor is a responsible position, but it is the dullest work imaginable, managing the accounts and contracts of a province and its military establishment.

After about an hour of hearing reports, issuing commands, passing the watchword, and so forth, the meeting broke up. Caesar indicated that I should remain behind, along with Vinius.

"First Spear, we need a place to put Decius Caecilius Metellus the Younger. Where do you suggest?"

The man looked me over with the casual indifference professional soldiers usually show for amateur junior officers. Only proficiency in battle ever won any respect from the likes of this one.

"We already have more officers than we need, Proconsul. What we do need is more legionaries."

"We shall lose a few of both before much longer," Caesar remarked. "In the meantime, Decius needs a battle station."

Vinius stooped and picked up his helmet from where it lay beneath the table. "The cavalry," he said. He wanted me out of his way, for which I could hardly blame him. Inexperienced officers, especially green tribunes, are the bane of a centurion's existence. I might have told him that I was not unacquainted with military life and campaigning, but he would not have been impressed.

"Excellent. Decius, you may report to the praetorian *ala*. Their present commander is a Gaul named Lovernius, but he needs a Roman superior. As a praetorian you are attached to my personal staff, so you will probably spend a good deal more time with me than with your *ala*."

"I don't suppose they are Spanish cavalry?" I had a good deal of experience riding with Spaniards.

"Gauls," Caesar said. "But deadly enemies of the Helvetii." Which didn't mean much since all the Gauls feuded with each other constantly. Well, any cavalry had to be better than Roman cavalry, which historically had been as pitiful as our infantry had been formidable. Like seafaring, mounted warfare is just one of those things for which we have no aptitude.

"Proconsul, with your leave, I'll go and inspect the watch." Vinius tied the laces of his cheekplates beneath his blue-shaven chin. His helmet was as plain as the others I had seen in this legion, except for its horsehair crest, which ran from side to side instead of front to back, another distinguishing insigne of the centurionate.

"Do so," said Caesar, returning his salute. When the man was gone, he turned to me again.

"You allow him much latitude, Caius Julius," I said, able to be less formal now that we were alone.

"I allow all of my centurions more latitude than I allow most of my officers. Centurions are the backbone of the legions, Decius, not the political time-servers in the sashes. Oh, a few like Carbo and Labienus are excellent soldiers, but my centurions, I *know* I can depend upon."

"Can you depend upon anyone else?"

He understood my meaning exactly. "What was the word in Rome when you left?"

"Well, I wasn't exactly in Rome. The City is unhealthy for me just now, so I was on my father's Tuscian estate just before . . ."

Caesar waved this aside impatiently. "I don't care if you were in Athens. You are a Caecilius Metellus and you know what's being said in the Forum. What is it?"

"That your enemies in Rome gave you this extraordinary command in full confidence that you would fail. That Crassus and Pompey rammed this command through the Assemblies and past the Senate for the same reason. That you and your army are going to wither and die up here in the wilderness like grapes on a vine when moles have gnawed away the roots."

He looked at me with deep-sunken eyes. "I am not ready to be a raisin yet. The first part is true enough, but not the rest. I have the full support of Pompey and Crassus, never fear."

"But what of that, Caius Julius? You know how Pompey operates. He'll let you do all the fighting and then take away your army at the last minute."

Caesar smiled frostily. "But that is politics, and I am far better at politics than Pompey."

"Well—that is true enough," I allowed.

"Decius, why do you think I worked so hard to secure this proconsulship?"

"Because the Gauls have been stirring up trouble for years and are probably allowing Germans to cross the Rhine," I said. "It's the only big war in the offing and war is where the glory and loot and triumphs are to be found."

He now smiled a bit more warmly. "That is blunt enough. You don't think patriotism is my motive?"

"I wouldn't insult your intelligence by saying so."

"Good. Most of my tribunes are lickspittles." He stepped close and took my arm. "Decius, there is far more to this command than just dealing with the Helvetii. There are tremendous opportunities here in Gaul! Back in Rome, people think it means nothing except whipping some brutish, half-naked savages, but they are wrong. Crassus wants a war with Parthia because he thinks only conquering wealthy, civilized enemies will enrich him and Rome. He is wrong too."

"I fully intend to avoid Crassus's war, when he gets it."

"Good. Stay with me here in Gaul. I am telling you, Decius: the men who support me here these next five years will dominate Rome for the next thirty years, as those who supported Sulla have dominated her for the last thirty!" These were vaunting words, delivered with intensity.

Of course, he was not speaking to me. He was speaking to *gens* Caecilia, whose support he desperately wanted. His appeal was none too subtle, either. My family had been among Sulla's supporters, with consequent beneficial effects upon our political prominence.

"You know I am not much of a soldier, Caius."

"What of that? Rome produces plenty of soldiers. You are a man of uncommon quality and unique talents, as I have frequently remarked in company of all qualities." This last was true. Caesar had been known to speak highly of me to people who denounced me as a mere eccentric if not an utter fool.

This was not the Caesar I had known in Rome. He sounded like a man possessed by the urge to conquer. He certainly didn't look like a conqueror. Tall, thin, and rapidly bald-ing, he looked far too frail to take the weight of an army upon his narrow shoulders. He wore a plain white tunic, with only his legionary boots and *sagum* to proclaim his status. Between tunic and boots his legs stretched as skinny as a stork's. "I shall consider what you say," I told him, inwardly vowing to get out of Gaul as rapidly as I could.

"Excellent. Now go and join your *ala*. They are quartered in the northeast corner of the camp. Draw whatever equipment you require from the supply tents. Then come back here for dinner. All my officers who are not on watch or other duties dine in my tent."

I saluted. "I take my leave, then, Proconsul."

He returned the salute and I walked away.

"And, Decius?"

I about-faced. "Sir?"

"Do get out of that ridiculous rig. You look like a statue set up in the Forum."

Abruptly, I realized how absurd Caesar would look in a dress uniform, like a mockery of a general in one of Plautus's comedies. That was why he insisted on soldierly plainness. Cae-sar's vanity was as famous as his debts and his ambition. He was having nobody near him who looked better than he.

2

M ORNING IN A LEGION BEGINS FAR
too early. Somewhere a *tuba* bellowed like an ox in mortal pain.
I awoke on my folding camp bed and tried to remember where
I was. The smell of the leather tent told me. I reached down
and shook Hermes, who was sleeping on a pallet next to me.

"Hermes," I said groggily, "go kill that fool blowing the
horn. You can borrow my sword." He just grumbled and rolled
over. Someone threw open the door flap. It was still dark outside, but I could vaguely make out a man-shape against the
glow of a distant watchfire.

"Time for morning patrol, Captain dear." It was one of my
Gallic troopers.

"Are you serious? The horses will be as blind as the rest
of us in this murk." I sat up and kicked Hermes. He mumbled
something incomprehensible.

"It shall grow lighter anon, and soon the little birds will be singing. You may trust my word in this matter, beloved." He ducked back out and let the flap fall. There is really no way to describe how a backcountry Gaul talks, but this is a sample. I grabbed Hermes with both hands, raised him, and shook him as hard as I could.

"Wake up, you little swine! I need water." My head throbbed. Caesar's field table had been austere, but he was liberal with the wine. Hermes had managed to sneak himself some of it.

"But it's still dark!" Hermes complained.

"Get used to it," I advised. "Your days of lazing around until sunup are over. From now on, you get up before me and you have hot water and breakfast ready." Eating breakfast was one of those exotic, degenerate habits for which I had been condemned in Rome. Hermes stumbled outside. Immediately there came a thud and a curse as he tripped over a tent rope.

I laced on my boots, stood, and lurched outside. The camp was coming to life all around me. The altitude and the earliness of the year put a bite in the air and I wrapped my *sagum*, which was also my blanket, closer around me. Soon Hermes returned with a bucket of icy water and I splashed my gummy eyes, rinsed my foul-tasting mouth, and began to feel marginally better.

"Get my gear," I told Hermes, but he was already there with it. He helped me pull the mail shirt over my head and the twenty pounds of interlinked iron rings slid down my body to hang from my shoulders to just above my knees. I belted on my sword, drawing the belt tight to take some of the weight off my shoulders. With my helmet beneath my arm, I went in search of my troop.

I found them gathered around a watchfire, a basket of loaves in their midst, a stack of wooden cups by the basket. A copper cauldron steamed over the fire. A ruddy-haired young man caught my eye as I drew near.

"Join us, Captain," he said. "Have some posca. It will clear the fog from your head."

"Good morning, Lovernius. If there's nothing better to be had, I'll take some."

He picked up one of the bowl-like wooden cups, dipped it in the cauldron, and handed it to me. I took a drink, winced, and made what must have been a comical face, for Lovernius and the others laughed. It takes years in the legions to actually enjoy hot vinegar and water, but at least it truly does wake you up.

Lovernius was an Allobrogian aristocrat educated in Roman schools. He was clean-shaven and short-haired in the Roman fashion, but his face was tattooed with horizontal blue stripes. The day was, as predicted, growing lighter, and in that dim light I inspected my men. There were around a hundred men on the praetorian *ala*, and about twenty in this particular troop. Most were long-haired and wore the dangling mustaches that civilized people find repulsive. They were tattooed fancifully but at least none of them were painted. Over their bright checked and striped tunics they wore short, sleeveless mail shirts. The belts that cinched their shirts were decorated with bronze plaques worked in intricate designs. They all had beautifully made iron helmets crested with fanciful little horns and upright wheels. I hate to admit it, but the Gauls are much better metalworkers than the Romans. Each man wore an open-ended torque of twisted bronze, silver, or gold around his neck.

Despite their tattoos and mustaches and barbaric ornaments, they were a handsome lot, as Gauls tend to be. They were well above the average Roman in height, their height emphasized by their upright, arrow-straight bearing. As warriors, they were by definition wellborn. As horsemen, they knew themselves to be superior to any mere foot soldier.

It is not true, as many think, that all Gauls have blond or red hair, although fair hair predominates. About half of these men had the hair we think of as Gallic. The rest were in varying shades of brown, and one or two had hair as black as any Egyptian's, but even these were fair of skin.

The loaves were legionary bread; heavy, coarse, and dry. I tore one in two and dipped it in the posca to make it more edible. The men were giving me the same once-over I was giving them.

"Would you care to address the men before we ride out, Captain?" Lovernius asked.

"All right," I said. I choked down a last bite of bread and tossed my cup to the ground. "Listen to me, you hairy-lipped scum. I am Senator Decius Caecilius Metellus the Younger, and by will of the Senate and People of Rome I have power of life and death over you. I ask little except absolute obedience and I promise little for failure except instant death. Watch out for me in the field and I will watch out for you in the praetorium. You'll never go short of loot while I'm your captain and you'll never go short of punishment if you aren't the best troop of the best *ala* attached to this legion. Keep arrows out of my back and I'll keep the stripes off yours. Is that understood?"

Soldiers like it when you talk to them like that. It makes them feel tough and manly. These grinned and nodded. I was making a good impression.

The horses were somewhat small and rough to Roman

24

eyes, but we are accustomed to the showy beasts we breed for chariot races. The Gauls never trim the manes or tails of their horses and these were still shaggy from their winter coats, so the impression they gave was not one of beauty. But I saw immediately that these creatures were ideal for the terrain we would be traversing.

The men began to stroke their mounts and talk to them. Gauls love horses to the point of worship. Indeed, they even have a horse goddess named Epona, a deity we Romans sadly lack. Most of their festivals involve horses in one way or another.

The youngest of the warriors, a boy named Indiumix, was detailed to care for my horse and see to its grooming and saddling. He displayed the beast to me proudly, enumerating its many virtues while he stroked it. When I was satisfied with my horse and the others, I mounted. Immediately, the skirts of my mail shirt bunched uncomfortably around my hips. I made a mental note to go to the armorer and have slits cut at the sides, cavalry-fashion.

We left the camp by way of the Porta Decumana, the northern gate. I accounted myself an excellent horseman, but my Gauls made me feel clumsy. They all rode like centaurs, each man with his longsword, his lance, and a sheaf of javelins tied to his saddle, with his flat, oval shield slung across his back. (I should note that the names we used for them were only approximations of their real names, which we found hard to pronounce and impossible to spell. The Gallic language has sounds for which there are no Latin letters. That is why one Gallic chief may seem to have a dozen different names, depending upon who is writing the history.)

We turned to the east, toward the lake. Lovernius explained that it was our duty every morning to inspect the great earthworks and receive the reports of the sentry officers. Thankfully, we would not have to ride the whole nineteen miles of it. The officers of the western half would ride to meet us somewhere in the middle. Every mile along its length a detachment of auxilia lay encamped. No doubt these men were nervous, for their camps were far more vulnerable to attack than the great legionary camp. But then, it is good for sentries to be nervous.

The guards at the swampy lake end of the wall reported no incursions the previous night. And so it went for seven or eight miles; no enemy action except for curses and spells screamed from the darkness beyond. The sentries spoke contemptuously of these ineffective assaults, but it was daylight now. I knew that it had been different the night before, when these same men had clutched their weapons and strained their wide eyes toward those uncanny voices in the outer gloom.

About noon, we came to a clear pool and dismounted to let the horses drink. I handed my reins to Indiumix and walked around the pool to stretch my legs. The muscles of my inner thighs were tight from clamping the barrel of the horse all morning. As I was about to turn back, a glimmer in the water caught my eye.

I stepped out onto a flat rock in the water and bent to look more closely. Something gleamed from the shallows. Getting down on my knees, I fumbled for it, my efforts made clumsy by that magical property of water that made my arm seem to bend beneath the surface. But soon I had it out. It was a beautiful fibula, a Gallic cloak-pin of fine gold. Exultantly, I took it back to show my troopers.

"Someone's lost a good pin," I said holding it up for them

to admire. "Bad luck for them, good luck for me!" To my surprise, they looked shocked and angry.

"Throw it back, Captain," Lovernius said quietly. "A water sprite lives in there. Someone threw that in as an offering before embarking upon some dangerous feat, perhaps preparing for battle."

I looked at the brooch regretfully. "He may be dead and no longer need the sprite's protection."

Lovernius shook his head. "It is death to take gifts pledged to the gods. It may have lain there a hundred years in full view, but no one would touch it."

I had seen Gauls toss small coins into pools for luck, but I did not know that it was taken so seriously. With a sigh, I threw the fibula back into the water, where it made a small splash. I was not about to offend the local gods. The men grinned and nodded, pleased that I respected their customs. It was also prudent. They probably would have killed me before we got back to the camp and made up a story about an enemy ambush.

As we rode on, Lovernius told me just how seriously the Gauls took this aspect of their religion. Sometimes, before a battle, they would pledge a whole enemy army to their gods in exchange for victory. After the battle, no enemy was spared. Not only were their bodies cast into a pool or marsh, but their weapons and armor, their baggage carts and treasure, their horses, cattle, and slaves were all destroyed or killed and thrown in as well, so that not so much as a cloak or a copper coin remained as loot for the victors. All was given to the gods.

There were places in the deep forests where great heaps of these strange battle trophies spent centuries slowly sinking into the mud. He also explained to me the horrible punishment meted out to anyone who took even the smallest item from one of them. I vowed never to go within spitting distance of such a trove.

It was afternoon when we rode back into the camp. I tendered my report to Titus Labienus, Caesar's *legatus* and deputy commander, then went in search of a legionary barber for a shave. I was not about to trust Hermes' inexpert hand at so delicate a task.

Freshly shaved, my stomach growling, I was walking back through the rows of legionary tents toward my own quarters and lunch when somebody hailed me.

"Patron!"

I looked around. I stood near the corner of a century block not far from the praetorium. The camp buzzed with the usual activities of such a place. Men in full gear marched to relieve the sentries, others swept and cleaned the streets, others carried supplies hither and yon. Little leisure is allowed in a legionary camp in the daytime. It is constantly being improved. There are always latrines to be dug, a bathhouse to be erected if the camp is to be occupied for a long time. And, it goes without saying, it never hurt to have that encircling ditch another foot deeper, the rampart another foot higher. Men with nothing else to do could always whittle a few more sharpened stakes to set in the bottom of the ditch.

"Patron!" Now I saw a work detail tightening the ropes of a tent larger than the others and generally policing up its area. Doubtless it was their centurion's tent, the lofty centurion being excused all such undignified labor. One of the men left the detail and trotted up to me. It took me a moment to recognize him.

"Young Burrus!" I grasped his hands. He was the son of

one of my clients, an old soldier who had served with me in Spain. "I was going to look you up. I have letters for you from your family." I also had letters for a half dozen or so other soldiers in the legion, sons of other clients of my family. Any time word gets out that an officer is going out to join a particular proconsul or propraetor, he becomes a mail carrier. But Burrus was an especially close client, having backed me in some decidedly rough situations.

"How is Father?" He grinned, showing that he had lost a tooth on one side.

"As mean as ever. He swears that you're living easy up here, that soldiering isn't what it was in his day."

"That sounds like the old brute." Lucius Burrus had been a boy when I had last seen him. Now he was a handsome young man, of medium height, well knit and with the enduring strength of the Italian peasant, just the sort every recruiter looks for. He was a bit the worse for the wear, though, with bruises on his arms and neck and anywhere else his skin showed.

"They must be training you hard here," I commented.

He winced and looked sheepish. "It isn't that. It's . . ." His voice tapered off and his gaze went to the entrance of the tent. So did mine. There was an abrupt cessation of activity around the tent as the door flap swept aside and a goddess walked out.

How does one describe perfection, especially when it is barbaric perfection? She was taller than any woman should be, taller than any man there. She was about an inch taller than I, although my thick-soled military boots put our eyes on a level. Her face was made up of features that should have robbed it of beauty: her jaw too long and narrow, her eyes set too close beside a nose that was too long and thin, her mouth too wide and full-lipped, her lips pushed outward by teeth that were too large. Taken together, the effect was devastating.

Her thick, gold-blond hair fell over her shoulders and to her waist, contrasting with her straight, level, dark brows. Her eyes were ice blue, paler even than a Gaul's, her skin whiter than a candidate's toga, her body as slender as a charioteer's whip, and as strong and supple. That body was rendered abundantly visible by her scanty tunic, which was made of red fox pelts.

You may take it from this that the woman made a powerful first impression. You would not be wrong. Outside the tent she stood there, a flat-bottomed jug balanced on her shoulder, quite aware of the attention she drew and quite contemptuous of it. She didn't just look like a goddess, she *stood* like one. Any athlete can look good in motion, but few mortals have the ability to stand superbly. Roman statesmen struggle for years to achieve such dignity and self-possession.

And yet, here was near divinity embodied in a German slavegirl.

My somewhat addled thoughts were interrupted by an ugly smack of wood against flesh and the thud of a falling body. I turned to see young Burrus on the ground. Titus Vinius stood over him with his vinestaff raised. Down it came across Burrus's shoulders. The stick must have been soaked in oil, because it bent without breaking.

"Don't have enough work to do, you lazy little shit?" The stick came down three more times.

An officer is never supposed to interfere with a centurion disciplining one of his men, but this was too much. I grasped his wrist before the stick could descend again. He wore a silver bracelet, a decoration for valor in some past battle, and it flexed slightly beneath my fingers.

"Enough, Centurion! He is a client of mine. I was giving him news from home."

The eyes that glared into mine were not quite sane. "I don't care if he's the high priest of Jupiter and I saw what he was doing! Now release my arm, Captain. You are interfering where you have no business." He seemed to have regained self-possession so I let him go. He lowered the vinestaff, but he kicked Burrus in the ribs with his hobnailed boot.

"Get up, Burrus! If you've nothing better to do here than stand and ogle my property, then go join the latrine detail." He turned his wrathful gaze on the others. "Shall I find work for the rest of you?" But they were already working furiously, looking anywhere except at him or the woman. I noticed that they all bore bruises, although none of them was as extravagantly marked as Burrus. The slave girl herself walked past us without a glance, as if we did not even exist. Even under the circumstances, I had to force myself not to stare after her.

Burrus got to his feet, stooped with pain, his face flaming with rage and humiliation. He would not look at me and I was acutely embarrassed to have witnessed his degradation. He gathered his arms from one of the pyramidal stacks and trudged off.

"That was excessive, Centurion," I said, making an effort to keep my voice level. "It's not as if he was asleep on guard duty."

"My men are mine to handle as I please, Captain," he said, giving the word an unbelievably contemptuous twist. "You had better remember that."

"You are getting a little above yourself, Titus Vinius," I said, as haughtily as I could manage. Being a Caecilius Metellus, that was haughtier than most.

His lip curled slightly. "This is Caesar's army, Metellus. Caesar understands that the centurions run things. It is we who will bring him victories, not the political flunkies in purple sashes."

I would have drawn my sword on him then, but Caesar could have had me executed for it. Under military law, Vinius had done nothing wrong. I tried an appeal to reason.

"If you don't want your men ogling your slave, give her some decent clothes. That woman is a menace to the morale of the whole army."

"I do as I like with my own property."

"You didn't take your vinestaff to me, Vinius," I pointed out. "I was staring as hard as he was."

"You're not one of my men," he said, grinning crookedly. "Besides, you are a Roman officer. You may stare all you like. Just don't touch."

Pulling rank hadn't worked. Reason had failed utterly. Well, where centurions were concerned, there was always greed. I reached into the purse at my belt. "All right, Vinius. How much to leave the boy alone?"

He spat at my feet. "Keep your money, aristocrat. He's mine, the woman is mine, and if the truth be told, this legion is mine. I am First Spear of the Tenth. Proconsuls come and go, but the First Spear is always in charge."

I was stunned. I had never known a centurion to turn down a bribe. "I shall speak to Caesar about this."

"Go ahead. That's what you politicians are good for, isn't it? Talking?" Behind him I saw a dwarfish little man standing in the doorway of the tent where the German girl had stood before. He was grinning at my discomfiture with wide-gapped teeth. He had beastly red hair sticking out in all directions. I looked away. Things had come to such a pass that I could not even stare down a malformed slave.

I turned and walked away. I had a powerful urge to say something biting, but it would only have made me look even more weak and ineffectual. At least Vinius did not laugh aloud as I retreated.

This exchange may seem incredible to people who live their lives around the Forum, but the army is another world entirely. A man who has earned the position of centurion is almost as untouchable as a Tribune of the Plebs. He is expected to be a harsh disciplinarian, so he cannot be reprimanded for cruelty. He may do anything with his men short of killing them. Accepting bribes to excuse men punishment or onerous duties has been allowed for centuries as one of the perquisites of the rank. Only cowardice in battle is cause to punish a centurion, and while they may be many things, they are rarely cowards.

As for force of character and moral ascendancy, such a man has few peers. People usually think that street gangsters and gladiators are tough, but that is because they have never met a Roman centurion with twenty years of brutal campaigning behind him. There is a centurion in command of every century, and there are sixty centuries to each legion. The First Spear is always the toughest of the lot.

No longer hungry, I went to the armorer to have my mail shirt altered and cool down in the meantime. I knew it would be foolish to go to Caesar with anger-fogged thoughts. While the armorer worked, I went over his stock of used weapons. By the time I had found suitable arms, I was back in my customary

33

state of philosophical equanimity. I bought a good Gallic long-sword that was far better for mounted combat than anything I owned, and an old but sound gladius, together with sheaths and shoulder belts to go with them.

In front of my tent I found Hermes awaiting me. He had laid out my lunch on a folding table I had brought, along with a folding chair. There is no more useful object in a military camp than a comfortable folding chair. I sat and dropped my burden beside me while Hermes poured watered wine from my stock. He seemed oddly excited.

"Master, I think I saw a goddess in the camp today! It must have been Venus. Doesn't Caesar claim to be descended from Venus? Maybe she was visiting him."

I took a long drink and sighed. "Hermes, do you really think Venus goes around dressed in animal skins?"

"It did look sort of odd, but the immortals aren't like the rest of us."

"What you saw was a German slavegirl. I saw her, too." The sight was as real as the cup before me. Even the barbaric custom of wearing furs did not mar her beauty.

Hermes grinned. "Really? Then these Germans can't be all that bad!"

"You think not? That woman could probably snap you across her shapely knee. Imagine what the men must be like."

"Oh. I hadn't thought of that."

I held up an admonitory finger. "And, Hermes, I cannot stress this strongly enough: Do not, I repeat, *do not* get caught staring at her."

"Are you serious?" he said, refilling my cup. "Tongues dragged on the ground wherever she passed."

"Nonetheless, keep your eyes and tongue firmly in your

head when she is around. In fact, keep your eyes lowered just as I tell you to when I have distinguished visitors, not that you ever listen to me, you loathsome little wretch." I bent, picked up the short sword, and tossed it to him. He caught it by the sheath and gave me a puzzled look.

"You want me to clean this up for you? It's not as good as the sword you're wearing."

"It's for you," I said. "I'm going to enroll you with a sword instructor here. It's time you learned how to handle weapons."

He looked dazzled, thinking he was Horatius already.

"Don't get any foolish ideas," I warned him. "I am doing this because you have to accompany me into war zones and bandit-infested areas. You cannot wear weapons in any civilized place and you must *never* touch arms in Rome, unless you want to grace one of the many picturesque crosses planted outside the gates."

He went white the way slaves usually do when you mention a cross. "Never fear, master!"

"Good. Now, what's for lunch?"

3

THAT AFTERNOON WE RODE OUT
in full strength, something just short of a hundred troopers.
From the camp we passed through the long earthworks into the
grassy, brushy lakeside plain beyond. We conducted a sweep
to catch any ambitious Helvetian warriors who might try to work
themselves close enough for an ambush after dark. We spread
out in a wide line and rode slowly forward, paying special attention to the frequent areas of good cover.

Several times we flushed two or three young, blue-painted
braves from a clump of brush and my men would give chase,
whooping and hallooing like men hunting hares. And the Gauls
ran like hares, too, their colorfully clad legs flashing as they
leaped and dodged, actually laughing as the horsemen chased
them down. I have never liked seeing warfare treated as sport,
but it was sport played in earnest. A couple of my men rode

back with fair-tressed heads hanging at their saddles.

In the middle of all this we saw a party of Gauls riding in, preceded by white-robed heralds bearing rods wreathed in ivy. These were the Helvetian envoys come to treat with Caesar. They rode with impressive dignity, ignoring the veritable human fox-hunt as it swept by them. Among them I noticed a few that didn't look like the usual Gallic aristocrats: They were bearded men in white robes and wearing silver diadems, and others, also bearded, but wearing animal skins. These last might almost have been Gauls, but Gauls are clean-shaven except for their mustaches, and these were neither tattooed nor painted.

I rode up to Lovernius. "Who were those other men with the envoys?"

"The graybeards in the white robes are Druids," he told me. I had heard of these priests and soothsayers but these were the first I had seen. "The others are Germans, Ariovistus's men."

"Isn't he the king of the Germans? I heard his name mentioned in a Senate debate. What are his men doing on this side of the Rhine?"

"Is that all they know in Rome?" He laughed bitterly. "Captain, Ariovistus and about a hundred thousand of his warriors have been living west of the Rhine for a number of years now."

"What! How did this come about?" A great dread lowered itself over me like a shroud.

"Surely you knew that most of Gaul is divided into two factions, one led by the Aedui, my own people, and the other led by the Averni, who live along the Rhine?"

"That much I knew. And I heard that you Aedui were winning until the Averni brought in some German mercenaries on their side. That was one reason why Caesar got this extraordinary command. But nobody said anything about a hundred thousand savages and their king! What possessed the Averni to do such a thing?"

"They were losing and men will do desperate things at such a time. Besides," he shrugged his mailed shoulders, "they and the Germans are cousins."

Perhaps I should explain something here. We Romans usually assumed that everyone west of the Rhine was a Gaul, everyone east was a German. That was roughly but not completely true. The fact is, they could be difficult to tell apart. They had been living in close proximity for centuries, and in the border areas they intermarried and swapped customs. In one place you might find a village where the people wore colorful clothes and tattoos and mustaches but only German was spoken. Likewise, in some areas the Gauls were bearded and wore animal skins.

You see this sort of thing all over the coastal areas surrounding our sea, where over the course of four centuries people of many lands have adopted the customs, grooming, and dress of the Greeks. More recently, we see imitation Romans everywhere. Primitive people often find a more sophisticated culture attractive and seek to join it, while those who feel their race has lost its warrior virtues will sometimes adopt the customs of a more primitive but more fierce and manly culture.

"An oddly mixed party," I commented. "Why Druids?"

"They will be advisers to the Helvetii. They are consulted on all matters of importance."

I guided my horse around a mud hole. "We do the same. It is always a good idea to consult the augurs for signs and make sure all the proper rituals are observed before you commit yourself to crucial action."

"It isn't quite like that. The Druids serve as advisers in worldly matters and they retain the history and lore and traditions of the people."

This was the first I had heard that the Druids were anything more than priests. "Are they politically influential?" I was not sure how a Gaul would interpret such an expression.

"The kings listen to them."

"Even German kings?"

He laughed. "Never! The Germans have only fierce gods they can see: the sun and the moon, lightning and thunder and the storm."

Then we started up another group of warriors and were off on another chase.

When we returned to camp that evening, we found that a pack of merchants had arrived and a veritable market day was in progress. The camp's forum had sprouted booths and the off-duty soldiers were allowed, a cohort at a time, to go there and purchase necessities or waste their money as they saw fit. I dismissed my *ala* and the men who had taken heads rushed away to show them off to their friends. Gauls set great store by these grisly trophies and even decorate their shrines and homes with them. They fancy the head to be the repository of many virtues such as courage and wisdom. We Romans hold that these qualities reside in the liver. Personally I am neutral, but I would regret losing either of them.

That evening Caesar entertained the envoys at dinner and I got a good look at them. The Helvetii were elders dressed in richly patterned cloaks and a profusion of massive, golden jewelry. The Druids, differing from the usual Gallic fashion, had long beards, white in the case of the two elder priests, short and red on a younger man. Unlike the other two he wore no silver diadem around his temples, so I took him to be an apprentice or acolyte. All three had slender, long-fingered hands that had never been hardened by labor or practice at arms. In their long, white gowns and holding their staffs they might have been heralds.

The three Germans were tall, burly men, whose hair and beards ranged from dark gold to near white. Their pale complexions were reddened and roughened by constant exposure. The evening had turned cold, but they wore only brief tunics of wolfskin and fur leggings that came no higher than their knees. Longswords hung at their belts and they leaned on spears forged entirely of steel. They gazed about them with fearless eyes that were of a blue so pale that you almost took them for blind men until that eagle gaze fastened on you.

Once, in the big, stone amphitheater at Capua, I had seen a Hyrcanian tiger, the first ever brought to Italy. When it ambled into the arena, I was struck by its great beauty, but its size and the way it ignored its surroundings made it seem as slow and lazy as a big, male lion. Then it noticed the massive fighting bull that had been matched with it. Like a streak of golden light it was across the arena and had the much larger animal down so swiftly that it looked like magic. The tiger was a sensation and fought there for many years. To me, it was feral deadliness personified.

When I saw those Germans, I thought about that tiger. These were not the semi-Gallicized Germans who dwelled along the river. They were the real thing; savages from the deep forests far beyond the Rhine.

The dinner was somewhat less austere than that of the evening before, but it was not exactly a banquet. A few delicacies had been purchased from the merchants and a hunting party had brought in a wild boar, but the envoys had no taste for olives and seemed to be repelled by our fermented fish sauce. Well, there is no accounting for tastes. I noticed that the Druids ate no animal food, not even eggs.

When the dinner was over, Caesar held audience. First to speak was the head of the Helvetian delegation. He wore a voluminous cloak woven in a dazzling pattern of checks and lines that intersected and overlapped bewilderingly. He had it wrapped about him against the chill of the evening. It was fastened at his shoulder by a golden brooch at least eight inches in diameter. His speech was translated by a respected Roman merchant who had lived in Gaul all his life, but I kept Lovernius close by me to make sure that the translation was accurate.

I will not try to reproduce here the many and extravagant images, figures of speech, and circumlocutions employed by the envoy, for the Gallic love of rhetoric exceeds even the Roman fondness for that art. Instead, I shall convey the gist of his words, which shortens his speech tremendously.

"Honored Proconsul of Rome, I, Nammeius, chieftain of the Helvetii, speak to you here on behalf of the glorious, the powerful, the ever victorious nation of Helvetia; ever just in her dealings with other nations, vigilant in peace and fierce in war, fair of face and form, sonorous of voice, generous, noble, and proud." From this you may imagine how tedious it would be if I wrote down everything he actually said.

"Rome listens." Caesar's vividly contrasting acknowledgment was in that spare, laconic style with which we were all to become so familiar. Nammeius was nonplussed. He had expected something more fulsome.

"Noble Caesar, for a final time, I protest that your interference with our migration is unjust and uncalled for. We are a nation of true men, and only persons lacking in manliness and spirit dwell in a single place forever, wearing out the land and fighting only the same neighbors. In the honored tradition of our ancestors we intend to burn our towns and farms behind us and pass through the land of the Allobroges and through your province into the territory beyond, where Rome and her allies have no interests.

"We promise to undertake this migration peacefully, and to cause no damage to the lands through which we must pass. No one will be killed or enslaved, no property will be stolen or harmed in any way. We have no need of plunder, for our movable goods will be on our wagons. We need not forage for provisions, for we will carry with us all the grain we need for the march. You must permit this, Caesar. Already, the smoke of our towns, our *oppida*, and our farmsteads rises to the heavens. Already the wagons are loaded and the folk have massed along the river. The season draws nigh when we must begin our migration, or it will be too late when we arrive at our destination.

"Caesar, when last we spoke, you asked for time to consider our request. This seemed reasonable to us and we granted you this interval. Now we find that you have employed this time in building a great rampart, the sort of thing for which you Romans are famous throughout the world. I must urge upon you the futility of this thing, for we are not Greeks to be terrified by a wall. When the Helvetii move upon their chosen path, no little heap of earth and logs will slow them in any way, for they sweep all obstacles before them like chaff before the wind. Once again, Caesar, and for the final time, I urge that you remove yourself from before us." With this the envoy resumed his seat.

"Honored Nammeius, I have considered your nation's proposal with great patience, despite the many provocations that I, and the friends of Rome, have received from your warriors. To begin with, I find your reasons for undertaking this migration to be totally unreasonable.

"Aeneas, son of the goddess Venus, whose son, Julus, was the founder of my house, led his people from a city burned by his enemies. He did not burn it himself." That was Caesar; always reminding people of the divine origins of his family. "Romulus, descendant of Julus, founded Rome 696 years ago. We have not budged since that time and feel no less manly for it." He smiled and the Romans present laughed at his witticism. I could see what the Gauls were thinking: that we had simply expanded our territory and founded colonies instead of migrating. But it was not their turn to speak.

"Your assurances that you can accomplish this movement of a nation through the territory of several others without causing harm I cannot accept. You are, as you have so eloquently stated, a nation of warriors, and while you can lead your warriors, you cannot control them. They will be in force in the land of ancestral enemies and will never be able to restrain themselves from plunder, rapine, and slaughter.

"As for the feebleness of my rampart, it is true that a ditch and a heap of earth are not daunting to athletic young men. And the wooden palisade atop the wall is not more than can be scaled by spirited warriors. But behind that palisade you will find the ultimate barrier: the Roman soldier. All the nations of the world have learned that his shield is the firmest of ramparts, and all enemies fall before his sword. Boasts will avail you nothing should you dare to match arms with him."

The other Helvetian envoy stood. "I am Verucloetius, war chieftain of the Helvetian canton of the Tigurini. I do not fear the Romans, and neither do my people. When the consul Lucius Cassius marched against us, we killed him and his army passed beneath our yoke!"

Caesar's face reddened but his voice rang low and cold. "Forty-nine years ago all Gaul was on the move, not just a single people. It was one reason we determined never again to allow such movements near our territory. You will find that our military organization has much improved since that time. My uncle, Caius Marius, saw to these improvements personally and he tested them by putting your kinsmen to the sword."

The Gauls reacted to the name of Marius as if they had been slapped. Two Gallic nations simply ceased to exist when they tangled with Marius, and several others were badly shredded. His was a name with which the Gauls frightened small children into obedience.

One of the Germans indicated that he wished to speak. Caesar nodded and the man stood. His wolfskin tunic was encircled by a belt six inches wide studded with bronze nails, and it creaked as he rose and hooked his thumbs into it.

"First Spear," Caesar said, "summon your interpreter."

Vinius clapped his hands, producing a sound like a large catapult hurling a missile. I smiled in anticipation, expecting to see the German slave girl. Great was my disappointment when instead the ugly, gnomish, fox-haired slave I had seen standing in the doorway of Vinius's tent walked through the guarded opening in the praetorium wall. He stood by the envoy and the man looked down his long, German nose as at a toad or other lowly, unattractive creature, and said something in a language that sounded like wolves fighting for leadership of the pack.

The slave translated, grinning insolently, displaying a

mouth in which teeth and gaps associated equally. "Is this proper? My people drown all such creatures at birth."

Caesar laughed richly. "In a truly well ordered world, nothing so ugly would be suffered to live. However, we live in the real world, not in Plato's. Sometimes uncomeliness must be overlooked in favor of utility. Molon was a slave east of the Rhine for many years, so he is fluent in your language. He fears the whip too much to tamper with the translation. He will render our words with precision. Pray continue."

After this the Germans behaved as if the slave was not there. "I am Eintzius, nephew of King Ariovistus, and with me is my brother, Eramanzius." Again, these are at best approximations of their names. "For some time now my king has been in contact with the councilors of the Helvetii and it has been agreed among us that our cousins, the Harudes and the Suebi, are to move onto the land vacated by the Helvetii. Those tribes are already on the move and preparing to cross the Rhine. If the Helvetii are not permitted to migrate, severe hardship will result. The Harudes and the Suebi will be greatly angered."

I heard a hiss beside me and Lovernius muttered: "I thought so! Those Helvetii aren't migrating because they have itchy feet. They are being *pushed!* These Germans have told them to clear out or be exterminated."

Caesar leaned forward in his proconsul's folding chair, his arms relaxed along its elaborately carved arms. "Honored envoy, I am not pleased by this news. Rome is not pleased. Rome has two policies which are not to be flouted and which I am here to enforce: the tribes of Gaul are to stay within the borders of their own ancestral territories; and the Germans are not to cross to the west bank of the Rhine."

"Caesar, we are already west of the river, and have been for years, and intend to stay." For all his barbaric aspect, Eintzius spoke with the effortless authority of an envoy of the Senate ordering some Oriental despot to cease and desist from whatever activity displeased Rome. Between him and Caesar I sensed a collision of two implacable forces. Suddenly, the Helvetii did not seem to be such a threat. I could almost pity them, caught between the millstones of Rome and Germania.

"That I will deal with when the matter of the Helvetii has been settled," Caesar said.

The other German stood. "Go fetch more men. What you have here will not provide a morning's amusement for us." For a skin-clad savage, Eramanzius was unbelievably arrogant. Of course, it helped that he was close to seven feet tall. People that tall tend to assume far more importance than they actually possess.

Nonetheless, both of them were intimidating in the extreme, in a way that the colorful Gauls were not. Partly, it was their outlandish habit of wearing furs. Gauls, and Romans visiting cold climates, sometimes wear fur inside their clothing, for warmth. But Germans wear it on the *outside*, as if they were trying to imitate the appearance of their totem animals. Among civilized people this is done only for purposes of ritual, as with the leopard-skin capes of Egyptian priests and Greek Bacchantes, or the lion, bear, and wolfskin worn by legionary standard-bearers. It is unsettling in the extreme to see people wear animal skins as their everyday attire.

Caesar regarded the man coldly. "Do not provoke me. There is no power on earth like Rome. From the soil of Italy the legions rise up like grain after the spring rains. If you truly wish it, we will provide you with entertainment up to your highest expectations, although we must forego the pleasure of hearing your applause afterward."

These were fierce words for a man with a single legion and some auxiliaries, but Romans love to hear that sort of talk. Even knowing the reality of the situation, I felt a jolt of good old-fashioned Roman steel stiffening my somewhat nervous backbone.

Nammeius stood, and with him stood the Gallic contingent. "We have accomplished all that words may accomplish, and it has been nothing. Henceforth, we shall speak with arms."

The Gauls and the Germans swept out. Last of all went the Druids, who had not spoken a single word. Caesar glared angrily after them, but I saw that his most malevolent expression was not directed at the chieftains. It was reserved for the Druids. When they were gone, he addressed the officers.

"Gentlemen, from now on we may expect serious hostilities. However, work on the rampart is now complete and we are receiving daily reinforcements of troops levied from the Provincials. These will man the strongpoints along the rampart. The legionary guard is to be doubled. Go now and rejoin your units and prepare for action."

I got up to leave with Lovernius, but Caesar beckoned me. "Decius Caecilius, attend me."

I waited while the other officers left. Titus Vinius favored me with an ugly smile as he walked out with his even uglier slave. Caesar went into his tent and I joined him there. It was divided into two sections, the smaller being Caesar's sleeping quarters, the larger containing a long table for staff conferences when weather should preclude holding them outdoors. A silver pitcher stood in the middle of a platter with cups and at Caesar's gesture I poured for us. It was first-rate Falernian. Caesar wasn't denying himself all of the pleasures of life while on active service.

"Word has come to me of your little run-in with Titus Vinius," he said without preamble.

I had been expecting it. "A legion is like a small village. Everyone knows everyone else's business."

"In this Province there is only my business," he said. "You are not to interfere with my centurions in the performance of their duties."

"Duties! Caesar, the brute was flogging a boy, a client of mine, for no reason whatever. I could not permit it."

"That was no boy, nor is he your client. He is a Roman soldier, bound by his oath of service like every other legionary. When he returns to civilian life in some twenty years, he will become your client again. In the meantime, he is under the authority of his centurion, unless he attains the centurionate himself and gets to flog his own subordinates. I'll not have Vinius provoked. He is my most valuable soldier."

"He is an oversensitive man, where his property is concerned."

Caesar smiled faintly. "Ah, you've met our Freda, I take it. A stunning creature, is she not?"

"She is that. Why do you permit him to keep her in camp? He is so jealous he needs his own personal executioner to follow her around and behead gawkers."

"I permit my centurions a certain latitude, including a small number of personal slaves, even mistresses."

"Every general does, but in barracks and winter quarters, not in a marching camp."

"When we march, they walk with the baggage train. If they

can't keep up, they are abandoned. Not that there is much danger of that happening with Freda. I suspect she can outrun a racehorse." He waved a hand to dismiss the subject. "I did not call you here to justify my policies, Decius. I have duties for you. I mentioned when you arrived that you would have more work here in the praetorium than with your *ala*."

"Whatever you command," I said, always alert for a nice, cushy staff job while other people were out slogging through the mud, getting things stuck in them. Heroes belong in poems and old myths, not in the boots of Decius Caecilius Metellus the Younger.

"Soon I will be leaving for Italy by the most direct route, over the mountains. Labienus will be in charge during my absence. My fine, ringing defiance of the barbarians will prove most hollow without the legions to back them up. I am going to find them and drag them up here by the nose if I have to."

"A couple more legions would be a comforting presence," I agreed.

"While I am away, I want you to organize my dispatches to the Senate. I intend to provide a detailed history of the campaign for the Conscript Fathers, as Cicero likes to call them, and you are the only man here with the education to be of assistance. Also, I know that you detest the Asiatic style of rhetoric as much as I do, so you won't be tempted to throw in a lot of nymphs and obscure Paphlagonian deities and salacious affairs of Zeus."

So I was to be a glorified secretary. No argument there. At least I would be under a roof when it rained. "You speak as if it will be a long campaign."

"Why do you think I wanted five years to finish it? The Helvetii were already on the move when I reached Gaul. Now the Germans are involved. Before I am done, I may have to subdue Gaul all the way from the Rhine to the Pyrenees. I may have to go all the way to Britannia."

I almost choked on my Falernian. "That is a large chunk of territory to take on. Not to mention a large population of extremely warlike barbarians."

He shrugged. "Alexander used to take as much territory in a year."

There it was: Alexander again. I wished the little Macedonian bastard was alive so I could kill him all over again. Just one such maniac in all of history and he inspired fools forever after. Well, Macedonia is part of the Roman Empire now, which ought to teach people something.

"Gauls aren't Persians."

"No, and I thank Jupiter for it. I doubt that Persians would ever make good citizens."

It was as if he had abruptly switched to a language with which I was not conversant. "I don't believe I follow you, Caesar."

He fixed me with that intense, lawyer's gaze. "Rome needs new blood, Decius. We are no longer the people we were in the days of Scipio and Fabius. Once, we could raise ten strong legions from the regions within two or three days' march around Rome. Now we have to scour all of Italy to make up three or four good legions. In a generation or two we may not even have that. Where, then, will we find our soldiers? Greece? That is absurd. Syria; Egypt? The idea is laughable."

What he said was not totally unreasonable. "If we could just clear the multitude of foreign slaves out of Italy and put natives back to work on Italian soil, we would not have this problem," I asserted.

He shook his head. "Now you sound like Cato. No man can undo history. We must seize the moment and bend the present to our will. You have served in Spain. What is your impression of the Iberians?"

"Wild and primitive, but they make first-rate soldiers."

"Exactly. And many of them are Gauls of a sort. I think these people of the Gallic heartland can be civilized. If they can be made to give up their seminomadic habits, settle down and stop fighting one another, and acknowledge the mastery of Rome, they could contribute immeasurably to our strength and prosperity."

This was radical thinking. To conquer barbarians was one thing: everyone approved of that. But make *citizens* of them?

"They can't even make good wine, although I admit their racehorses and charioteers are as good as any bred in Rome."

"I knew I could depend on you to have a firm grasp of the essentials."

"But, Caesar, not so long ago we fought a bloody war over the right of *Italian* communities to hold the franchise! Those were our cousins, most of them Latins or at least Oscans who shared most of our customs and traditions. If it took a war to give those people full citizenship, what would it take to convince Romans that Gauls deserve the honor?"

"Good sense, I would hope," he said impatiently. "That, and fear of the Germans." He had a point there. "You know as well as I do that they are not howling savages, they just look and sound like it. They are marvelous artificers and halfway decent farmers. They even have rather attractive architecture, although they don't build in stone. But they are politically primitive, still in the tribal stage, feuding endlessly with one another."

"And they have no writing," I pointed out.

"No, they do not. What they have instead is Druids."

"I fail to make the connection."

"How powerful would a priesthood be if it had a monopoly on literacy, Decius? Think about it. I know that you are not as dense as you pretend."

It was flattery of a sort. "You mean like the Egyptians before they learned Greek writing?"

"Something like that. But imagine a society in which only the priests could read and write while even the nobles and the kings were illiterate. The Druids have a position almost like that."

"Lovernius told me they were repositories of law and tradition as well as intermediaries between the Gauls and their gods."

"Exactly. And as such they are arbiters on all matters of contention between the petty kings and chieftains, not that they stop much of the fighting. They wield great influence where the Gauls must cooperate to deal with a non-Gallic people such as the Germans. Or Rome. There are twenty or more major Gallic nations and a hundred petty chieftains and their tribes, with no unity among them. But there is a single cult of Druids from the Pyrenees to Britannia all the way to Galatia. They are the sole unifying force among the Gauls. If I am to subdue the Gauls, I may first have to break the power of the Druids."

Well, I held no brief for the Druids. Hereditary priests have always struck me as a parasitical lot. Our forefathers showed great foresight in making the priesthoods a part of political office.

"Good riddance to them, then," I said.

Caesar sat and leaned forward. "And, Decius, they are not

just bards and lawgivers. Their religion is a dark and bloody one. Their great festivals involve human sacrifice. In their groves they erect great effigies of men and beasts made of wicker. At important rituals these are filled with men and women and animals and set afire. The screams are said to be appalling."

I felt the thrill of horror that we usually feel when the subject of human sacrifice is mentioned. Of course, the Gauls would have to exert themselves to come up with human sacrifices as horrifying as those of our old, implacable enemies, the Carthaginians. But these wicker immolations would certainly suffice to characterize the Gauls as savages. Our own very rare human sacrifices were always carried out with great dignity and solemnity, and we used only condemned criminals for the purpose.

"Your plans do not lack grandeur," I admitted. "But then, ambitious men predominate in Rome just now, not safe, conservative plodders like my own family."

"Nonetheless, I would welcome the support of the Caecilians." This was the Caesar I knew; the Forum politician who was so adept at building a coalition to back his schemes.

"You are talking to the wrong one. I am by far the least of my family. Nobody listens to me."

He smiled. "Decius, why must you always behave like a dutiful boy? The great men of your family are getting old and soon will step down from public life. By the time you hold the praetorship, you will be high in the family councils. Bonds forged in the field are lasting, Decius."

It was a fine sentiment but not altogether true. Old soldiers cherished a certain good fellowship, but only as long as their ambitions did not clash. Marius and Sulla and Pompey had all been great comrades-in-arms in many campaigns. Until they vied for power, at which time they became deadly enemies.

4

THE NEXT DAY I BEGAN MY TE-
dious work in the praetorium while Lovernius and the rest of
my *ala* conducted their patrols and sweeps and escort duties.
Most of these duties were performed by the regular auxiliary
cavalry, of which we were acquiring a prodigious number. Caesar wanted an immense cavalry force for this campaign and was
most insistent that the province provide every able-bodied man
and beast for this service. We Romans have always been rather
contemptuous of cavalry, but the more horsemen you have, the
more Gauls respect you.

At least my duties kept me safe. As safe as one may be
in a tiny legionary camp in the wilderness surrounded by overwhelming multitudes of howling barbarians. They were not yet
ready to mount a concentrated offensive against us, but that
was only a matter of time. In the meantime, it was certain that

their nocturnal assaults would grow in frequency and boldness. Everyone's principal worry was that they might call upon German reinforcements to help them drive us from their path.

In obedience to Caesar's orders, I had to wear my armor and keep my weapons handy even when engaged on clerkly tasks. To make things worse, he forbade any drinking during the day. I thought this was carrying things a bit far, but I knew better than to protest.

Before settling down to my papyrus, pens, and ink, I found one of the legion's sword instructors and arranged for him to teach Hermes the rudiments. Like most such men he was an ex-gladiator and the fact that he had lived to retire proved his proficiency with weapons. The scar-faced brute immediately set the boy to thrusting at a six-foot stake like any other tyro on his first day in the *ludus*. I knew that within minutes he would feel as if his arm was ready to fall off; but the instructor would not be satisfied until he could keep it up all day, and hit a spot the size of a silver *denarius* every time. He was already starting to sweat when I left for the praetorium.

From all around I heard the bawling of the centurions and their *optios* as they drilled their soldiers. The hammers of the armorers made a continuous din and the hooves of the cavalry clopped on the hardened surfaces of the streets as they rode out to patrol or back in to report. I smiled to hear it all, because I was no part of it. I had a task that would keep me sitting, and it would not be in a saddle.

While Caesar and Labienus conferred with a delegation of semi-Romanized Allobrogians, I sat in a folding chair at a field table and drew my *sagum* close against the chill morning breeze. Clouds blocked what little warmth might have been gleaned from the remote, Gallic sun. Thus wrapped in cold iron and warm wool, I opened the first scroll of Caesar's reports to the Senate.

It contained bald and uncomplicated notes concerning Caesar's doings from the time he left Rome: how he took charge of his legion in Italy and marched north into Gaul, picking up his auxilia along the way. At first I took this to be the sort of preliminary notation any writer may make in preparation for the serious work of writing a history or a speech.

I despaired of the task Caesar had set me. Not only were these mere, skeletal notes, but there was a difficulty I had not foreseen: Caesar's handwriting was astoundingly bad, so that I had to strain my eyes just to make out the letters. To make things worse, his spelling was more than merely atrocious. Among his many eccentricities, he spelled some of the shorter words *backwards* and transposed letters on many of the longer words.

I thought of the times I had seen Caesar at his ease, usually with a slave reading to him from the histories or the classic poems. Of course, most of us employ a reader from time to time, to spare our eyes, but I now realized that I had rarely seen Caesar with his nose buried in a scroll. It was an incredible revelation: Caius Julius Caesar, Proconsul and darling of the Popular Assemblies, would-be Alexander, was nearly illiterate!

I decided that I would first have to copy Caesar's notes verbatim. His literary oddities were so distracting that making any sort of sense of them was a daunting task in itself. I spent most of the morning copying the first scroll into my much more polished hand. When I had it rendered into acceptable form, I went over it again. Then a second time, then a third.

After the third reading I put the scroll down, aware that I

confronted something new in the world of letters. Having copied the notes into readable form, I realized that I could do nothing to improve them. I was, as Caesar had said, no admirer of the ornate, elaborate, Asiatic style, but Caesar's prose made mine seem as mannered as a speech by Quintus Hortensius Hortalus. He never used a single unnecessary word and nowhere could I find a word that could be excised without harming the sense of the whole.

The First Citizen has granted Caesar apotheosis, elevating him (and himself by family connection) to godhead. Caesar was no god, but the gods played some extraordinary tricks with him. How a man who could barely read or write could create the most beautiful, flawless Latin prose ever written is a mystery that plagues me to this day. I had seen some of his juvenilia, and those scribblings were as wretched as the works of most beginners. His mature style might have been the creation of a different man entirely.

I was musing upon these matters when a shadow fell across the table. I looked up and there stood the German slave girl, proud and self-possessed as a princess. I was huddled into my woolen cloak, nearly freezing, yet she stood in her scanty tunic and the cold breeze didn't even raise goosebumps on her bare limbs.

"Ah. Freda, is it not?"

"Freda," she said, correcting my pronunciation. Actually, this simple name sounds almost the same in German as it is written in Latin letters. The first consonant is given a little more voice as it comes out between the upper teeth and the lower lip, and the second has a bit of buzz to it as it is made with the tip of the tongue between the upper and lower front teeth instead of touching the front of the palate.

"For Caesar from Titus Vinius," she said. Her voice was low and husky and aroused uncomfortable sensations.

"You mean for the Proconsul from your master?" I said, pretending to be annoyed by her casual, disrespectful tone. Actually, I just wanted to hear her speak again, barbaric accent and all.

"For His Worship from Himself, if it makes you feel better." She wielded the old-fashioned slave jargon with a sarcasm Hermes would have envied.

"Why does the First Spear send a personal slave to deliver a message? It is customary to use soldiers as runners." It was a stupid question, but I did not want her to go just yet.

"I do not care, and neither do you," she said, radiating equal parts contempt and seductive musk.

"I don't care for your tone, girl."

"So? You are just another Roman. If you want to punish me, you will have to buy me from Titus Vinius. I doubt that you have the money."

"I have never heard such insolence!" What a liar I was in those days.

"Decius Caecilius," said Caesar from behind me, "if you will let Freda complete her errand, she can go to pursue her duties and we can continue with ours."

Embarrassments always seem to come in batches. She walked past me so close that I could tell she wore no artificial scent. No mare in heat ever smelled better to a stallion. I did not turn around as she handed her message to Caesar, and she did not glance at me as she walked away. She was as beautiful from behind as she was from in front, especially in motion.

Caesar walked over to me and looked down. "I never knew a man could look so much like a statue of Priapus while sitting down. Right through armor and a heavy cloak, too."

"If Titus Vinius is such a jealous man," I said, "why does he allow her to parade all over the camp half-naked?"

"It is customary to display extraordinary possessions, Decius. If you own a splendid work of art, you place it where people can admire it and envy you its possession. Many men enjoy being envied." He turned and walked back into his tent.

"Freda," I said to myself, practicing the sounds. I learned later that the name comes from their word for "peace"; an oddity considering how little interest the Germans have in the subject. It must result from their custom of sealing an alliance between tribes by marrying the women of one tribe to the warriors of the other.

With an effort, I forced myself back to the task of making Caesar's scrolls readable.

That evening Hermes was of very little use to me. Both his arms hung limply at his sides and his face was a mask of pain. I could sympathize, almost. My father had sent me to the *ludus* when I was sixteen to learn swordwork and that first day was among the most memorably painful of my life. Of course, I gave him no hint of any such tender feelings.

"I have officer of the guard duty tonight," I informed him. "That means that I will not be sleeping. Neither will you. Because of my duty I can't touch wine. Neither shall you. Do you understand?"

"You must be joking," he groaned. "I couldn't lift a cup if I was dying of thirst in Libya."

"Excellent. I want a lamp lit inside the tent and one before the tent all night long. Surely that is not beyond your capacities?"

"As long as they're small lamps," he said.

Not being utterly heartless, I rubbed his shoulders with liniment before I left for guard mount. After all, his torment would start all over again the next morning.

Officer of the guard was a duty traditionally delegated to the cavalry, I suppose because infantry officers were more important and needed their sleep. It was a duty I always hated, but not only because it meant that I went without sleep. I was always afraid that I would come upon a man who had fallen asleep at his post. Then I would have to report him. Even in peacetime in the middle of Italy the punishment for that infraction was brutal. In the presence of the enemy, it was worse than brutal. Before the whole legion, the men of his own section beat him to death with rods, a process that could take a long time even when the sticks were wielded by strong men.

As with so many other virtues, I failed to match our ancestors in the hardheartedness so highly esteemed in military men. Our old tales are full of commanders who condemned their own sons to death for disobeying orders, even when the disobedience brought victory. This was supposed to prove something about Roman justice and martial sternness. It never proved anything to me except that Roman fathers are a bad lot.

I mounted the wall surrounding the legionary camp at the main gate and began to walk the circuit, making more noise than absolutely necessary. To my relief, the increased guard Caesar had ordered meant that the sentries stood in pairs. That way they could help keep each other awake. There were watchfires inside the camp, but none along the rampart, lest the night vision of the guards be ruined.

As I made my way west along the southern wall, then north along the eastern wall, I found the men commendably alert, whipping around with leveled weapons the instant they heard me, giving the challenge and not lowering their points until I replied with the watchword. Everyone knew that negotiations with the Helvetii had broken off and the barbarians could be upon us at any moment.

When I got to the northern wall, I found the guards even more nervous. They were closest to the Gauls.

"You'll have plenty of warning before they come," I said to the first set of sentries I encountered on that wall. "There's still the great rampart between the camp and the enemy."

One of the soldiers spat eloquently. "Maybe. But it's just manned by auxilia. Those buggers are worthless!"

"Most of 'em would as soon kill us as the barbarians. Not a citizen in the lot. And the cavalry are all Gauls themselves. How can we trust that pack of savages?"

I knew better than to argue with prejudice like that.

"What cohort is this?" I asked.

"First," said one of them. "The First Cohort always has the honor of guarding the wall nearest the enemy, and the right end of the battle line."

Being on the right end presented their unshielded sides to a flanking movement by the enemy. Naturally, the last place any sane man would want to be on a battlefield is considered the post of honor. Not that any sane man would want to be on a battlefield at all. It is by means of these spurious distinctions that men are duped into behavior contrary to their best interests.

"Any activity from the barbarians?" I asked.

"Not a sound yet, sir. But they're out there, you can be sure of that. We'll be dodging arrows and javelins and stones before long. That rampart's too thinly guarded, even if the auxilia were good for anything. The savages can make it across by ones and twos. Can't do any real damage that way, but they can harass us."

"Keeps us on our toes," said the other phlegmatically.

About the middle of the north wall I found a pair of sentries muttering in low-voiced conversation.

"You'll never hear the barbarians coming if you keep that up," I said when I was ten feet away. They turned around rather stiffly and raised their weapons.

"Watchword!" one of them challenged, barely above a whisper.

"Hercules unconquered," I replied as quietly. No sense making the enemy a gift of the watchword.

"Patron!" said the challenger. "I didn't know you had officer of the guard tonight."

"Burrus? Is this the First Century's section?"

"It is tonight. Each man is supposed to pull sentry duty every third night. Nobody will get much sleep now that the guard's doubled." He jerked his head toward the other man. A *pilum* in one hand and a massive *scutum* on the other arm limit the possibilities for gesticulation. "This is Marcus Quadratus. He's in my *contubernium*."

The other man's helmet bobbed. "Good evening, Senator. Burrus never tires of telling us that his family are clients of the Metelli."

"Arpinum?" I hazarded, guessing at his accent.

He grinned. "That's right. Home town of Cicero and Caius Marius."

"What was it Homer said of Ithaca?" I mused. " 'A small place, but a good breeder of men.' " The man moved as stiffly as Burrus and I presumed it was for the same reason. "You seem to have received the personal attention of your centurion just like Burrus."

Quadratus glanced sidelong at Burrus, who nodded.

"He's broken three vinestaffs over my back in the last five days. His *optio*'s taken to carrying a bundle of them under his arm and passing him a new one when he breaks one over somebody."

"Is the whole century getting this treatment?" I asked. Even for a senior centurion this was extreme behavior.

"He's rough on everybody," Burrus said, "but it's just our *contubernium* that's singled out for special punishment."

"But why? Is it always the woman? Is your tent closest to his, giving you more opportunity to appreciate her?"

Quadratus managed a rueful smile. "No, she's just an excuse. He'll find a speck of rust on our mail at morning inspection, or somebody's marching out of step. The woman's the best reason to get flogged, though. At least then you're getting something for the punishment you absorb."

"Why does he have it in for your *contubernium?*"

"Don't think we haven't asked ourselves, sir," Burrus said. "Some think he's just insane, but I think he's using us to make a point and cement his control of the Tenth."

"How is that?" I asked, mystified as always by legion politics, which can be every bit as complicated and cutthroat as the Forum kind. Burrus enlightened me.

"He's only been *primus pilus* since Caesar took over a little more than a month ago. That was when Caius Facilis, the old First Spear, retired. It always takes a while for the men to accept a new man as the one with the power of life and death. I think he's trying to drive us to mutiny."

"Executing a whole *contubernium* would drive the point home pretty thoroughly," Quadratus said. "I don't think anyone would question his authority after that."

I had heard horror stories like this before, but it was disquieting to run across an example firsthand, if they were correct. The oddest thing was that they did not act as if this were anything especially atrocious: just one of the many hazards of soldiering, like wounds and inclement weather and being captured by barbarians for torture and human sacrifice.

"It's happened before," Burrus said, reading my thoughts. "But never in the Tenth."

"Has Vinius always been here in the Tenth?" I asked. Some men spent their whole careers in a single legion, but senior officers were sometimes transferred.

"No," Burrus said. "He was with Caesar in Spain a few years ago, one of the first order centurions in the Seventh." This meant he had been one of the centurions of the First, Second, and Third cohorts, who were senior to the other centurions of the legion. At least, this was how it was back then. I understand things have changed since the First Citizen's military reforms. I hope the changes have been for the better, but I doubt it.

"Why did Caesar want him in particular?"

"You don't make the first order without being good at your job," Quadratus opined. "He's a good soldier, at least on the march and in camp. We haven't seen him in battle yet."

"And," Burrus added, "he has a set of *phalerae* that he wears for ceremonial parades. They don't award those for good behavior."

Phalerae are massive, circular medallions worn mounted on a strap harness and worn over the armor. They are decorations awarded for extraordinary valor, so awe-inspiring that men who won them actually wore them into battle, although they were nothing but an encumbrance and extra weight.

Something whizzed past my head and I brushed at my ear, thinking it was some night-flying insect. Both sentries swung around to face the outer darkness and raised their shields to just below eye level. They did this so perfunctorily, seeming bored by yet another military chore, that at first its significance escaped me.

"That was an arrow, Patron," Burrus informed me. "You'd best duck below the palisade or get behind us, seeing as you're not carrying a shield." Even as he said it I heard an arrow *thunk* solidly into the chest-high wood of the palisade. From the gloom outside the camp came the sound of Gauls hooting and shouting.

I edged behind them. "I'm going to have a few words with Carbo," I said. "He was supposed to stop this sort of thing." I was appalled at how badly my military instincts had eroded. In a Roman alley I could sense danger coming from any direction. Here, it seemed I was as helpless as a tribune on his first day of service.

"Not much chance of that," Quadratus said. "These Gauls get around in the dark like bats." A slingstone smacked off the hide-sheathed wood of his shield with a crack that rang in my ears.

"Shouldn't we raise the alarm?" I asked, embarrassed that I, an officer, had to solicit advice from a couple of common legionaries.

"It will have to get a lot worse than this," Burrus told me. "We don't wake the whole camp for a few arrows and stones.

The barbarians aren't even very close, or we'd have been catching javelins by now."

"It's what the Gauls want, you see," Quadratus added. "It's to keep us on edge and wakeful. The less sleep we get, the worse shape we'll be in on the day we fight them in force, in the open." Another stone clanged loudly off the bronze-sheathed rim of his shield. He felt for damage. "Damn! Put a dent in it. No, Captain, we only raise the alarm if they make an assault on the camp, and they can't get past the rampart in big enough numbers for that, so it's just this petty harassment every night."

"At least it's every third night for you two," I said.

"Don't we wish," Burrus said. "Vinius said he found leather mold on our tent this morning. We stand sentry every night until he tells us otherwise."

"After a full duty day?" A stone hurtled over my head, making a sound like a large bee hurrying to a distant flower. "I'll speak to Caesar about this."

"Don't bother," Burrus advised. "He'll just back his First Spear and you'll only annoy both of them."

"He's right, sir," Quadratus affirmed. "Vinius can deal with just about any staff officer he doesn't like. You'd best stay out of it."

"We'll see. I have to finish my rounds. I'll see you men again before daylight."

"Bring your shield next time, Patron," Burrus said, chuckling. How a man in his position could see humor in anything was mystifying, but I was impressed enough to overlook his little insolence.

An officer is never supposed to show fear before the ranks,

so I waited until I was out of their sight before I ducked under the protection of the palisade and made my way to the next sentry post in a ludicrous, bent-kneed crouch. I straightened again only when I came in sight of the next pair and resumed my fearless swagger.

All along the north wall the sentries were answering the Gauls' windy war cries and challenges with the many rude noises of which Italians are the world's masters. Darkness and their equipment deprived them of the eloquent gestures that everyone born south of the Po considers to be a part of the national arsenal.

It was with great relief that I concluded my inspection of the north wall and worked my way down the west wall, where enemy action was far less intense, and then to the south wall where all was quiet once more. At the main gate I descended into the camp and walked up the Via Praetoria to its intersection with the Via Principalis where the main watchfire burned. It was there that the guard relief gathered and there that I found a slave tending the water clock that timed the reliefs.

"How long until the next relief?" I asked the slave, a gray-haired man whose long service with the legion had earned him this cushy if somewhat sleep-deprived duty.

"Two hours, sir. They stand four on, four off in this legion. First night watch goes on an hour before sunset, the last is relieved an hour after sunrise."

I looked at the water clock. It was a clever Greek contraption like an ornate bronze bucket filled with water. There was a hollow float in the water, which drained out through a small tube in the bottom. As it descended, the float tripped a lever at hourly intervals, and each time the lever would drop a bronze ball into a shallow dish of the same metal, producing a loud *clang*. I had seen the gigantic one in Alexandria, which produces a noise so loud you can hear it all over the city. I could never figure out why, since Alexandrians never pay any attention to what time it is.

"What do you do in winter, when it freezes?" I asked.

"Move it closer to the watchfire, so it doesn't freeze. If the wind's blowing hard and it freezes anyway, you watch the stars. If it's cloudy, you just guess."

"That must make for some hard feelings," I mused. "Every man is sure to think he stood a longer watch than the other reliefs."

The slave nodded. "Winter's a bad time this far north, that's for sure."

I went to my tent, where I found Hermes dutifully tending the lamps. He handed me a flask. His arms and shoulders seemed to be recovering, since he could raise the flask waist-high. Its warmth felt good to my chilled hands.

"It's that awful vinegar stuff the soldiers drink," he said apologetically, "but it'll sure wake you up." I took a drink and he was courteous enough to wait for my eyes to stop watering before he asked me the inevitable question: "Are those bar-barians making all that noise outside?" My tent was close enough to the north wall to hear them clearly.

"It certainly isn't reinforcements from Rome. But don't worry, they're just entertaining us tonight."

"If it's all the same to you, I'll worry anyway." Then he lowered his voice, although he was already speaking in low tones for Hermes. "We're really in the middle of it, aren't we? I've heard the soldiers talking and they say we're unsupported in the middle of barbarian territory and it's only a matter of time before about a million of them come down on us all at once."

My face must have been as sour as the posca as I nodded. "It's true, and that's not the worst of it. I think there's a man in the camp as dangerous to us as anything outside."

"How do you always find people like that?" Hermes asked.

"The gods are not without a sense of humor. This is their little joke on me."

"Then they're laughing hard up on Olympus tonight," He said. "They've matched you up with the meanest crucifier in the legion."

To a slave, "crucifier" is the most powerful epithet of fear and opprobrium. Hermes also had the slave's facility for keeping his ears open while the free men all around ignored him and talked as if he wasn't there. My peers often upbraided me for listening to slave talk, but it saved my life a good many times.

"More soldier gossip?"

"It's all over the camp. Next to the barbarians, the First Spear and his German woman are the favorite subjects around here. Everyone's talking about how Vinius and the new officer are going at it shield to shield."

"Poor Caesar," I said. "He's used to everyone talking about him. Are bets being laid?"

He shook his head. "No. Everyone says you'll be squashed like a bug."

I took another drink of Posca and choked it down. "It's going to get worse very quickly. I want you to ask around tomorrow, see if you can get odds on me to win."

He looked at me pityingly. "You don't expect me to bet any of my money, do you?"

"You're a slave. You're not supposed to own money. Have you been stealing from me again?" By law, slaves are not supposed to own property, but the gulf between law and reality is as wide as that between Hades and Olympus. Actually, Hermes rarely stole from me, but it did him good to know he was under suspicion at all times.

He dodged the question. "Are the odds about to go up even higher?"

"Yes, they are. I am about to make Titus Vinius even angrier at me. With luck, he may drop dead from pure rage."

5

I ARRIVED AT THE WATCHFIRE
just as the bronze ball clanged into the dish. The watch relief
stood in two orderly lines. At their head was a man whose
helmet was tinned so that it shone silver instead of bronze, and
it sported a crest of white horsehair. His eyes widened a bit
when he saw me, then widened a bit further when he saw that
I was not alone. He saluted with a professional's easy disdain.

"Aulus Vehilius," he said, introducing himself, "*optio* of
the First Cohort and tonight's relief commander." So this was
Vinius's right-hand man, the one who carried his spare vinestaffs.

"Decius Caecilius Metellus, Captain of the praetorian *ala*
and officer of the watch."

"Who are these?" Vehilius said, nodding his crest toward
the men standing behind me.

"My troop of the praetorian *ala*."

"Auxilia have no place on the camp wall. That's for legionaries only."

"Consider them my personal bodyguard. I fear assassination by political rivals."

He looked at me as if I were insane, an entirely understandable attitude on his part, then snapped: "We are wasting time. Guard Relief, march!" He spun on his hobnailed heel and strode off. The relief stepped out smartly, with a fine, martial clatter. I saw that some of them were grinning at the *optio*'s discomfiture.

I walked up alongside Vehilius, who sternly ignored me. Behind me, Lovernius and the others ambled along in far less formal order. After all, not only were they Gauls, they were cavalrymen, and could not have marched in step to save themselves from crucifixion.

At the top of the wall, starting from the Porta Praetoria, Vehilius began relieving the sentries. As we reached each sentry post the challenge was given and the watchword rendered, then the *optio* received the report of the senior man, after which the two men at the front of our line took the places of the two on watch. The relieved men then fell in at the rear of the line.

So it proceeded until we reached the north wall. The noise and missile-hurling had stopped, to my great satisfaction. I decided the Gauls must be getting tired, too. Besides, they had to be well away before daylight when we would be after them again with the cavalry.

When we reached the post where Burrus and Quadratus stood, we went through the usual challenge-and-watchword business and Quadratus reported on the night's activities. Then Vehilius ordered the column to march on.

"A moment, *Optio!*" I said.

He paused. "Yes, Captain?"

"Aren't we going to relieve these men?" I demanded.

"No, we are not. These two, and the men of the next three posts, belong to the sixth *contubernium* of the First Century, First Cohort. They are to stand watch all night as punishment."

"I see. I presume that is for this night alone?"

"They stand all-night watches until the First Spear instructs otherwise."

"And does that not endanger the security of the whole camp?"

"That is not for me to judge. And now, Captain, if it is all right with you, and even if it buggering well isn't, I am going to continue with my duties."

"Don't let me keep you, *Optio.* Good evening to you."

Stiff as a spearshaft, he whirled and clumped off, followed by soldiers whose broad grins vanished when he turned to glare at them.

When he was gone, Lovernius made a very Gallic gesture. "Captain, I have always heard how adept you Roman politicians are at making friends. Could I have been misinformed?"

"There is going to be great trouble over this!" said Indiumix delightedly. Gauls just love trouble.

"Patron, what are you up to?" Burrus asked.

"Burrus, Quadratus, you are relieved. These two men," I pointed at two of my Gauls, "will take your place. Stay here on the wall, but I want you to get some sleep."

"But they aren't legionaries!" Quadratus protested.

"I take the responsibility upon my own head," I assured them. "I am officer of the watch, and I am ordering you two to get some sleep. You'd better do it now, because I won't have this duty for another three or four nights."

Soldiers have a remarkable ability to sleep anywhere, under any circumstances. They laid their shields carefully atop the earthen wall, then lay down and pillowed their heads on them. In full armor, belted with sword and dagger and cuddling their spears, they were out like a pair of extinguished lamps.

We proceeded to the next three sentry posts and relieved the remaining six men of the *contubernium* in the same unorthodox fashion. Then Lovernius and I leaned against the palisade and contemplated the now quiet night. Springtime insects were making noise out there, and an occasional owl hooted.

"Five sesterces says he'll come after me before sunrise," I hazarded.

"Ten says he'll wait and denounce you in front of Caesar and the whole staff in the morning."

"Done." We clasped hands on it and Lovernius smiled, shaking his head admiringly. Gauls have an entirely inexplicable admiration for reckless, suicidal fools. As it turned out, he won the ten sesterces.

The sun rose in good time, warming our chilled bodies and raising a picturesque ground fog from the lake, so that for a few minutes the camp seemed like a great ship afloat on a sea of wool. I wondered whether this was how Jupiter felt, seated among the clouds. The air held the inevitable smells of a legionary camp; the odors of fresh-turned earth and woodsmoke. These are agreeable smells, quite unlike the many stenches of the city. At that moment, though, I would gladly have exchanged it all for an ugly, smelly town.

The men of the unfortunate *contubernium* rose and resumed their places at the wall. My own men stood down and came to gather by me.

"Go on back to your tents," I told them. "You've done your duty for the night."

"But we'd rather stay and see what happens next," Lovernius protested.

"I know you would, but it's almost time for the morning patrol. There are probably Helvetii hiding out there in that fog. Go get them. They were very annoying last night." They smiled, saluted, and walked off. Whatever was coming, it was none of their doing and I wanted them out of it.

The sun was almost above the mountain crest to the east when the new guard relief arrived. It was in the care of a different *optio* this time; a man with a thoroughly broken nose and an engaging, lopsided grin who threw me a salute that was sloppy enough to look respectful, coming from a professional. The cheekplates of his bronze helmet were decorated with stylized little shrines made of sheet silver; a design intended to bring good luck. From the knob on the helmet's top sprang a tuft of short, blue feathers.

"You're relieved, Captain," he said as two of the men he brought took the place of Burrus and Quadratus.

"Any special orders for me?" I asked him.

"None that I was given to relay, though if I were you I'd be planning what I'd say to Caesar."

I fell in beside him as he proceeded on his rounds. "I've been thinking of little else for the last four hours."

"Any good ideas?"

"None yet. Any suggestions?"

"Run. The Gauls might take you in. But then, they might just trade you back. The Germans might be a better idea. If they don't kill you on sight they'll probably protect you. Their laws of hospitality are very strict."

"I don't suppose Caesar would just send me back to Rome in disgrace?"

"Hah! If he did that, half his staff officers would pull the sort of idiotic stunts you've been entertaining us with, just to get out of the coming war. I've never seen such a spineless pack of bluebloods." He spat over the palisade, in which were stuck several arrows.

"What do the blue feathers mean?" I asked him. "Second Cohort?"

"Correct. I am Helvius Blasio, *optio* of the Fourth Century of the Second. I already know who you are."

"Word does get around, doesn't it?"

"Decidedly. Everyone knows everyone else's business in a legionary camp. Doubly so when it involves someone flouting the First Spear's authority. Such persons attract great attention and admiration. For a very brief time, anyway."

I accompanied him as he finished his rounds, being in no rush to meet my fate. We discussed the enemy and the upcoming campaign. Blasio maintained his professional's nonchalance, but I sensed his unease. The whole camp vibrated with the tension of a legion deep in enemy territory and about to plunge into action.

I took my leave of Blasio and got myself shaved and barbered, then I went to my tent. Hermes had my breakfast already laid out.

"One of your Gauls told me you're in trouble," he said cheerfully.

"That is correct. Now run along and report to your sword instructor."

He groaned. "I thought it was the one on the receiving end of the sword who was supposed to hurt!"

"Every accomplishment comes at a price. Off with you, now." Grumbling, he did as he was told.

All too soon, I heard a *tuba* sounding the officer's call. I was abominably weary, but there was to be no rest for me. With my helmet beneath my arm I strode smartly toward the praetorium. One advantage of belonging to a family like mine is that one is given a very thorough schooling in all the rhetorical arts. These include not only the art of public speaking but also of presenting oneself, both standing and in motion. Since a man bent upon high office must serve with the legions, he is taught how to show himself before the troops. There is a genuine art to getting the rough military cloak to flutter behind you as you walk, and draping it casually over the slightly raised arm when you halt so that it bestows the dignity of a toga.

Vinius might be able to outshout me, but he could never match me for poise and sheer, aristocratic style. And I was certain that I would have to carry this off on style alone, since I had nothing else at my disposal.

The faces gathered around the staff table wore a wide variety of expressions, from the carefully noncommittal to the violently hostile. The only smile present was my own, and that was as false as a whore's. Caesar looked as grim as death, but maybe, I thought, he was just thinking about all those Gauls.

"Decius Caecilius Metellus," he said, destroying another of my fond delusions, "the First Spear has leveled some extremely serious accusations at you. You must answer them."

"Accusations?" I said. "Am I supposed to have misbehaved?"

"You would do well to acknowledge the gravity of your situation," Caesar said. "Foolishness that can be overlooked in peacetime, in Rome, is not to be tolerated in a legionary camp at war."

"Ah, yes, foolishness," I remarked, my eyes not on Caesar

but on Vinius. "I think forcing sentries to go night after night without sleep in the presence of the enemy is foolishness of the most dangerous sort."

"Proconsul," Vinius said, keeping a tight rein on his voice, "this officer has interfered with my sentry postings. Since his arrival here, he has sought to coddle his precious client who happens to be a member of my century. Last night that man and the rest of his *contubernium* slept on guard duty. I want them executed."

There was a collective indrawing of breath.

"Those men slept at my command. Their guard posts were not deserted. I manned them with troopers from my own *ala.*"

"He let *Gauls* guard a legionary encampment!" Vinius said witheringly. "It's worse than treason!"

"The offense is grave," Caesar said. "Even so, capital punishment at this point would be excessive. The men were acting on instructions from a superior, however idiotic those instructions may have been. We must, after all, consider their source. No, the fault lies not with the legionaries but with this officer."

Vinius stood there fuming. Nothing looks sadder than a man cheated of a few executions.

"I believe that I acted with perfect . . ."

"Silence," Caesar said, without special emphasis. I shut up. Caesar had that admirable ability to make a common spoken word sound like thunder from Jupiter.

"Decius Caecilius, what am I to do with you? I could pack you off to Rome in disgrace, but that is what I suspect you most dearly wish. I could reduce you in rank, but you are already about as low as a man can get and still be an officer in this army. I could make you a common soldier, but you are a Senator and I would not offend the Senate by making a member of that august body serve as a foot-slogger." This may have been the very last time Caius Julius Caesar ever worried about offending the Senate.

"There is always beheading, Caesar," Labienus murmured. "It is a gentlemanly punishment, worthy of a lordly Caecilian."

Caesar stroked his chin as if he were giving the suggestion serious consideration. "There is his family to consider. The beginning of a war might be a bad time to alienate the most powerful voting bloc in the Senate and the Assemblies."

"Oh, we won't miss him," my cousin Lumpy assured Caesar. "We have plenty more where he came from." Some men will stoop to anything to get out of paying off a hundred sesterces.

"The idea is tempting," Caesar said, "but an execution before hostilities have properly commenced might be viewed as severe. No, I shall have to devise something else. No matter, I'll think of something. First Spear, rest assured that this officer will never again interfere with your men or with your performance of your duties."

Vinius was far from satisfied, but he knew better than to argue. Even a First Spear could not demand the execution of a superior officer.

"As the Proconsul wishes," he said, not quite churlishly.

Thus far I seemed to be getting away with my pose of aristocratic disdain, but I was far from easy about it. This chit-chat about execution was almost certainly just scare talk, but I could not be perfectly certain. A military commander is permitted tremendous leeway in the measures he deems appropriate to secure order and discipline within their forces. He could be hauled into court when he returned home and laid down his *imperium*, but juries in such cases usually sided with the commander. All citizens understand that the security of the State and the Empire depend utterly upon the discipline of our soldiers, a discipline that is unique in all the world.

Lucullus had declined to execute Clodius (still called Caludius back then) when he had every right to. Clodius had incited officers and men of Lucullus's army to mutiny against their commander. But he had not wished to offend the powerful Claudian clan, and Clodius hadn't accomplished much, anyway. Other commanders were less tolerant.

Caesar ignored me for the rest of the staff conference, during which he sorted through the mundanities and complexities of the army's situation with great efficiency, dispensing duties and special assignments in a crisp, clear tone that left no questions as to exactly what was expected. Once again I was impressed. I later learned that it was Caesar's opinion that more military disasters had occurred because of unclearly worded orders than from all other causes combined.

Once his duty was assigned, each man saluted and left to carry out his orders. Last to go was Titus Vinius. He was glaring pointedly at me and Caesar was not unaware of the fact.

"That will be all, First Spear," Caesar said. "You have leave."

Vinius almost said something, thought better of it, saluted and left, trailing a miasma of hatred so palpable you couldn't have heaved a spear through it.

"Well, Decius Caecilius, what am I to do with you?" Caesar said when Vinius was gone. It was a good question. The duties of tribunes and staff officers are seldom clearly defined. Everyone knows what a legionary is supposed to do, likewise with *optios* and centurions. A general and his *legatus* have a clear commission from the Senate and People. The rest of the officers are pretty much the general's to dispose of in whatever fashion pleases him. Sometimes, a general will think a tribune capable enough to be given command of a legion. More often, a tribune is expected to keep out of the way.

"Am I to take it that I have already forfeited my cavalry command?"

"You could forfeit much more than that. Do not provoke me, Decius. I am not favorably inclined toward you just now. I requested your presence here as a personal favor. I know that I had at the time what seemed like a good reason for wanting you with me on this campaign, but I confess that the reason escapes my memory."

He pondered for a while and I sweated. I was sure that there had to be some loathsome duty he could put me to. There always is, in an army.

"It is clear that you have too much time on your hands, Decius. You need something to keep you busy and at the same time remind you of the discipline required of a soldier's life. From now on, you are to report to an arms instructor at first light every morning and you are to exercise at arms, interrupting only for officer's calls, where you are to stand in the back and say nothing. At noon, you are to return to your clerical duties here. At night . . . well, I shall find something for you to do at night—something that does not involve the sentries."

So I was in for humiliation. It could have been worse.

"It may seem to you that I am showing unwarranted leniency with you. It is only because I, too, consider Vinius's treatment of that *contubernium* to be unwise. However, he knows the men and he knows the legion and you do not. If he wishes to make an example of them, that is not unreasonable, at the beginning of a campaign. That way, the other men will know exactly what to expect. However, I voiced no such doubts to Vinius, and if his general deems it unnecessary to reprimand a centurion for measures he employs to discipline his men, it is certainly not the job of a newly arrived officer of cavalry to countermand his instructions. I am not accustomed to explaining myself to subordinates, Decius. I trust you appreciate this extraordinary privilege."

"Certainly, Caesar!" I said fervently.

"I do this only because I know you are an intelligent man, despite your many deceptively stupid actions. As to your *ala*, I will leave you in that position, but you are to ride with them only for parade until I instruct otherwise. A combat command is entirely too dignified and serious for you at the moment, and Lovernius is perfectly capable of handling them in the meantime. That will be all, Decius. Report to the arms instructor. One of the legionary trainers, not just a sword instructor. I want you to regain your feel for the *pilum* and the *scutum*."

I winced, knowing what I was in for. "As you command." I saluted, whirled on my heel, and marched away. I was quite unsatisfied, but that was no concern of his. I wanted to talk to him about Vinius's actions and my reservations about the man himself, but Caesar was clearly not interested. It struck me that Vinius had distracted attention from his questionable behavior by making this a personal clash of wills between him and myself. I knew then that I had made a far more dangerous enemy than I had supposed. I had thought that I was past underestimating men because of their low breeding and boorish attitudes, but I have frequently been wrong about myself.

Hermes was surprised to see me show up at the training compound between the legionary camp and that of the auxilia.

He was even more surprised when I submitted myself for arms training. The young recruits paused to gape at the unexpected sight until their instructors barked at them to resume their monotonous exercises. The repetitious *clunk* of practice swords against shields resumed.

"You've done this before, Captain," the spear instructor said, "so you know the drill. You can warm up for a while with the javelins, then you start in with the *pilum*. The shields are over there."

My shoulder twinged with anticipation, knowing what was to come. Javelin throwing is an agreeable enough sport, one at which I excelled. Of course, there is a major difference between tossing the things out on the Campus Martius, without a shield and dressed in a tunic, and going through the same exercise wearing armor with a legionary's *scutum* on your left arm.

The *scutum* is nothing like the light, flat, narrow cavalry shield, which is called a *clipeus*. The *scutum* covers a man from chin to ankles and is as thick as a man's palm. It is oval in shape, made of three layers of thin wood, steamed and glued so that it curves around the body, giving protection to the sides and improving the balance. It is backed with thick felt and surfaced with bullhide, and completely rimmed with bronze. The long, spindle-shaped boss makes a spine down the center, its widened middle section hollowed out to accommodate the hand. The boss is sheathed with bronze: this tremendous contraption has to be managed with a single, horizontal hand-grip in its center, behind the boss.

In truth, the *scutum* is not so much a shield as a portable wall, turning a line of legionaries into an advancing fortress. In the famous "tortoise" formation a unit of cohort size can advance with *scuta* overlapped in front, back, sides, and overhead like roof tiles, invulnerable to anything smaller than a boulder hurled by a catapult.

In ordinary use, the *scutum* doesn't have to be maneuvered much, because it leaves so little uncovered to begin with. In a stand-up, toe-to-toe fight, it need only be raised a few inches from time to time to ward off a thrust to the face. But when hurling the javelin, it has to be raised high for balance, placing great stress on the left wrist and shoulder. That will only happen a few times in the course of a battle, but in practice it just goes on over and over—and so it was that morning.

Javelins are about four feet long, lightweight weapons to soften up the enemy before the battle lines clash. The *pilum* is another matter entirely. It is man-height, made of ash or other dense wood, and as thick as your wrist up to the balance point, where it flares to form an area as long and as thick as a forearm. The rest of its length is an iron shank terminating in a small, barbed head. Compared to a javelin, it has all the flight characteristics of a pointed log.

Military tinkerers are always coming up with ways to improve the *pilum*, the idea being to make it difficult for an enemy to throw it back at you, always a hazard with missile weapons. Marius slotted the iron head into the wooden shaft, fixing it with one rivet made of iron and another made of wood. The idea was that, upon impact, the wooden peg would break and the shank would then rotate on the iron one, rendering it useless for throwing. Caesar's innovation was to temper only the point, allowing the relatively soft shank portion to bend. This must have made him popular with the armorers, who had to straighten them out after the battle.

Of course, the *pila* employed for training were of a more

permanent nature. The target was a man-sized straw bale fifty feet away. The *pilum* is never thrown farther than that. This is primarily because there is hardly a man alive who *can* throw one farther than that. Most centurions instruct their men to get within ten feet before hurling the *pilum*. That way you can scarcely miss and the effect is devastating.

The purpose of the *pilum* is not so much to kill the enemy as it is to deprive him of his shield. With the massive thing firmly lodged in the shield and bent past further use, the warrior can only abandon the shield or else employ it very inefficiently. The commonly taught technique is to nail the enemy's shield with the *pilum*, draw your gladius, step in, give the shaft of the *pilum* a kick to uncover the unfortunate wretch, and stab him. Most barbarians are too lazy to pack around heavy shields of the Roman type, so as often as not the *pilum* goes right on through the flimsy shield and impales the man behind it. Then there is nothing left to do except to find another barbarian to stab. Sometimes barbarians try to endure the first storm of missiles by huddling behind overlapped shields, only to find all their shields nailed together by *pila* so that all have to be abandoned, leaving them defenseless.

In short, although the sword gets all the glory, the *pilum* is our battle-winner.

The drill with the *pilum* was always the same: step out, raise the spear over the shoulder, then, at the proper range, take one very long step. Back goes the *pilum*, up comes the *scutum*, and heave. To get the massive spear fifty feet you have to use your whole body and you feel the strain from your right wrist to your left ankle. And in training, this goes on hour after hour. The instructor encourages you with his wittiest line of patter.

"Not very good, sir, but at least you won't have to walk so far to fetch it, will you?" Or: "I think you scared him that time, sir, but I hear the Germans don't scare so easy, so you'll have to do better than that." Or: "Not quite like making speeches in the Forum, is it, Captain? See if you can do it without nailing your own foot next time." Or: "What did you do in your last legion, sir? Did you have your slave heave your toothpick for you?" At least he was ruder to the recruits.

Just when I was about to welcome death from exhaustion, it was time for sword drill.

"There's your enemy, sir," the ex-gladiator said, pointing to the straw-wrapped post in front of me. "Now kill him! You've trained in the *ludus*, unlike young Hermes here, so you should be able to dispatch this barbarian without fuss. Here, just to make it easier for you, I'll give you an aiming mark." He took a piece of charcoal and drew a circle as big around as the tip of my little finger at throat level. "There. Can't miss that, can you? Now, to the throat, *thrust!*" The last word snapped out like the bow of a *ballista*, powered by twisted rope, launching an iron bolt.

If I hadn't already destroyed my arm and shoulder hurling the *pilum*, I probably could have managed it. As it was, I could hardly raise my sword high enough to make the thrust. My point lazed upward along a wobbly course like a very sick fly, eventually striking the stake about five inches to one side and six inches below the mark.

The swordmaster cupped his chin and clucked, to the vast amusement of an assortment of idle bystanders, of whom there were far too many for a well-run army encampment.

"Sir, I think I detect a certain basic flaw in your technique. Shall I tell you about it? Yes? Well, for starters, it's best if you thrust quickly. Once your swordarm is out in front of your shield, it is completely unprotected. This is why we gladiators wear the *manica* when we fight in the Games." He referred to the heavy wrapping of leather and bronze gladiators wear to protect the unshielded arm. "Your point should go out, strike, and be back behind your shield before your enemy sees anything coming.

"But that is not what you just did. Between the time you launched your thrust and the time that your point missed its target, not only did your barbarian have ample leisure to hack your arm off, but several of his friends sauntered over to have a go at you as well. Now, let's try that again, and this time, try not to disgrace yourself utterly, eh?"

I was, if I may boast, a good swordsman. But I was out of practice and dreadfully fatigued from the *pilum* drill and I had had no sleep the previous night. All this combined to make me look worse than the rawest recruit. Recall that I was doing all this in full legionary gear: helmet, mail shirt, *scutum*, bronze-plated weapon belts, and so forth, with a combined weight in excess of fifty pounds.

If truth be told, most Roman legionaries are at best competent swordsmen. A soldier has a vast number of duties to perform and several weapons to master, so sword drill occupies only a small part of his time. Battles are won by masses of men working in close formation to bring the greatest strength to bear against the proper part of the enemy line at the proper time. Single combats of the Homeric sort are a relative rarity and the gladius is more often used to finish off an enemy already wounded by something else than it is employed in duelling with a specific opponent fighting with similar armament.

But gladiators do nothing except train for single combat

all day long. They don't have to pitch tents or dig ditches or stand guard duty or any of the hundred other duties of a soldier. Thus the best of them are artists with the sword, and this instructor was going to be satisfied with nothing that fell short of his own standard of perfection.

And so the long morning dragged on, until I felt like a statue made of wax, slowly melting in the heat. Most of my audience tired of the sorry spectacle and wandered off in search of other diversion. When the instructor finally called a halt to my sufferings, I dropped my shield, sheathed my sword, and pulled off my helmet. A cloud of steam rose from the helmet into the cool air like smoke from an altar.

I heard girlish laughter and looked around for its source, but the sweat pouring into my eyes blinded me for a while. When I blinked and swept the worst of it away, I saw Freda standing there watching me. Beside her was the ugly little slave, Molon.

"It is ancient custom," I said, "to endure the rudeness of military instructors, who have the authority to upbraid trainees of whatever rank. Insolence from slaves is not so easily overlooked. Do not overestimate your privileged position as the property of the First Spear."

"No need to be modest, Senator," said the wretched Molon. "Pretty soon you'll be fit to match against your slave boy there." He nodded toward Hermes, who was gaping at the German slave girl with a lovestruck expression, utterly ignoring his master's humiliation. I would have killed Molon, had I been able to raise my sword.

"And what gives you license to speak to a Senator in this fashion?"

"From what I hear, there are about six hundred of you

Senators, and not many of you amount to much."

That was damnably true. "But I am an exception." What a liar I was. I hoped the German girl would be impressed, but I thought it unlikely that she knew what a Senator was.

He quirked a misshapen eyebrow at me. "Really? From one of the big families?"

"You mean you are unaware of the *gens* Caecilia?"

He shrugged his humped shoulders. "I've never been to Rome. But now I think of it, there's been a Caecilius or two in charge here in Gaul."

"There? You see?" It may seem odd that I should stand there, drowning in my own sweat, trading idle chitchat with a grotesque, insolent slave. I can only say that my situation had departed somewhat from the path of strict sanity and even this odd diversion was welcome. That, and the presence of the German girl.

"Romans," she said, as if we were something amusing, incomprehensible, and slightly distasteful. To my disappointment she turned and sauntered away, doubtless to inspire erections wherever she passed. Molon stayed where he was. He looked around, then came closer to me.

"Look, Senator, would you happen to need a new slave?"

I was astounded. "You mean Freda? I doubt that I could afford her, and Vinius would surely never sell her to me!"

"Not her, me! Would you consider buying me?"

"Whatever for? Hermes gives me worry enough as it is."

He nodded and assumed a crafty look. "Just so. I can keep an eye on him for you, beat him when he steals, things like that. You have the look of a master too softhearted to flog a slave."

"I can see why that would make me attractive to you. Why should I want you?"

"I know this country, Senator. I know the land and all the tribes, I can speak the languages. The local people think the world of me, sir."

"I could see in what high esteem those German envoys held you. If you are so valuable, how could Vinius bring himself to part with you?"

"Well, Senator, my master has plans that don't include me, and I think he'd sell me cheap. You could use an intermediary if you don't want to haggle with him."

"Listen here, my man. You don't fool me. I've seen every Latin and Greek comedy ever written, and I know that slaves as ugly as you are always conniving rogues. Go try to sell yourself elsewhere."

He grinned slyly, but then all his expressions were sly. "Just think it over, Senator. I think you'll realize what a bargain I am." He turned and walked, or rather lurched, off.

"You're not going to buy him, are you?" Hermes said, aghast.

"I might," I warned him, "if you don't make yourself more valuable."

That night, after finishing my day's work on Caesar's reports, I sat in my folding chair and gave the matter some thought while I digested a frugal dinner, helped along by some heavily watered native wine. I found it surprisingly good. It was getting so that anything that didn't taste like vinegar was agreeable.

Did Molon really expect me to buy him? If so, why? It was easy enough to imagine that he would not want to be the slave of a man like Titus Vinius. If the man treated his soldiers in such a fashion, what must the lives of his slaves be like? But did he expect Vinius to entertain an offer from me?

There was an obvious interpretation, of course: Vinius had put him up to it, wanting to plant a spy on me. I have always resisted such trains of thought. I have known too many men to dwell upon subversive enemy plans of this sort until they saw plots, spies, and conspiracies no matter what direction they looked.

On the other hand, in typical Roman political life of the day there *were* plots, spies, and conspiracies everywhere. One just didn't expect to find anything so sophisticated and sinister in a legionary camp.

And what did he mean about Vinius's "plans" which did not include him? I would have thought that a man like Vinius, having no further use for the probably unsellable Molon, would just knock him on the head and leave him in a ditch somewhere. Probably, I thought, it was just more meaninless verbiage intended to obscure his real purpose. This practice is not restricted to speeches before the Popular Assemblies.

Mostly I was wondering how I could get my hands on Freda, and this clouded all my other thoughts. I was around thirty-two years old that year, and should have been past such schoolboy passions, but some things you never truly outgrow. That an entire, battle-hardened legion seemed to share my condition alleviated somewhat the embarrassment of my situation. But not much.

6

THE NEXT FEW DAYS FOLLOWED the same pattern: up at an absurd hour, attend officer's calls, attend arms drill in the morning, work on Caesar's papers in the afternoons, drop into exhausted sleep at night, endure the jabs of my fellow officers and the smirks of the legionaries in the meantime.

It was a life that was not entirely without its compensations. Being the laughingstock of an entire army prevents the sort of overweening pride that draws the wrath of the gods. Whenever I chanced to pass men of Vinius's century, they saluted respectfully and alone among the legionaries they did not find me a source of merriment.

My Gauls visited frequently and showed a surprising sympathy with my plight. For a pack of unlettered savages they were pretty decent men. I only rode with them once during this time, when Caesar called for a review of the mounted auxilia, of which he was collecting a prodigious force, having scoured all of Rome's nearby holdings and allies.

Handling Caesar's papers had another advantage: I was learning everything about his army and its management. Actual fighting takes up only a small part of an army's time, unless there is a siege. The rest of it is taken up in training and waiting, and the army's officers have to keep it fed and equipped and paid the whole time. The army's morale depends upon how well these activities are carried out.

The process of keeping the army supplied and fed was an eye-opener. It meant, primarily, dealing with civilian suppliers. What went on between them and the supply officers was even better than the dealings of the Censors and the *publicani*. The kickbacks were both amazing and blatant, and it came as something of a shock to see how many officers of the army, both legionary and auxilia, owned productive farms or workshops in the Province.

"Do you conceive that this has somehow escaped my notice?" Caesar said one evening when I pointed this out to him.

"It has occurred to me to wonder whether you understood the sheer comprehensiveness of the corruption," I said. "For instance, here we have one Nazarius, commander of the auxilia archers and skirmishers. He is also the owner of the largest tanneries in the province. Upon arrival here, Caius Paterculus, Prefect of the Camp, deemed all of the tents owned by the Tenth to be unfit for service and replaced them with new ones. The contract for the necessary hides was granted to Nazarius. A legion uses something in excess of eight hundred tents. At approximately twelve hides per tent that calls for"—arithmetic was never my greatest talent—"well, a lot of hides, anyway.

Between the allowance for tentage and what actually passed between Nazarius and Paterculus, I believe that a substantial sum now rests in the purse of the Prefect of the Camp." This officer had authority over everything having to do with camp management and had actual command of the camp when the legion marched out.

Caesar, who had been dictating notes to a slave, sighed and folded his hands over his slightly protruding belly. "Decius, this is ancient military practice, begun, I suspect, by Romulus. After all, we must buy hides from *somebody*, and who if not the largest supplier in the district? Now, if somebody were selling us inferior hides and passing them off as serviceable, that would be genuine corruption and I would punish it accordingly. But I have inspected all of our tentage and it is first-rate. There was no question that tents meant for the Italian climate were not fit for service in Gaul. As long as the Republic is not being cheated, what is the harm?"

"That is only one instance, and not the most egregious of them. There is . . ."

"Decius," Caesar interrupted, "I am certain that I know every instance you are about to cite in the most sordid detail. You can do nothing about these practices. You are a Roman statesman who will never spend more than a year or two at a time with the Eagles, as a part of your political career. The men who actually run the legions spend every day of their lives with the standards."

"And a piece of every transaction stays with the Prefect of the Camp and the First Spear," I said with perhaps more bitterness than was truly justified.

Caesar smiled slightly. "Now you know why Prefect of the Camp is an office held for only a single year, by a centurion on his last year of service before retiring. It is his final chance to line his purse and the theory is that he can't do any lasting damage in a year. Whatever he can get away with is his reward for twenty-five years of the most brutal, demanding service imaginable. It isn't a perfect system, but it works."

"I suppose the same could be said of our whole government," I remarked.

"Precisely. Now run along, Decius." He returned to his dictation as if he had not even seen me.

Indeed, I was a bit astonished that Caesar had granted me that much attention. Worry had put new lines in his face and his eyes were growing hollow. There was still no sign of his new legions and the campaigning season was wasting as the barbarians grew stronger. He would not be able to delay his trip to Italy any longer. He had hoped to avoid it, for it might look as if he were abandoning his army just as the war was about to commence.

The foreboding among the soldiers was getting worse. The combination of danger and inaction was corrosive. Rumors began to sweep the camp: the enemy was at hand; they were just across the river; they had a spell of invisibility. Fortunetellers and charm-sellers did a lively business in the camp forum until Caesar ordered them driven out.

Men saw omens everywhere, from the flight of birds to the direction of thunder to odd behavior in their many animal mascots. Caesar was finally driven to address the entire army from his praetorium platform like a general haranguing the troops before a battle. He told them that not only was he *pontifex maximus* of Rome but that he was an augur of many years' experience and was perfectly capable of reading the omens for the army. It did little to settle their minds, and every night there were false alarms when overexcited sentries thought they saw hordes of Gauls massing in the gloom. A few exemplary floggings did nothing to improve things.

It looked as if Rome's best legion was falling apart.

"WAKE UP!" SOMEBODY HISSED. I pried an eyelid open. It was utterly black outside.

"Hermes, is that you?" Then I heard Hermes snoring on the ground beside me, undisturbed.

"Forget about your slave," the voice said urgently. "The Proconsul wants you to report to him right now, and be quiet about it!"

"Who is that? Identify yourself." We might as well have been conversing in the bottom of a mineshaft.

"It's Publius Aurelius Cotta," he said. This was a mere boy of a tribune, bearer of an ancient name and destined to do it no honor, to judge by his excitability.

"What's this about?" I demanded, sitting up in my cot, feeling about for my boots.

"Something important," he said, displaying a firm grasp of the obvious.

"I don't suppose you brought a lamp? I can't find my gear."

"Forget that," he said. "Caesar's orders."

This had to be big. Caesar had decreed stiff punishments for so much as walking around without your helmet. I located my sword belt by touch and wrapped it around my waist. Hands outstretched to find the entrance of my tent, I stumbled out. Cotta caught my arm and I could just make out the low glow of distant watchfires.

"I don't hear any alarms," I said. "I presume we aren't

under attack. If Caesar wants me to copy some more of his damned reports to the Senate, I'll desert."

"I think it's rather more important than that," Cotta said, trying for an air of aristocratic nonchalance. He needed a few more years to pull it off.

"Then what is it?"

"I'm forbidden to say. He even told me to keep my voice down when I came to summon you."

"Doesn't want the soldiers to hear about it, eh? This must be something more than ordinarily disgraceful. Probably forgot to post sentries and the Gauls crept in and took over the camp and now he wants me to fix . . ." I tripped over a tent rope and fell on my face. After that I confined myself to muttering curses and imprecations. Cotta seemed grateful for the relative quiet.

We found the enclosure of the praetorium unusually torch-lit and near the table stood a knot of officers, wrapped in their woolen cloaks and looking as sour as I felt. I recognized Labienus, Caesar's *legatus*; Paterculus, the Prefect of the Camp; and others I did not know well. Carbo was there, and beside him was a Gaul. The man was shorter than most, dressed in a dark tunic and trousers, his arms and face smeared with dark paint.

"Is that Metellus?" Caesar said, ducking through the doorway of his tent. "Good, then let's go."

"There may be raiders outside the camp," said one of the officers."

"What of it?" Caesar said. "Aren't we all armed? Come, gentlemen. This is a serious matter and I want it handled with utmost care and discretion."

We all trooped along behind Caesar. I was burning with questions but I knew better than to ask them. We walked straight north and left the camp by way of the Porta Decumana in the middle of the northern wall. The gate guards gaped at us, but Caesar ordered them sternly to hold their tongues, on pain of death. He sounded like he meant it. These portals are not true gates, with doors and bars. Rather, they are overlaps in the camp wall. There are several ways of arranging them, but the idea is always that an enemy cannot get through them without coming under fire from above on both sides.

Once outside, the Gaul took the lead. He strode along as if he had eyes in his toes, crouched and looking as if he wanted to break into a run. I was reminded of a hunting dog chafing at the leash.

I did not like being away from the security of the camp. Even with the great rampart out there somewhere, we would be easy prey for some raiding band. Even a single young glory hound could rush in and cut one or two of us down before the others could react. Romans have always detested night fighting, and for good reason.

As near as I could judge we were heading northeast, in the general direction of the lake. Soon the ground began to squish beneath my boots and I knew we were getting near it. This was the area of marshes Caesar had charged Carbo with keeping clear of Gallic infiltrators. From ahead of us I heard a mutter of voices and then we were passing through a semicircle of light-armed auxilia.

"This is the place," Carbo said. We stood by water. I could hear its faint lapping and I could just make out the glittering reflection of stars on its surface. There was that wet, fecund smell that always dominates wherever water and land meet. There was an underlying smell, too, one not nearly so pleasant. Why had we come to the lake in the middle of the night?

"We can see nothing," Caesar commented. "Somebody strike a light and get some torches burning."

"The Gauls will be able to see us for miles," said Labienus.

"Let them come!" Caesar said testily. Apparently he did not relish being awakened at such an hour any more than I did. There came a clicking like the chirping of crickets. That was the auxilia. Every man had taken his firekit out and they were breaking the monotony of their long, nocturnal watch by seeing who could get a fire going first with flint and steel.

"Hah!" said a man, with the satisfaction of one who has just won some money off his fellows. A kneeling Gaul had managed to land a spark on a little nest of tinder laid upon his shield. He blew upon it carefully and the glowworm of smoldering tinder burst into a small but definite flame. Someone held a torch to it and soon we had a tolerable light.

"Bring the torches here," Caesar ordered. He stood at the edge of the water, and now I could see that something floated in it just off the bank. I was sure it was a man. What else would draw them out here at such an hour? But what man?

"The Gaul was right," Labienus said. "Must have eyes like an owl to recognize him in this gloom."

"Get him out of the water," Caesar said. "Decius Metellus, attend me."

I stepped up to his side as two of the auxilia waded into the water and began to haul the corpse out. They were Gauls and Gauls lack the Roman distaste for handling the bodies of the dead. Head-hunters cannot be too finicky.

"Proconsul?" I said.

"Decius, I've just remembered why I wanted you here. It was for situations like this."

The body was out of the water, lying on its back. Two of the Gauls held their torches low so we could get a good look. The features were contorted and slightly swollen, probably the result of having been strangled by the noose that was visible around the neck. Still, they were recognizable.

It was Titus Vinius, First Spear of the Tenth.

I straightened. "All right, I'll kick in for the funeral fund, although I'll wager there aren't any decent professional mourners to be hired in these parts."

"Don't try to provoke me, Decius!" Caesar snapped. "This is more than a serious loss to the legion. The men's spirits are low enough as it is, and now the First Spear has been murdered! This could be catastrophic!"

"I should think it would raise morale enormously."

"Don't be facetious. I want the killers exposed so that they can be executed without delay."

"Why do you think this is murder?" I asked him. "And what was he doing out here anyway? If the fool was wandering around alone at night, he was probably caught by Gallic raiders and killed. That isn't murder, it's enemy action."

Caesar sighed. "Decius Caecilius, I thought this sort of thing was your specialty. Even I, lacking your unique talents, have noticed that Titus Vinius still possesses his head."

"That is something of an anomaly, but far from conclusive. It may be . . ." Then I was interrupted, not an unwelcome thing since I had no ready answer for him.

"Caesar," Paterculus said, "may I speak frankly?" He was a grizzled old sweat with a face like an Alpine cliff.

"Please do so."

"You don't need this . . . this philosopher to guess who killed Titus Vinius. It must have been the men of his own century. They all hated him."

"Assuredly," I said, not liking the way this was going. I knew who the prime suspects were the second I saw Vinius' dead face. "They just asked him to take a stroll with them out by the lake in the middle of the night, unarmed. He acceded to this request with the bluff joviality for which he was famed wherever the hobnailed boot of Roman soldiery has trod."

"Don't talk nonsense," Paterculus said. "They must've killed him in the camp or up on the wall, then dragged him out here."

"And they did this without anyone noticing?" I demanded.

"Easy. The First Century has the north wall tonight."

"Eighty men can't keep a conspiracy secret."

"Wasn't the whole century," Paterculus said. "Just that one *contubernium* that was giving him so much trouble. That boy . . . what's his name? Burrus? Let me have him for an hour. I'll have the whole story out of him."

This was getting ominous. "Caesar," I urged. "If the death of the First Spear is a blow, what would this do to the Tenth? If men of the legion murdered their own centurion it could be worse than damaging to morale. It could inspire imitation."

Caesar stood for a while in silent thought. Then he spoke in a voice that was low, but it was one all of us could hear.

"What you say is very true. Decius, I am appointing you investigating officer. If this murder was not committed by men of the First Century of the First Cohort, you must find out who did commit it and you must do it quickly. You are hereby excused all other duties. In the meantime I must take certain disciplinary measures."

"Have I your authority to interrogate anyone I think fit; legionary or officer, free or slave, citizen or barbarian?"

"This is my province and you have my authority as Proconsul of Gaul and Illyria to interrogate any human being within the limits of my *imperium*. Just handle the investigation with utmost discretion."

"No, Caesar," I said. The mutter of low-voiced conversation halted.

"What?" Caesar said, unable to believe his ears.

"I want to conduct this investigation, but I cannot be hampered by considerations of discretion. However ugly or messy this crime proves to be, I will expose it. I want no one to think that I may fail to act for fear of embarrassing you. I must have your decree, stated before these officers, that I have full powers of investigation and arrest. If not, I will return to my arms drill."

Caesar glared at me for long seconds amid the dead silence. The flickering orange light of the torches made his face a frightening sight. Then he smiled so faintly and nodded so slightly that it might have been a trick of the uncertain light.

"Very well. I will leave two of my lictors with you as insignia of your authority. This afternoon I will conduct funeral rites for Titus Vinius. After that I leave for Italy to collect my legions. Labienus will be in charge during my absence. I want you to have the culprits apprehended by the time I return. If you have not discovered them by that time, then I must take unwelcome but necessary steps to restore the order and discipline of the Tenth Legion."

"Caesar, do you want my men to carry his body back to the camp?" Carbo asked.

"Please leave him until daylight," I said. "I want to study the body and the site as soon as the sun is up."

"Very well," Caesar said. "Best he were not brought in at night anyway. The wake-up trumpets will sound soon and the soldiers will be up. I don't want all sorts of wild rumors flying through the camp while it's still dark and men's minds are prey to primitive fears. Carbo, bring all your men over here to guard the site, but keep them at a distance. Come, gentlemen. We have plans to discuss." He turned to go.

"By your leave, Proconsul," I said, "I'll stay here until daylight. I want to make certain that no one interferes with the scene."

"As you wish," Caesar said. He began to walk back toward the camp. Carbo went off to summon his men and the others went after Caesar. Each of them eyed me in utter mystification. None had any idea what to make of me. Labienus lingered later than the rest.

"Metellus, what sort of man are you? I have never seen a man behave with such shameless gall. Are you a hero or just some sort of lunatic?"

"A woman once called me a male harpy. I hound evildoers to their doom."

He nodded. "That settles it, then. You're a lunatic." With that he walked away.

The auxilia were whiling away their time with a torchlit dice game. "Where is the man who found the body?" I demanded. One of the dicers called something over his shoulder and the man came in from the outer gloom, looking like a piece of the night detached from the whole and made animate.

"Tell me how you found him," I said.

"We were performing the nightly sweep—"

"First identify yourself."

"I am Ionus of the Gallic Scouts, part of the Second Cohort," he began, his accent so dense that I could barely understand him. The auxilia are organized only as cohorts, never as legions. "We are under the command of Captain Carbo; valiant as a lion, cunning as a serpent, virile as a wild boar . . ."

"Yes, yes, I am well acquainted with Captain Carbo's virtues. We are old friends. Tell me how you found the dead man."

"Each evening, just after dark, we conduct the sweep to catch any Helvetii who might come in through the swamp. Beginning at the legionary camp, the light-armed skirmishers extend in two lines from the great rampart on the left. Captain Carbo commands from the right flank. Upon his signal, they begin walking toward the lake. We Scouts go out ahead of them at a hundred paces. We are picked men, known for our keen night vision and our skill at moving silently in the dark. My own tribe, the Volcae, are famed for this skill."

"I take it you are great cattle raiders?"

"The very best!" he said, smiling proudly. Just as the Greeks of Homer considered piracy a proper calling for gentlemen and our own ancestors of Romulus' time thought it quite correct to appropriate other people's women, so the Gauls believe that cattle thieving is both fine sport and a legitimate means to augment one's material wealth.

"Go on, then. You set out on the evening sweep. Did you start any infiltrators?"

"We found none this night, and that seemed odd, for we usually net anything from three to a score of them. Perhaps this night is one ill-omened for the Helvetii and they deemed it a bad time to go adventuring."

"You swept all the way to the lake?"

"Yes. Then Captain Carbo told the Scouts to make a careful check of all the nearby bodies of water. Sometimes the raiders hide among the reeds until the sweep passes. I led these spearmen," he gestured to the dice-playing skirmishers, "and we came here. That was when I saw the dead man."

"Then this is not the lake itself?" I asked him, surprised.

"No, we are about five hundred paces from the lake proper. This is a pond. There are many of them around here. The reeds make this one a good place to hide. The skirmishers had just begun poking their spears in the clumps of reeds when I noticed something floating out in the water. At first I thought it was a dead Helvetian, perhaps one wounded the night before who went to hide in the pond and died there. His tunic was dark. But then I saw that his legs were bare, like a Roman's."

Most Gauls wear trousers. Often they fight bare-chested or wearing a brief cape over their shoulders, and some of them fight stark naked, dedicating themselves to their gods and trusting to no other protection. But very seldom do they wear tunics leaving the legs bare, like civilized soldiers.

"When did you recognize him?"

"He floated facedown and I waded out to him, thinking to take his head should he prove to be an enemy. But then I saw his short hair and knew he was a Roman. I rolled him over and I knew his face instantly. The First Spear always stands on the platform next to Caesar during reviews and we had one just two days ago."

"You did not lie about having good night vision. Was there anything else?"

"I told the spearmen to stay and guard the body while I ran to report to Captain Carbo. We went to tell Caesar. He would not believe me at first, but he sent for the First Spear and he couldn't be found. So he summoned his officers and I led the lot of you here."

The rest of Carbo's men arrived and I was busy for a while arranging them into a cordon around the site. I told them to come no closer, my main concern being to preserve the site as best I could. Not that there was likely to be anything to read from the signs, with the way half the Empire had been trampling all over the place for hours.

Gradually the eastern horizon turned pale. Imperceptibly, a bit at a time, distant objects became discernible. In time I could see that I did, indeed, stand beside a pond. It covered perhaps three acres, half of its area choked with dense weeds. In the distance I could see Lake Lemannus itself. Satisfied that I had sufficient light, I went to the body and crouched beside it.

Death had rendered Titus Vinius no prettier. His mouth was twisted in a wide-open snarl, as if he had been gasping for breath when death overtook him. The cord of braided hide around his neck would account for that. It was buried deeply in the flesh of his neck and had been tied off over the spinal cord.

He wore a dark tunic of coarse wool, such as slaves wear. As the light improved, I noticed a thin slit about the width of three fingers just over the heart. I grasped the neck opening and ripped the garment halfway down. There was a stab wound two inches to the left of the sternum, probably through the heart. There was no blood, but then the body had been in the water for hours. In any case, penetrating wounds to the torso bleed internally. My old friend Asklepiodes had taught me that and I wished fervently that I had him by my side just then. He could read wounds the way a huntsman can read the signs left behind by animals.

All I could tell was that the wound had been made by a double-edged dagger. Every soldier in both camps carried just such a dagger at his belt. I wore one myself. At least two killers, then. I could visualize it: One man looped the garotte around

Vinius's neck from behind and drew it tight. Perhaps he struggled too fiercely and a confederate in front stabbed him, or perhaps the noose was just to hold him so that the knife man could do the real execution.

Then I saw that there was something wrong with his scalp. I fought down superstitious revulsion and felt the damp hair. Beneath the dense, curly, goatlike hair, I felt a skin laceration. With a little pressure, I could feel bone shift beneath my fingers. Someone had smashed Vinius's skull with a club or some similar object. Three killers now?

Not necessarily. Men do not always die easily and a man like Vinius could be counted on to die harder than most. Perhaps the daggerman or the strangler had bashed him on the head to make doubly certain. One would think, though, that the knotted cord would be enough. And if there was uncertainty, why not just stab him a few more times? Men willing to stab other men are usually not reluctant to do it repeatedly.

A theory began to take shape in my mind, and it was not one I liked. It pointed straight at the First Century and most particularly at one special *contubernium*.

There was little more to be read from the corpse. It was unarmed and without a purse or ornaments of any kind. That meant little, since Gauls would have stripped Titus Vinius of any valuables. I was still hoping for Gauls, although the continuing presence of his head argued against that.

I examined the ground near where the body had been found, but it was so thoroughly trampled by hobnailed boots that there was nothing to be learned. Surely, I thought, a man as strong and battle-hardened as Titus Vinius must have put up a terrible struggle, even if only for a few seconds. I hoped for bits of clothing or ornaments or weapons torn from the killers, but I found none. A single foreign dagger would serve to direct suspicion away from the legion. I found only a scrap of dirty white linen.

A score of questions tore at me: Why was he dressed in a dingy, slave's tunic? Why was he here? Why that particular night? And for which of several exceedingly good reasons had he been killed?

My musings were interrupted when a solemn procession came from the direction of the camp. Most were soldiers, but they glittered more than those I had seen so far. Then I saw the flashing greaves on their shins and I knew that these were the surviving centurions of the Tenth. They had donned their dress uniforms for this duty. With them came a small group of slaves. Among these was Molon, wailing extravagantly and bearing a great bundle upon his back.

The man in front halted the procession. "I am Spurius Mutius, centurion of the Second Century, First Cohort of the Tenth, and now acting First Spear. We've come to take the body of our comrade back to the camp for his funeral."

"Has the Proconsul informed you of my special authority?"

"He has." I looked at fifty-nine hard, closed faces and I knew what I was in for. I was the outsider here, just another political interloper. These were the professionals of the Tenth. They were closing ranks the way the old military maniples used to, when the *principes* and the *hastati* and the *triarii* merged their squares into one massive, impenetrable block to face the enemy.

"You may have him," I said. "I've learned all I can here."

Mutius turned to the slaves. "Do your duty." These were funeral slaves, of which every legion keeps a staff. On campaign, they dispensed with the archaic trappings they wore in

Rome and looked like any other army slaves. The priest, also a slave, performed a *lustrum* to purify the corpse. Foreigners are sometimes shocked to find that slaves can be priests among us, but our gods are not the snobs that some people's are.

The funeral men stripped the dingy tunic from Vinius's body and Molon, still wailing and weeping, dumped his bundle on the ground. He threw open the wrapping blanket to reveal his master's glittering dress uniform. With swift efficiency, the slaves dressed the corpse.

"Molon, go mourn somewhere else," I ordered. "But not too far away. I want to speak to you presently." He nodded and walked off, wailing. It was annoying, but we are all bound by tradition and there was nothing to be done about it.

Within minutes Vinius was laid out on a shield and clad in his finery. His silvered helmet bore a magnificent side-to-side crest of scarlet horsehair and his greaves were polished brilliantly. His armor was especially splendid: a shirt of small scales, plated alternately with gold and silver so that they resembled the plumage of a fabulous bird. The *phalerae* were arranged over his body on their strap harness: nine thick, silver disks as broad as a man's palm, each decorated with the head of a different god in high relief. In all, he looked greatly improved from the sordid, waterlogged corpse the Gaul had discovered. The funeral slaves had even been able to settle his face into an expression of stern serenity.

"What god has laid us under a curse?" mused a grizzled old veteran. "The First Spear murdered at the outset of a campaign! Was there ever a worse omen?"

"Quiet there, Nonius," Mutius said. "Let's take him back." Three spears had been arranged beneath the shield and six centurions bent to grasp their ends, but at that moment I noticed something.

"Wait." The six paused and I pointed to a band of pale skin around Vinius's right wrist. I had grasped that wrist a few days before to stop him from flogging Burrus further and had felt a bracelet beneath my fingers. Among Romans only soldiers wear bracelets, and then only as awards for valor. "He wore a bracelet. Where is it?"

"You're right," Mutius said, rubbing his stubbled chin. "He won that in Africa when he was a common legionary. It was his first decoration for bravery. He always wore it." He turned slightly. "Molon!" he barked. "Come here, you ugly cur!"

Molon shuffled over to us, trying to wail and smile at the same time. "Sir?"

"You were instructed to bring all your master's decorations. Where is his bracelet?"

Molon was caught short. "But I brought everything! I don't . . ." His protestations ended in a yelp of pain as Mutius's vinestock slashed across his shoulder.

"If you've stolen that bracelet I'll have every inch of hide off your back, you misshapen wretch!"

"But it was not in his chest!" Molon cried, now huddled on his knees with his arms above his head, shielding it. "He never took it off! He even slept with it!"

"That's enough," I said as sternly as I could. "The killers probably took it. I want all of Vinius's belongings put under seal and brought to the praetorium immediately."

"It will be done," Mutius said. "Let's go."

The six raised the shield to their shoulders and began to walk back toward the camp. The rest of the centurions followed in double-file and I walked behind them.

"Sir, do you want this?" I looked up and saw one of the funeral slaves holding out the braided noose. I was about to wave it away in disgust, then thought better of it. I took it and tucked it under my sword belt. If nothing else, I could add it to the macabre little collection of murderous souvenirs I kept at home.

I saw Molon shuffling along with the slaves, his head hanging in mock sadness. I signaled him to come to me.

"Well, sir," he said, "that's another one gone, eh?"

"Molon, I am only going to tell you this once: You are to keep yourself handy because I am going to question you. If I hear that you have run away, I shall use my special new authority to have our entire cavalry force run you down and bring you back in chains. As far as I am concerned, you are a suspect in your master's murder. Do you know what that means?"

He shrugged. "It means the cross, of course. That may frighten slaves in Rome, but in this part of the world they really give some thought to torture and colorful executions. Every soldier in this army faces worse than the cross if he's captured alive. Besides," he smirked, "do you think these old vinegar drinkers will believe that someone like me could overpower someone like Titus Vinius?"

"Whoever did it wasn't acting alone," I said, "and it doesn't take a giant to wield a dagger."

"You're stretching now, sir," he said, sounding not quite so confident.

"Just keep in mind that you are under suspicion and behave accordingly. How many slaves did Vinius have?"

"You mean here in the camp with him?"

"Yes."

"Just me and Freda. He has—had an estate back in Italy, but I never saw it."

"No cook, valet, mule handler?"

"I'm all of 'em. And interpreter, too."

"And what does Freda—well, I suppose I don't need to ask what services she performed for him." Molon grinned insinuatingly and I punched him in the side.

We came into the camp and I reflected that, at the very least, I wouldn't have to report to the arms trainer that morning. Secretly, though, I was glad that Caesar had sentenced me to that torment. I had not realized how far out of condition I was, and that is not a good way to be when going into a war. I was now almost back to my old level of skill and endurance and I resolved to spend an hour or two each day at drill until I was as good as ever, if not better.

I told Molon to report to me at the praetorium along with the rest of Vinius's property and he promised to do so. As I walked through the camp to return to my tent, I tried to judge the state of the soldiers. They were sprucing up their equipment for a formal parade, but there was nothing festive about them. They spoke in low voices and their expressions were downcast and fearful. They looked at the sky too much. That is a bad sign among soldiers because it means they are looking for omens, betraying a lack of confidence.

They were arranging the crests on their helmets, which among ordinary soldiers are worn only on parade and in battle. Likewise, they were stripping the oiled covers from their shields. Because of its layered construction, the *scutum* is very vulnerable to soaking. Thus it is kept covered much of the time, but on parade and in battle the covers are removed, revealing the brightly painted and decorated faces. But no amount of paint and gilding and feathers and horsehair could make this legion look like Rome's best. The Gauls had not even showed up in force and already the Tenth looked like a beaten army.

I found Hermes waiting for me with breakfast, hot water, and decent wine. Sometimes he was not really such a burden.

"Is it true what I've been hearing?" he asked as I launched into breakfast.

"If you've heard the First Spear's been killed, it's true," I said around a mouthful of hot bread. "Whether he was murdered hasn't been established, but if the Gauls did him in they got him to dress oddly beforehand."

"This is a strange army and an odd war," Hermes pronounced. "I think we should go home."

"If that were possible you'd have a hard time keeping up with me. And believe me: it's bad to be with an army even in the best of wars. Now go along to your weapons drill and let me think."

So I sat there in my folding camp chair and tried to think, but no thoughts would come. Exhausting days and short nights were taking their toll. The night before had been even shorter than most, with no more than an hour or two of sleep, and much excitement. And now another day was starting. And I did not like what I was facing.

Thus far, I had been no more than an oddity to the Tenth Legion. That was nothing new. I was something of an oddity in Rome. Now I was chief investigator and I would be the most unpopular man in Gaul. My investigation was likely to send several men to the executioner. My well-known sympathy with Burrus and his *contubernium* was going to cast my investigator's impartiality into serious doubt. Everyone would assume that I was looking for a scapegoat to take the blame and exonerate my client.

Worst of all, everything so far pointed to that *contubernium:* they certainly had a motive to kill Vinius. I had seen with my own eyes the brutality with which he treated them, and I knew that they feared he was hounding them toward a mutiny that would earn them execution. They were on the north wall that night and had the opportunity to drag him out and throw him in the pond undetected by the rest of the legion. There were eight men, all of them tough, trained soldiers, well able to overpower and kill even such a man as Titus Vinius.

It left some questions unanswered but it was enough evidence for almost any jury in Rome to convict them. Here their lives were in the hands of the Proconsul. At least, in Caesar, I was dealing with a lawyer who understood the nuances of evidence. That was why I now had a few days to investigate. Many commanders would have ordered some executions already. And I think I amused Caesar. Something about the way I pursued criminal investigations struck him as entertaining.

But how many days did I have? I already knew that Caesar could move an army with unprecedented speed. A trip across the mountains into Italy and back again with two legions would have taken weeks for most men, even if they were waiting at the foot of the pass on the other side. I had a feeling that those legions would be burning *caliga* leather all the way to Lake Lemannus.

And what other suspects did I have? The Gauls? They would certainly have killed him had they caught him, but how would they have done that? And why would they leave him his head, surely one of the more prestigious trophies to be had from this war?

Molon? I knew he wanted to leave the service of Vinius, but murder is an extreme step to take, and he would need at least one confederate. It occurred to me that Freda was a large, strong young woman, perhaps capable of wielding the garotte

117

and immobilizing Vinius long enough for Molon to finish him off with a dagger. It was conceivable that the two of them might have been able to haul him out to the pond. Dwarfish men like Molon are often far stronger than they look. But how would they have gotten him out of the camp?

And I did not want to suspect the German girl, although I had no good reason for this.

I shook my head. This speculation was taking me nowhere. What I needed more than anything else was rest. With a full stomach, my head pleasantly buzzing from the wine, I went into my tent and collapsed.

It was past noon when the trumpets woke me. At just that time Hermes arrived, sweating and breathing hard. With his assistance I got my parade uniform on. At least this time I wouldn't be laughed at for wearing it. After days of living in my field gear, it felt stiff and uncomfortable. Helmet on and plumes nodding, I made my way to the praetorium.

I arrived just as Caesar was mounting his platform. I joined the officers on the lower platform atop the surrounding rampart. I looked out over the legion, drawn up in rigid formation, the ten cohorts turned out in their best finery. All except one.

The First Cohort wore no plumes or crests and their shields were still in their covers. Separated from them was the First Century, and I gasped when I saw them. They stood disarmed, their weapons and armor piled on top of their shields, which lay on the ground at their feet.

Before that century stood eight men who had been stripped to their tunics, their hands bound behind them. I did not have to guess who they might be.

Just before the platform a funeral pyre had been raised

and atop it lay Titus Vinius. Around the pyre stood the standard-bearers with their standards swathed in dark cloth in token of mourning. Flanking the *aquilifer* were two trumpeters with their great *cornicens* looped over their shoulders. When Caesar reached the platform, they sounded the assembly call on their instruments.

"Soldiers!" Caesar began without preamble. "The First Spear of the Tenth Legion is dead, and there is every indication that he was murdered. Until the culprits are exposed, I decree the following punishments: the First Cohort, of which Titus Vinius was senior officer, is in disgrace and will be denied all honors until the demands of justice have been satisfied. They will perform no military duties and are restricted to menial labor. They may not salute their officers or their standards and none are to salute them in return.

"The First Century of the First Cohort, for failing to preserve the life of their commander, are to be denied association with honorable soldiers. They are to pitch their tents outside the camp walls and are to abide there until the demands of justice are satisfied." At this a collective gasp went through the assembled legion. This was a terrible punishment, the next thing to decimation. Even worse, in a way, for every man of them could be killed by the Gauls. But Caesar was not through.

"This *contubernium*," he pointed at the disarmed men, "is under arrest and will be held in confinement. They lie under the deepest suspicion. This day I depart for Italy to find and bring back our reinforcements. If they are not proven innocent by the time I return, they are to be executed. They are citizens and may not be crucified, but their crime merits worse than beheading. Therefore this is the form their punishment shall take: The balance of the First Cohort will form two lines facing

119

each other, each man armed with a vinestock. These men will walk between the lines, naked, to be beaten by their fellow soldiers. Any man who is still alive when he reaches the end of the line will turn and make the same journey, repeating the course until he is dead."

He paused for a while, then he began the funeral rites. "Let us now set to rest the shade of our fellow soldier, Titus Vinius." He pronounced the invocations, the language of them so archaic that nobody could understand more than one word in five. Then he performed the funeral oration. It followed the standard form, listing Vinius' distinctions, the high points of his career and his many awards for valor, finishing with an appreciation and regretting that his services would be sorely missed in the campaign to come. That may have been true militarily speaking, but personally I wasn't going to miss him a bit. I only regretted the mess his death left behind.

With a last call to the gods, Caesar descended from the platform and thrust the first torch into the oil-soaked stack of wood. Soon it was blazing merrily and the whole army stood at attention while the flames leaped upward and consumed the body of Titus Vinius along with some very valuable armor and equipment.

As the flames began to burn down, the *cornicens* blew the dismissal and the legion dispersed. I went to join a knot of officers who stood before the praetorium awaiting Caesar's officer's call. The disconsolate army marched past us. Last of all came the First Cohort. On their faces was a miserable admixture of fear, rage, and shame.

"There go some unhappy men," I remarked. For once I was not trying to be flippant, but there must have been something wrong with my tone, because a man nearby whirled and stalked up to me. He was one of the centurions, the great, horseshoe-shaped crest atop his helmet striped brown and white. He planted himself a foot before me and barked in my face:

"Of course they're unhappy! They're the First of the Tenth, best soldiers in the world, and they're in disgrace! You Forum politicians don't know what disgrace is because you've forgotten what honor is! Well, we haven't forgotten in the Tenth!" I was utterly dumbfounded to see tears coursing down his weather-beaten cheeks. Then he whirled and strode off, yelling for his decurio.

Carbo walked up to me. "Best tread softly, Decius," he advised. "Odds are good that you'll be the next man killed in this army."

"I'm all too aware of it. The only men I'm getting along with these days are barbarians and the disgraced. How can he banish an entire century from the camp? It's outrageous!"

"So is the murder of the First Spear. An example has to be made, Decius. At least they have a chance. He could have ordered decimation. He could have ordered the lot of them to march into Germany and not return until he sent for them. Maybe it will be best just to let those eight men be executed. The legionaries won't be perfectly satisfied, but it would return the legion to some sort of normalcy."

I shook my head. "No! I don't know about the others, but I am sure that Burrus didn't kill his centurion, richly as the man deserved it, and I won't allow him to be punished for it."

"Then you have a very large task," Carbo said. "It is more than just saving Burrus. These men want their honor back, and if that *contubernium* is not to be executed, you must give them something better."

As he spoke these words, the officer's call sounded and we passed within. Next to Caesar's tent I saw Molon standing beside some chests and bales; the belongings of the late Titus Vinius. And on top of the heap sat Freda, looking as disdainful as always.

"Gentlemen, I must be brief," Caesar began. "I need every hour of daylight I can get to ride to Italy. This sorry business has already cost me half the day. Treasurer, your report."

The legion's treasurer was an *optio* chosen for his excellent memory, good penmanship, and a head for figures.

"Titus Vinius never married, had no children and never informed me of any family. He left behind no will. Therefore, according to custom, the Proconsul is executor of his estate until a family member comes forward to make a claim. Word will be sent to the steward of his Italian estate, who will presumably inform the family, if any. He paid regularly into the funeral fund and this, along with a generous contribution by the Proconsul, will pay for a fine gravestone. Massilia has excellent Greek stonecavers and a monument will be commissioned immediately.

"The aforementioned steward visited Titus Vinius twice each year and at those times the First Spear made his banking arrangements, presumably with an Italian banker. He kept at all times a balance of one thousand sesterces with the legion bank." This was a tidy if not a princely sum. A senior centurion could be a modestly wealthy man, what with pay, loot, and bribes.

"Very well, Treasurer. Gentlemen, I hereby take charge of the movable goods of the late Titus Vinius. They shall stay here in the praetorium while Decius Caecilius Metellus conducts his investigation. There remains his ambulatory property: his livestock and his slaves. His horse and pack mules will stay with the pack train animals for now. That leaves his slaves. Accommodation must be found for them and I have a full staff."

Slowly, every head turned until we were all staring at Freda, who ignored us.

"Actually," Labienus said, "I have room in my tent . . ."

"You know, I could use a cook . . ." and so on. Everyone found that he had room for just one more slave. Everyone except my cousin Lumpy. Maybe the family rumors about him were true.

"Recall, gentlemen, that Molon goes with her." Even that dismal prospect did not slow down the offers of accommodation. Caesar silenced everyone with a wave and a look of utterly malicious humor came over his face.

"Decius, you may have them." Instantly, every man in the meeting was glaring at me, even my old friend Carbo. This was perfect. Now everybody but the Gauls hated me.

"And now, gentlemen, I must ride. I shall take only a small escort of cavalry. I intend to be back here, with our reinforcements, in no more than ten days."

"Is that possible?" asked Labienus, incredulous.

"If not, I intend to make it so," Caesar said with that confidence of which only he was capable. It was a trick he knew how to use well. He could almost convince even me that the gods were truly on his side. "You are dismissed. Decius Caecilius, stay here."

The others left as the small cavalry escort arrived. I was glad to see that Lovernius and my *ala* were not among them. I needed friends at that moment.

"Decius," Caesar began, "I cannot impress upon you too strongly just how much I depend upon you to solve this murder.

Even with the reinforcements my army will still be very small. I *need* the Tenth! And I must have it in top fighting order, not weakened by suspicion and dishonor and fear of evil omens."

"Caesar, Vinius was a prodigious wretch. There are six thousand suspects within these walls."

He waved it aside with a gesture. "Men do not achieve the centurionate by being mild. Nobody loves a centurion. But they are seldom murdered. You must find the murderers for me, Decius. If you do not, I will be compelled to execute Burrus and the others, guilty or not. This war is about to commence and there will be no time for niceties." A Gaul led up his horse and boosted him into the saddle.

"A moment, Caius Julius," I said.

"Yes?"

"Why did you give me that woman?"

He sat there for a moment, savoring his peculiar jest. "First of all, you deserve something for the misery you are going to endure. Then again, the man who has her will have the jealous resentment of the others and all my other officers are more valuable than you. I would as soon their efficiency not be impaired. But most of all, Decius, someday you may be very valuable to me and I will be able to hold this over your head."

I knew exactly what he meant. I was betrothed to his niece, Julia, and she would never forgive me for having owned this woman.

"Caius Julius," I said bitterly, "you are an Etruscan punishment-demon in human form!"

Caesar rode off laughing.

124

7

I FACED, QUITE PROBABLY, THE most demanding task of a decidedly checkered career. In Rome I would have known where to begin, but here I was in all but alien territory. Not only was I not in Rome, I was in a legionary camp, and that camp was in Gaul, and Gaul was in a state of war. All of these were distracting circumstances. Before I could even begin, I had to regain my equanimity. I needed to speak with the only sane, sensible people in the camp. I decided to call upon my Gauls.

Before I could do that, though, I had to make some domestic arrangements. I went to the heap of Vinius's belongings. Molon wore a nervous grin and Freda studied me as if I were some sort of odd new bug.

"You both understand that you belong to me now?"

Molon nodded vigorously. "Yes! I am very glad to be your property, sir!"

"How about you?" I asked Freda.

She shrugged. "One Roman is much like another."

I did not appreciate being likened to Titus Vinius, but I let it pass. "You," I said to Molon, "are to lay out your former master's belongings over there by the desk. I want to make a complete inventory this afternoon. You," I said to Freda, "are to go to my tent and busy yourself there; clean up or whatever it was you did for Titus Vinius when he was away. My boy Hermes is there now. If he tries to lay hands on you, you may beat him."

She stepped down from her perch and walked past me without a glance or another word. I could not restrain myself from following her with my eyes. What a view she presented.

"Did she act this way toward Titus Vinius?" I asked Molon. "He struck me as a man who had a short way with insolent menials."

"She's not your typical menial, sir," Molon said. "And she has, if you'll forgive me, an unerring eye for men's weaknesses. I think she's already sized you up."

"Thinks I am a man who will put up with anything, eh? Well, she shall learn otherwise." I pulled the tunic away from Molon's hunched shoulder. It was almost black with bruises. "I am not a centurion, so I do not carry a vinestock. I beat slaves only for the most serious infractions, but then I am merciless. Let us establish our relationship in this manner: See to it that you please me, or I shall sell you to a less easygoing master, and almost anyone in the world is less easygoing than I am."

"Oh, believe me, sir, I want to remain with you! But then,"

that crafty gleam came into his eye, "are you sure you can sell me? A relative of Titus Vinius might show up sometime and claim me."

"Molon, anyone with the brains of a snail would knock you on the head and leave you in a ditch rather than feed you all the way back to Italy. I may have some use for you as an interpreter. I will be in Gaul for no more than a year. Keep me happy and when I leave, I'll sell you to some genial merchant who needs your skills. You'll be out of the legion camps and living easy."

He nodded, rubbing his hands together. "That would be most acceptable."

"See to it, then. If anyone wants me, I will be with the praetorian cavalry for a while. Have everything ready for me when I get back."

"Just leave it all to me, master."

I have always found that slaves respond better to kindness than to severity, although they are quick to take advantage of perceived weakness. Molon knew what a soft position he now had and I was confident he would exert himself to please me. Freda was apt to be another question entirely.

I found my *ala* caring for their horses after their daily patrol. As non-citizens, they had not been required to attend the funeral. They welcomed my arrival with smiles and backslaps.

"Good to have you back, Captain!" Lovernius said. "Will you be riding with us again?"

"Not for a while, as luck would have it. Caesar has assigned me to investigate the First Spear's killing." Judging from their smiles and cheerful attitude, these men did not share the legionaries' poor morale. They were not a part of the Tenth Legion and the death of its senior centurion did not upset them at all.

"We've been talking to the spearmen," Lovernius said. "They tell us someone strangled him."

"Strangled him, stabbed him, smashed his skull, and threw him into a pond," I elaborated. Abruptly the Gauls frowned and one of them snapped something in their native tongue.

"What did he say?" I asked, surprised.

Lovernius looked mildly upset. "If you will pardon my saying so, Captain, they take it very ill that someone would dump a Roman carcass in one of our ponds. They are uneducated and superstitious men."

I was not pleased with the comment, but not for the reason he expected. "I am sorry to hear it. I keep hoping that I can pin the killing on the Helvetii, but I don't suppose they would have defiled a holy place in such a fashion."

"Undoubtedly not," Lovernius said. "And with such wounds it is unlikely that he would have crawled there and died. Why are you so anxious to blame the Helvetii?"

"Murder within the legion is bad for morale. That the victim was the senior centurion makes it worse. Not that anyone liked the vile brute, but these are men with a powerful sense of hierarchy and a centurion should be inviolate, killable only in battle. A whole cohort is in disgrace, a century banished beyond the camp walls, and a *contubernium* facing a truly vicious execution upon Caesar's return. To make it all worse, the prime suspect is a personal friend and client of mine."

"That is bad," Lovernius commiserated. "Cheer up. It may

have been the Germans. They have no respect for our sacred waters."

"Is this true? Not that I like the idea of Germans lurking about out there, but it would help things immeasurably if I could blame them. "Have they no sacred places?"

"Only groves in the deep forest, beyond the Rhine. The oak and the ash and the rowan are their holy trees. Places where lightning has struck are sacred to them. Not much else."

"This bears looking into. Indiumix, saddle my horse. Lovernius, I want you to ride out a short way with me."

"It will be my pleasure." He addressed the men at some length in their own language. They nodded somberly. I had not thought a dead man in a pond would put such a damper on their spirits, but barbarians can be odd.

When I was mounted, we rode out through the Porta Decumana in the north wall. The sound of tent pegs being hammered led us to a spot just northeast of the legionary camp where the First Century was setting up its new, unwalled camp. From the vantage point of my saddle I had no trouble spotting the silvery helmet of the *optio* upon whom I had made so poor an impression a few nights before. He was pointing and shouting orders at the tense-faced men, who were in for a very frightening night. He betrayed no expression as I rode up and dismounted.

"*Optio,*" I began, "I know you are extremely busy so I shall not detain you long. I wish to speak with you in the praetorium tomorrow morning concerning the activities of the late Titus Vinius."

He spat on the ground, narrowly missing my left *caliga*. "I'll be there, assuming I'm alive tomorrow morning."

"Well, there is always that unwelcome possibility."

"Half of us will be on guard at all times."

"This whole army is a conspiracy against a good night's sleep. Perhaps I can help you out a bit. I am giving my Gallic riders orders to provide continuous night patrols for this area. I'll talk to Gnaeus Carbo about sending out some of his skirmishers for the same purpose."

"We're being punished, Captain," said the *optio*. "You're interfering."

This seemed unreasonably obstinate even for a man like this one. "I happen to believe that this punishment is unjust."

"Nevertheless, it was ordered by our commander and we will endure it. You can bugger off, Captain. We'd rather guard ourselves than depend on barbarians." The stony glares of the nearby legionaries told me they shared their *optio*'s poor opinion of me and my Gauls.

Lovernius laughed at this. "So be it. Fools should die like fools."

"That's enough," I said. I had not expected my offer to be met with such ingratitude. But then, I have never understood professional soldiers. "Tomorrow, then, *Optio*." I remounted and we rode away.

"I still want you to provide night patrols," I told Lovernius. "They may be stiff-necked idiots, but they shouldn't be put into such danger just because a man like Vinius got himself killed."

"Whatever you say, Captain."

That evening I settled down to the task of sorting through the goods left behind by the late First Spear. These were not great in bulk. A legion has to march great distances, and even a senior centurion is allowed no more than four or five pack mules for his personal use. The chest that had held his dress armor and decorations was now empty, since those items had been cremated with him. I wondered if the puddle of melted silver and gold would go into the urn along with his charred bones, to be buried beneath the tasteful gravestone being commissioned from one of Massilia's more reputable monument firms.

There was a chest of clothing and another holding his field armor and weapons, which were almost identical to those of an ordinary legionary, but of higher quality. Another held preserved foods, pots of honey, and seasonings; the sort of little comforts and minor luxuries every campaigner takes along to ease the rigors of soldiering.

The smallest chest was heavy for its size. Its lid was fastened with a lock that appeared to be fairly elaborate. I could find no key among the miscellaneous belongings on the table.

"Molon!" I called.

"Here, sir," he said, right at my elbow.

"Where did Vinius keep the key to this?"

"He never allowed me in the tent when he opened that chest, but I saw him reaching for a little pouch at his sword belt on the occasions when he ordered me out."

Wonderful. Doubtless the key now rested among the other metallic debris in the ashes of Vinius's funeral pyre.

"Then run to the smithy and fetch me a crowbar. Be quick about it." He didn't exactly run, but he went into a fast lurch. A short time later he was back with the tool. The box was even stouter than it looked and it took the two of us levering the bar to break the lid open. Inside were papyri and folded wooden tablets, some of them with dangling leaden seals.

"This looks more like something a banker would own than a soldier," I commented. I picked up a tablet and opened it. It was a deed to an Italian estate in Tuscia.

"You'd think he'd keep his land deed in a temple closer to home," I said. I opened another. This, too, was a deed, to an estate in Campania, purchased just a few months before. I noticed Molon studying it over my shoulder. I pointed to the other belongings.

"Stack these things over by the big tent and find something to cover them with." He did not look happy but he set to the task. Quickly, I went through the documents. The bulk of them were deeds to sizable estates. It looked as if Titus Vinius had been determined to buy up Italy. I recognized the names of some of the sellers but that meant nothing. Many wealthy Romans owned lands they had never seen. They bought and sold them through intermediaries, as the wars and politics of the times caused values to rise and fall.

I glanced over the sums recorded for the various sales and made a quick estimate of the total, then I sat back, stunned. Titus Vinius had died a millionaire. Where had this money come from? Men from wealthy families did not make a career in the ranks. I knew that the Tenth had not been in on any of the great looting parties like the sack of Tigranocerta, Mithridates' stronghold, which fell to the legions of Lucullus some eleven years earlier. It had been stationed in Gaul or Spain for at least the last ten years, with occasional visits to northern Italy. The total of his pay and bribes and loot could hardly have amounted to a tenth of the fortune recorded in these documents.

"Will there be . . . ?"

I snapped a deed shut at the sound of Molon's voice. "Don't sneak up on me like that!" He hadn't been sneaking, but I was so absorbed in this incredible revelation that I was oblivious to everything else.

"If you don't mind my saying so, sir, your nerves are on edge. Shall I bring you some wine?"

"Do so." Suddenly, I realized that my mouth was dry. How did these deeds tie in with his murder? I was sure that there had to be a connection. Titus Vinius had died under very peculiar circumstances. Titus Vinius was incredibly rich for a career soldier. Any man may have one great anomaly in his character or his history. I was not prepared to accept two unless they were bound together in some way.

Molon returned with a pitcher and a cup and I drank gratefully. I began to put the deeds back into the chest, and as I did so I shifted it slightly. It still seemed to be exceptionally heavy. I decided to wait and investigate this when there was no observer present.

"Molon, I am going to return to my tent. Carry this chest."

"Excuse me, sir, aren't you going to add these items to the inventory?" He indicated the scroll that lay open by my elbow, one end weighted with a dagger, the other with my helmet. I had completely forgotten it.

"I'll finish up in the morning. It's getting too dark to write. What business is it of yours, anyway?"

"Oh, none, none. Have a little more of this wine, sir."

I did as he suggested. It soothed my agitation wonderfully. After all, what was there to get excited about? I couldn't help it: things were not as expected and that was always upsetting in a hostile environment. I was getting almost soldierlike in my yearning for an orderly existence.

We trudged back to my tent and I kept Molon in front of me the whole time, making sure that he had no opportunity to peek into the chest. I could see that I was going to have a problem with the thing. I wanted nobody to know what I knew until I had some answers to my questions.

Hermes looked as uneasy as I felt when we arrived at my tent. I took his chin between my thumb and forefinger and turned his head for a better view of his face. He had a fine black eye developing.

"You've made Freda's acquaintance, I see."

"Why did you buy him?" Hermes demanded, looking sourly at Molon.

"I didn't buy anybody. Caesar gave them to me."

"It's going to be crowded in this tent," he complained.

"No, it isn't. You and Molon can sleep out here under the awning. Spring is here and summer isn't far off."

"I'll freeze!"

"I shall miss you," I assured him.

The tent flap opened and Freda came out. Hermes' peeved expression changed to one of worshipful awe. It was going to take more than a black eye to dampen his ardor.

"I have set your tent to order," she reported. "You and the boy have been living like swine."

"I suppose it takes a nomad to know how to keep a tent tidy," I said. "Molon, take that chest inside and leave it under my bed." He did as I told him, and I kept my eyes on him the whole time to make sure he didn't look inside it. Then Hermes helped me out of my armor. I waved my arms around and flexed my stiff shoulders. I always felt as if I could fly when I was relieved of that weight.

"Hermes, fetch lamps and put them in the tent."

"There's already one in there," he said, referring to the tiny clay lamp that provided a minimal glow.

"I want more lamps and bigger ones," I told him. "Find me some." He went off muttering and I sat down to absorb some wine before getting to the night's major activity. Freda stood by the doorway, ignoring me while I spoke to Molon.

"Now that you belong to me, I need to know about you," I began. "Tell me about your history."

"Not much to tell," he began, meaning that there was not much he was willing to tell me. "My father was a Greek merchant who lived in Massalia. My mother was a Gaul, a Boian woman from the north, so I learned both their languages as a child. I went with my father on trading expeditions up the river valleys all the way to the Northern Sea." He said all this as if he were speaking of someone else, giving no indication whether it had been a happy time for him.

"I suppose I was about sixteen when we were captured by a party of German raiders. Ordinarily, Greek traders can pass through territory fought over by warring tribes in perfect safety. The Gauls never molest them. They value the foreign trade too highly. But these were Germans who had just come across the river and we were just more foreigners as far as they were concerned. They got into the wine we'd been trading and before long they were putting the men to death and having fun with the women slaves we'd bought. The next morning we were marched back toward Germany. My father was dead by that time, which was a great relief to him."

"Why did they spare you?" I asked him.

"Later on, when I learned their language, I found out that they thought I resembled a forest sprite of theirs; a mischievous creature that lives beneath the roots of trees and plays tricks on people. They thought it might be bad luck to kill me, so they made me their slave. At first they used me for hard labor, but I proved I could be more valuable to them as an interpreter."

"Why?" I asked. "There are German tribes that have lived next to Gauls for centuries. There should be no shortage of Germans fluent in both tongues. And they must have plenty of Gallic slaves."

"Very true," he nodded, "but these were a tribe from the deep forest, and they had little trust of the river-dwelling tribes, and none at all for Gauls, slave or free."

"What made you different?"

"I was Greek, or at least half-Greek, and therefore exotic. I wasn't connected to any of the local tribes, so I wasn't likely to betray them out of tribal loyalty."

"So how did Vinius acquire you?"

"My mas—that is to say, my former master was among the envoys sent by Rome two years ago to treat with King Ariovistus. He met with them on the east bank of the Rhine, in order to keep up the fiction that he was not maintaining a presence in Gaul proper."

"These Germans may not be as politically unsophisticated as we often think," I mused.

"They have little liking for subtlety," Molon said, "but they are adept at just about everything that helps to expand their power. They like to fight, but they would rather intimidate than fight, and they are quite willing to negotiate until they are strong enough to attack."

"You begin to prove your value already. Did Vinius buy you?"

"I was among the gifts given to the envoys. Titus Vinius asked for me personally and the others acceded willingly, since they thought me to be by far the least valuable of the presents."

"A pardonable mistake. Did he acquire Freda the same way?"

He looked at her with a smirk. She glared back. "No, she was given to him by a Suebian chieftain named Nasua a few months later."

"Why?" I asked him. "And who are the Suebi?"

"They are an eastern tribe who arrived on the Rhine about the time of that embassy. As to why, the German chiefs are great gift givers, and they are always trying to outdo each other in generosity. Nasua leads jointly with his brother, Cimberius. It seems Cimberius sent a splendid, jeweled goblet to the Roman Proconsul, so Nasua presented Freda to Vinius in front of all the chiefs and dignitaries. He said she was a captive princess of some tribe far in the interior, but I think she is just some cow tender's daughter he had tired of."

Freda snarled something and boxed him alongside the head hard enough to send him staggering several steps.

"What did she say?" I asked him. "It sounded uncommonly vile."

He grinned, exposing many gaps. "She told me how pleased she is to be the property of so handsome and noble a Roman as yourself, sir."

"And I was almost beginning to believe what you said. But tell me this: Why have you never sued to have your freedom returned? If your father was a citizen of Massilia and you were taken captive by raiders from across the Rhine, then your slavery is unlawful and may be set aside."

He shrugged. "My mother was just a concubine. My father had a legitimate son by his Greek wife and never acknowledged me. There is little point in suing. Freedom is a greatly overrated commodity, anyway. For most of us it just means freedom to starve."

I got up as Hermes returned with the lamps. While he arranged them inside the tent, I watched Freda watching me. No fear there, just a coolly fierce calculation.

"There you go," Hermes announced as he came out. "It's lit up like a forge in there."

"You and Molon make yourselves comfortable out here," I told them. "Freda, come with me." I ducked through the doorway and sat on the edge of my cot. The ropes creaked beneath me as I tugged at the laces of my boots. Freda came in. "Close the flap behind you," I told her. She did so, a slightly contemptuous twist marring the perfect beauty of her lips. In the distance I heard a trumpet call; a lonely sound, even in a crowded legionary camp.

With my boots off I lay back, lacing my fingers behind my head. It gave me a casual look and concealed their trembling from her. "Come closer," I said. The tent was not a large one. A single step brought her within inches of where I lay.

"What do you want?" she asked in a tone that said she knew very well what I wanted.

"Take your clothes off," I told her, keeping my voice amazingly steady. She hesitated, radiating defiance. "Freda," I said patiently, "there are three men before whom a woman should never be ashamed to undress: her husband, her physician, and her owner. Now get out of that barbaric costume."

With an even more extreme curl to her lip, she reached up and unfastened the fibula that held her hide tunic at the left shoulder. The swell of her breast kept it from falling and she tugged it down to her waist. Then she had to push it past the broad curvature of her hips. Beyond that resistance, it fell to puddle around her ankles.

The sight of a barbarian woman's body can be shocking to one of refined sensibilities. Highborn Roman women carefully remove every strand of hair that appears from their scalps on down. They often have even their slaves given similar treatment. Even Gallic men depilate themselves except for their scalps and upper lips. Germans think it best not to interfere with nature in these matters. Unlike many Roman men, I do not find a woman repellant in her naturally hirsute state. Rather the contrary, in fact, and never more so than in Freda's case. She looked like a raw young animal, not a polished marble statue.

"Turn around," I said, my voice barely betraying the sudden dryness of my mouth.

"Whatever my master wishes," she said, making a slow half turn. Her great, golden mane covered her to the cleft of her buttocks.

"Raise your hair," I told her. She gathered the mass of tresses atop her head and held it there with both hands, standing with her weight on one leg in the classic pose of the Aphrodite *Kallipygia*. She was a picture of youth, strength, and grace; a magnificent young beast perfect in every detail, including a flawless skin.

"All right, you can put your clothes back on."

She whirled and let her hair drop. "What?" It was the first genuine feeling I had been able to elicit from her.

"I've seen what I wanted to see. Put your tunic back on. Or leave it off, if you'd rather sleep that way."

She stooped and picked up her furry tunic. "You are easily satisfied."

"Titus Vinius did not beat you, Freda," I said. "Why was that?"

"I pleased him," she said, fastening the fibula at her shoulder.

"Don't be absurd," I said. "That vicious bastard beat anything that came within reach of his vinestock. You don't have a mark on your skin. Tell me why this is so."

She sank down onto the pallet recently occupied by the now-banished Hermes. "Men sometimes find their pleasures in strange practices. Especially men who have great power over lesser men. Sometimes, such men like to be beaten themselves." She smiled at me sweetly. "They like to be humiliated and degraded by women. By slave women best of all."

By Hercules, I thought, these Germans are far more sophisticated than I had imagined!

"And you performed these, ah, services for Titus Vinius?"

"Whenever he wished. And he never laid a hand or a stick on me, although he sometimes spoke roughly to me in front of others. He said that he had to do this for the sake of appearances. He always begged my forgiveness afterward and wanted to be punished for it."

Well, well, Titus Vinius, I thought. What an odd person you've turned out to be. I'd known politicians who didn't have as many strange quirks.

"You always obliged him?" I asked.

"Of course. I am a slave, after all."

"So you are. Go to sleep, Freda, I have a lot to think about."

She studied me incredulously for a few moments, then she lay down, pillowing her head on her bent arm. She closed her eyes, but whether she slept or not I could not tell. I snuffed out the lamps and lay back.

It had not been easy. I had longed to take her in both hands and bury my face in that fabulous hair, but I knew I would be lost if I did that. She might be a barbarian slave, but she knew her own power and I would be acknowledging that power by following my natural inclinations.

Whatever else I was, I was not going to be another Titus Vinius.

8

MY FIRST STOP THE NEXT MORN-
ing was the smithy. The smith, like many of the legion's arti-
sans, was a soldier who earned himself extra pay and exemption
from fatigue by practicing a necessary craft. Luckily, repairing
the lock on Vinius's chest and crafting a key for it was not
beyond his level of skill. I stood close while he did the work
and paid him a couple of sesterces for the effort. It was not
strictly necessary to pay him, but it is always a mistake to take
such persons for granted. I might need to have my horse shod
some day and it would be done more expeditiously if the man
remembered me fondly.

I left the chest inside the great tent of the praetorium,
where it would be about as safe as it could be under the circumstances. Then I went to speak with the men most immediately concerned with the success of my mission. I found them

under heavy guard in a pit excavated next to the tent in which the standards were kept. It was twenty feet on a side and twelve feet deep. A *contubernium* stood around its periphery facing inward, each man with a sheaf of javelins to go with his *pilum*. One of the guards had a white band painted around the lower rim of his helmet, signifying that he was the decurion.

"I am the investigating officer," I said, addressing the man with the white band. "I need to speak with the prisoners."

"We were told you are to have access," the decurion said. He turned to the man next to him. "Silva, run the ladder down for the captain."

"While I confer with them, I'd appreciate it if you and your men would step back from the edge here. I need to speak in private."

He shook his head. "Not a chance, sir. If one of them contrives to commit suicide, one of us takes his place. If they harm you, we all go in there. Just keep your voice down and we promise not to eavesdrop."

I went down the ladder and Burrus jumped up to greet me. The rest sat disconsolately on the muddy ground, their ankle-rings fastened to a single chain like a slave work gang. Men in their predicament could be forgiven for a lack of enthusiasm.

"Patron!" Burrus said. "What is happening? The guards are forbidden to speak to us."

"First off, I've been assigned to investigate the murder of Vinius."

He turned to the others. "You see? I told you my patron would get us out of this. He is famous for rooting out traitors and murderers. We are as good as free!"

I was touched by his faith in me, although I feared it might be exaggerated. I looked at the rest of the *contubernium* and they seemed to share my skepticism. Quadratus gave me a sour smile and nod. The rest looked me over warily. They were typical soldiers, most of them older than Burrus, a couple of them silver-stubbled veterans. It was the sort of balance considered ideal in the legions, with the veterans providing steadiness and the recruits the youthful boldness necessary to aggressive operations. A unit made up entirely of veterans is likely to be too cautious; one of recruits too reckless and easily panicked in adversity. It was a combination that had won us an empire.

"I am the only man in Gaul who can save you," I told them bluntly. "I do not believe that you killed Titus Vinius, but even I must acknowledge that you *look* as guilty as Oedipus."

"Who's Oedipus?" one of them asked.

"He was that Greek who put it to his mother," said a veteran.

"Well," said another, "that's Greeks for you. What do you expect?"

We were getting off the subject and I made a mental vow to avoid metaphors. "Listen here. If I am to prove that you men did not kill Vinius, I need to know everything you know about him. You don't need to tell me how vicious he was, I know all about that. But did he have, let us say, extralegionary dealings?"

"What senior centurion doesn't?" Quadratus said. "Naturally, he was dealing with the local merchants and suppliers. The First Spear and the Prefect of the Camp always live in each other's purses. It's always been that way with the legions."

"I'm looking for something more serious than the usual, petty institutionalized corruption. How was Vinius making himself rich?"

A veteran scratched his chin. "I never knew that Vinius was any richer than other men of his rank. We paid him what we could to get out of shit fatigues and punishments, but that's not going to make anyone rich. We used to figure most of his bribes went to buy him new vinestocks." At this the others laughed, showing a commendable resiliency of spirit.

"I've learned something about Vinius," I said, lowering my voice, "and I want you to keep this among yourselves."

Quadratus gestured toward the surrounding guards. "You think we're going to blab it all over camp?"

"In the last year," I continued, "Titus Vinius was investing heavily in estates in Italy. He spent or pledged in excess of a million *denarii* and I am curious as to just how he came by such a sum."

"It's news to me," Quadratus said. The others looked similarly dumbfounded. "Of course, he didn't consult with us about his financial dealings."

"I'll wager that he didn't confide in anybody," I said. "Not in this legion, at any rate. That's why I want to know what he was doing *outside* the legion. Molon tells me that he was on at least one or two embassies to the Gauls and Germans."

"Watch out what that ugly bugger tells you," said one of the older men. "A slave will never tell the truth when he can get away with a lie. But that much is true. Vinius went out just about every time the Proconsul here had to treat with the barbarians. He was in charge of the honor guard and the First Spear's advice was always sought in military matters. It's custom."

"Did Vinius ever consult with the Gauls or the Germans here?"

At that they all laughed. "Barbarians in this camp? Not likely, except for those praetorian auxilia."

This was getting like those dreams I sometimes had, where I was always running through the strangely deserted streets of Rome, trying to get home or to the Forum, and somehow never making it there, instead running into a succession of blind alleys.

"All right, then, tell me about what you were doing the night he was killed."

"Quadratus and I were on the same station on the north wall where you found us before," Burrus said. "We always had the same guard posts on our duty nights, which, as you know, was every night recently." He named the other six by pairs. He and Quadratus had manned the easternmost post, and the rest had the three successive posts to the west.

"When did you last see him?" I asked.

"At evening parade before guard mount," Burrus told me. "He was on the reviewing stand with the *legatus*, like most evenings."

"Caesar wasn't there?"

"The Proconsul usually appears only at formal parades," said a veteran. "Often as not, morning and evening parades are reviewed by a tribune."

"You didn't see him on the wall that night?"

"We rarely do," Quadratus said. "Why work your way up to senior centurion if you're just going to tramp around the wall all night like a common boot?"

"Spoken like a true career soldier," I told him. "He was found dressed in a coarse, dark-colored tunic, like a slave's. Did any of you ever see him dressed like that?"

They looked at one another with embarrassed expressions, an odd sight on such hard-bitten countenances.

"Well, sir," a veteran began, "we all knew that Vinius and that German woman got up to some pretty strange games, but they kept it behind the tent flap. He never let anyone see him looking like anything but a centurion."

"Dressed like that, in public," Quadratus elaborated, "well, he'd've been a laughingstock, worse than when you showed up in that full-dress rig." They all had a good chuckle at my expense. "He would've lost respect, and a centurion can't afford that. A First Spear least of all."

"He was killed a few hundred yards from where you were standing guard," I said. "Did you hear anything?"

"Just the barbarians raising their usual racket," Burrus said. "Just like that night you were guard officer. They could've slaughtered a dozen Romans out there and we probably wouldn't have noticed. On top of that, we were all half dead from lack of sleep."

"That's one thing being shut up here is good for," Quadratus commented. "Mud and all, last night was the first decent sleep we've had in weeks."

I looked up. There was nothing above the tent except the cloud-scattered blue sky. "I'll see if I can persuade Labienus to put an awning over this hole."

"It's not too bad as it is," said one of the veterans. "Not like it was Libya."

I left them with further assurances that I would extricate them from what looked like certain doom. The younger men seemed eager to believe me. The rest had long ago learned the folly of expecting anything except the worst.

Walking back toward the praetorium I saw that a sizable

crowd had gathered in the camp forum. I sauntered over to see what was going on, passing as I did the scorched patch of ground occupied the previous day by the funeral pyre of Titus Vinius. In the middle of the crowd I saw Labienus seated in a curule chair on a low platform with a half-dozen lictors before him, leaning on their *fasces*. Spotting Carbo among the onlookers, I went to see what was going on.

"The *legatus* is holding court," he informed me. "A bunch of Provincial dignitaries and lawyers came in this morning and they need judgments on some long-standing cases."

"In a military camp in a war zone?" I said.

"Life goes on," Carbo told me, "even in wartime."

It is one of the many anomalies of our governmental system that, when we sent a propraetor or proconsul to the territories, we expect one man to be both magistrate and military commander. That is why he takes a *legatus*; so that he can concentrate on the more crucial function, leaving the other to his assistant. But sometimes, as now, the same man had to fill both roles. I was surprised to see well-dressed Gauls among the dignitaries, including some Druids who looked like the same ones I had seen earlier.

If nothing else, this seemed an opportunity to have the praetorium to myself. I took a shortcut over the wall by the speaking platform and found the big tent deserted. First I walked a complete circuit of the tent to make sure that there were no possible onlookers, then I went inside.

I lifted the heavy chest onto the table and opened it with my shiny new key. I took out all the deeds and made a list of them, with full particulars including purchase price. Then, with all the papers and tablets heaped to one side, I picked up the box. It was still far too heavy, even taking the thick wood and iron strapping into account. I carried it to the door opening and set it down with sunlight flooding into the bottom. It was perfectly smooth and without any projections. I tried shifting the heavy rivets that held the strapping, but none of them moved.

I turned it over and examined the bottom. The chest rested on four stubby legs about an inch high, with leather pads glued to their feet. These I twisted one by one. The third one gave slightly. I took the chest back to the table and grasped the leg. Lifting that corner slightly, I turned the leg again. There was a click before it had completed one quarter of a revolution. The bottom of the chest sprang up a bit. I managed to get my dagger point between the bottom and the side and levered it up. The wooden slab came up easily. I was looking at what seemed to be a second chest bottom, this one made of solid gold.

After a while I remembered to breathe and took a closer look. There was a cross-hatching of lines on the otherwise regular slab of gold. I stuck my dagger point into an interstice and pried up a miniature gold brick the length and width of my forefinger. It lay astonishingly heavy in my hand and I saw in the rectangular hole left by it another layer of gold.

I replaced the gold bar, closed the false bottom, and twisted the trick chest leg into alignment. Then I went to the tent's provision chest and helped myself to a goblet of Caesar's wine, proud that I didn't spill a drop.

Who knew about this treasure? Vinius seemed to have no family. Did he confide in that steward of his? If so, how intimately? Sneakily, unworthily, a compelling thought crept into my brain: There was wealth here sufficient to clear all my debts and finance my tenure of the notoriously expensive aedileship. I could repair the streets and renovate a temple or two and put on splendid Games and have plenty left over for fun. How difficult could it be to alter those deeds and transfer them all to my name? I could become a major landholder, completely independent for the first time in my life. The estates were widely scattered and no one would ever know about most of them. Wealth in land was rarely investigated. Wealth of any kind, for that matter.

"Into the wine supply a bit early, aren't you?"

I jerked around. Labienus stood in the doorway. "I find it helps my ponderings," I told him.

"Pour me a cup," he said. "I could use a little inspiration." He walked in. "I had to take a break before I ordered some summary executions that someone might sue me for when I return to Rome. Gods, how I detest provincial businessmen and *publicani*." He glanced at the stack of deeds beside the strongbox. "Did those belong to Vinius? A lot of paperwork for a centurion."

I handed him a cup. "He was a bit of a businessman himself."

"Do yourself a favor," Labienus advised. "Forget about this murder. I know that boy is one of your clients, but your family must have thousands of them. He won't be missed, and the sooner those eight are executed, the sooner this army will return to normal. Normal is what you want with a war starting."

"I can't let it rest until I'm satisfied," I told him. "And I'm far from satisfied."

"What is the great mystery?" he demanded. "The man was a brute and he treated his men like animals. That particular *contubernium* caught the brunt of his stick and it drove them to an act of foolish desperation. Completely understandable, if unforgivable. Let them pay for it and be done with it."

"It doesn't make sense," I said.

151

"What doesn't?" he said impatiently.

"The dagger, for one thing."

"The dagger? What about it? Good, traditional weapon for killing people. Done all the time. Explain yourself."

"We have here eight soldiers, at least three of whom would have taken part in the murder. Every one of them carries a gladius day and night. Why use a dagger when you can use a gladius? You know what a gladius stab is like. It looks like someone rammed a shovel through the body. People sometimes survive a dagger thrust, if no vital organs are pierced and the infection doesn't kill them. A gladius thrust is certain death, which is why we adopted the murderous thing in the first place."

"You have a point," he admitted. "But men in such extremity often don't think straight. And it was a conspiracy. Each may have wanted to deliver just a part of the killing so that the guilt would be evenly spread."

"A valid objection," I allowed, my lawyer's training coming to the fore. "But I find it hard to believe that they would be so incautious in eliminating a man as dangerous as Titus Vinius." This legalistic fencing was helping me to keep my mind off all that gold in the bottom of the box. Even so, my scalp was sweating. "And the business with the strangler's noose. It just doesn't sound soldierly. I think these men would have done the job neatly and quickly, had they been inclined to kill him. And there is the way he was dressed."

"That is an oddity."

"The accused men say that the last time they saw him he was with you on the reviewing stand at evening parade. Did you see him after that?"

"Let's see . . . he came back to the praetorium and conferred for a while with Caesar and some Gauls—"

"Gauls? What Gauls?"

"Some of the ones out there now. They were hounding Caesar for some decisions about their cases, because they know that once the war is on there'll be no time for holding assizes."

"What are their cases concerned with?"

"The usual," he shrugged. "Contracts for public works, which are in doubt because of this extraordinary five-year commission; some killings that would expand into blood feuds if we allowed these Provincial Gauls to revert to their ancestral ways; a number of land tenures that are in dispute, that sort of thing."

The mention of land made my ears twitch, but land in Gaul didn't seem to interest Titus Vinius. It occurred to me to wonder why. The province held splendid farmlands and they could be had cheaper than any in Italy. Labor was cheap as well. There was always the uncertainty connected with the upcoming war, but if that was his reason, it displayed a disappointing lack of confidence in Roman arms on the part of a senior centurion.

"Why did Caesar need him to confer with these Gauls?"

"I don't know. I was only there for a few minutes before I had to go to the camp of the auxilia to inspect the newly arrived cavalry. In any case, Caesar just told them to come back for court in two days. He didn't tell them that he'd be gone. He just wanted to fob it all off on me. In some ways he is as lazy as he ever was."

"You didn't see Vinius after that?"

"No. He probably retired to his tent with his German woman." He looked at me sharply, reminded of the grudge he and all the other officers had against me. "How did you rate her, anyway? If Caesar didn't want her, he should have given her to me. I'm his *legatus*."

"I have powerful friends in the Senate."

"Hm. He probably owes you money. Caesar is supposed to have cleared his debts at last but I don't believe it. They were just too enormous. Oh well, back to work." He set his cup on the table, next to the gold-laden box. "Take my advice, Metellus: Let those men be executed. It will be the best thing all around."

"Not until I'm satisfied they're guilty."

"It's your career." He stooped and went back outside.

I carefully stowed the documents back in the chest and locked it. Then I hung the key on a thong around my neck. Then I sat and stared at the chest for a while. I longed to take it to my tent, but I could not afford to draw attention to it. I certainly couldn't carry it about with me. I entertained wild visions of sneaking out of the camp under cover of darkness and burying it someplace, to return later to dig it up. I pushed aside this childish fantasy and decided that the praetorium was the best place for it. It was well guarded and I had already ordered Vinius's belongings transferred there.

How safe was it? For one thing, it wasn't safe from me. Never had such temptation been thrown my way. I was getting the bitter feeling that I could be just as corrupt as all those Senators I so despised. Maybe their opportunities had just come along earlier. Then I thought of Burrus and the rest of his *contubernium*. Might I have given in had the lives of men I believed to be innocent not depended upon me? I still do not like to think about it.

But what of the others? There was a strong likelihood that Paterculus, the Prefect of the Camp, was involved in these unsavory doings. Did he know about the chest? If so, what could I do about it? Damned little. In fact, if *any* of these military savages wanted that box, I would be well advised to let them have it, unless I wanted to end up facedown in a pool myself.

And what of Caesar? Oddly, for one of the very rare occasions in all the years that I knew him, I did not seriously suspect him of culpability. For one thing, he had taken charge of the Tenth only about two months previously, while Vinius' suspicious transactions went back at least a year. It was possible that Vinius had cut Caesar in on whatever he had going on, but I doubted that as well. If Caesar had something to hide he certainly would not have assigned me to investigate, knowing as he did my enthusiasm for snooping into things.

In the end I hauled the incredibly valuable box outside and stowed it with Vinius' other belongings, under the cover Molon had spread over them. Either it would be safe or it would not, and in either case I intended to stay alive and unhurt. The temptation still rankled, though. The sudden wash of greed had left me feeling unclean. I almost envied men like Crassus, who could make a whole career out of raw greed and feel perfectly wonderful about it. That was his public face, anyway. For all I knew, he woke screaming in the middle of the night with dream-Furies chasing him, like any other man with a guilty conscience.

In the midst of these unsettling thoughts I walked out through the opening in the praetorium rampart and collided with a white-robed man who was passing by outside. I started to stammer apologies and realized that he was the youngest of the three Druids I had seen when the Gallic and German envoys had called on Caesar. I switched from Latin to Greek, which I thought he might understand.

"Your pardon, sir. My thoughts were elsewhere."

He raised a hand to his breast and swept his staff to one side in a graceful gesture. "The fault was mine," he said in heavily accented but very passable Greek. "I was admiring the standards and failed to watch where I was going." He nodded toward where the eagle and the lesser standards stood in gleaming splendor, guarded by men draped in lion skins, near the pit where the provisionally condemned men waited for me to save them.

"I am Decius Caecilius Metellus the Younger," I informed him, extending my hand. He took it awkwardly, like one unused to the gesture. His hand was as soft as a patrician woman's. Clearly, these Druids had made an easy life for themselves.

"Caecilius Metellus? Is that not one of the great Roman families?"

"We are not without distinction," I affirmed, preening.

"I am Badraig, acolyte of the Singing Druids."

"You came here for the court?" I inquired.

"Yes. We had expected Caesar to be here." He looked annoyed at this. Apparently, Labienus had been correct about Caesar's ruse.

"Caius Julius can be unpredictable," I commiserated.

"I had thought he held us in higher esteem. Several times during the negotiations he has entertained us separately, and we have informed him of our religion and customs and practices." Clearly, he didn't realize that Caesar was gathering propaganda to use against them.

"Don't be upset. In the Proconsul's absence his *legatus* wields full authority. His every decision will be backed up by the Senate. If you don't mind my asking, what business do you Druids have before the court?"

"There are several border disputes to be settled here, and these require our presence."

"I am not well informed about your customs, but it was my impression that Druids owned no land." He fell in beside me as I strolled toward my tent. I had no objection to such interesting and unusual company and he certainly led my thoughts away from that troublesome box.

"Nor do we, although we have charge of holy places. But by ancient custom Druids must be present before any decision can be taken concerning boundary disputes. In the days before the Roman presence in the land you call the Province, the decision would have lain with us." I detected more than a hint of resentment in this.

"Well, that much less to trouble you, then. Ah, here we are. This is my tent. Will you join me for some refreshment?"

"You do me honor," he said, with another graceful gesture. Whatever the rest of the Gauls were like, at least the Druids were well-bred.

"Molon! A chair for my guest."

Molon came out of the tent and gaped in astonishment at my guest. "Right away, sir," he said, and scurried off to borrow one from another tent. He was back in moments, and then he and Freda proceeded to serve lunch. She regarded the young priest with the same cool disdain she seemed to hold for the entire male sex. As Lovernius had hinted, the Germans had little awe of the Druids or their sacred sites.

"We're low on wine," she announced.

"Can't have that, now, can we?" I reached into my pouch and handed her a few coins, wincing at the expenditure. No more worries about money if I can just get back to Rome with that box, I thought. I pushed the evil thought aside, knowing that it would return all too soon. "Run along to the camp forum," I bade Freda. "Doubtless a wine merchant has set up. A trial crowd is always a thirsty crowd."

Without comment, she turned and walked away. Badraig did not follow her with his eyes. These Druids were an unworldly lot, I thought.

Molon had come up with a passable hare, but Badraig passed it up in favor of fruit and bread. Likewise he declined to accept any wine, drinking water instead. More for me, I thought.

"That is an interesting staff," I remarked. It leaned against the table and I was admiring its intricate carving. It was about man-height, made of some twisted wood. "Is it a part of the Druidic regalia, like an augur's *lituus?*"

"Yes, every Druid carries one. It is used to mark out sacred boundaries and consecrate waters. But it is also a walking stick and is not sacred in itself. You may handle it."

I took it and found that it was heavier than it appeared. Its whole length was carved in a bewildering interlaced design, but the knotty top was the most interesting. A natural swelling in the wood had been carved into the head of a deity, only it had three faces, each facing in a different direction. The eyes bugged out grotesquely, as they usually do in Gallic art. I have often wondered why the Gauls, wonderful artificers though they are, choose to portray the human form in this grotesque and childlike fashion.

"Is this one god or three?" I asked him.

"You see three gods, yet they are one," he answered cryptically.

"Three or one, which is it?" I asked.

"Most of our gods have triple natures," he explained, "and

above them all are the great three: Esus, the Lord of all Gods; Taranis, god of thunder; and Teutates, Lord of Sacred Waters, the chief god of the people."

"Three gods, then," I pronounced.

"After a fashion. And yet they are one."

I hoped this was not going to turn into the sort of vague, mystical mumbo-jumbo in which foreigners delight. He would have to exert himself to exceed an Egyptian priest in tediousness, though.

"Each is worshipped in separate ceremonies, at different times of year, and each has his own ritual, his own sacrifices. But all three are one god, each aspect presiding over one season of the year."

"Your year has three seasons?"

"Certainly: autumn, winter, and summer. Autumn begins with the feast of Lughnasa, winter with the feast of Samain, and summer with the feast of Beltain, when the great bonfires are kindled." Clearly, these Gauls were a people who liked to do things by threes.

I tore off a leg of roast hare and dipped it in a bowl of *garum* sauce. Badraig drew back a bit, involuntarily. It seemed that, like most Gauls, he regarded *garum* with ill-concealed horror. I decided to throw tact to the winds.

"Is it true that you hold human sacrifices at these festivals?"

"Oh, but of course," he said, as if there were nothing at all peculiar about the practice. "What other sacrifice could be worthy of the great ones? To Taranis, for instance, we offer prisoners taken in battle. These are placed in holy images made of wicker which, after the most solemn ceremonies, are set alight."

Sorry that I had asked, I pinched the bridge of my nose between thumb and forefinger. "Yes, I had heard something of this."

"Now for sacrifice to Esus," he began, warming to the subject, "the victims are . . ."

At that moment I was saved from further enlightenment by Freda's return. She had a large wine jug balanced on her shoulder and she jerked her thumb at Badraig as she approached. "They want him at the court," she said curtly.

"Be more respectful," I said. "This gentleman is a priest of high rank as well as my guest."

She looked down her long nose at him. "He just looks like another Gaul to me." With that she swayed her way back into the tent. I stared after her, fuming, amazed once more that Vinius had never beaten her. She certainly made *me* want to beat her. I turned back to Badraig.

"A thousand pardons. That savage is recently caught and she hasn't yet been properly trained."

He waved a hand dismissively, wearing a broad smile. "That one is a German to her bones and she will never change. You would be well advised to free her or sell her to a trader traveling south. Her sort are always more dangerous than useful."

"I shall give it serious consideration."

He rose and took his staff. "And now I must go. Doubtless some legal precedent I have memorized is required. I thank you most gratefully for your hospitality."

"You have provided good company."

"You show an unusual interest in our religion. Would you like to attend a celebration of ours?"

I was astonished. "You allow foreigners to observe your rites?"

"Not all of them are great, solemn occasions. I will get word to you when there is to be a celebration nearby. I promise: no human sacrifices."

"Very kind of you to offer, but there is a war on and I am bound by duty."

He smiled again. "You never know. In war, there is always far more waiting than fighting. Good day to you, Decius Caecilius Metellus the Younger."

"And to you, Badraig the Druid," I answered, wishing I knew whatever string of honorifics he doubtless had to add to his name. I always hate to be outdone in courtesy by a barbarian. Still smiling, he turned and walked away, toward the camp forum.

9

I SPENT THE REST OF THE DAY IN-
terviewing officers and legionaries concerning the whereabouts
and activities of Titus Vinius on the fateful night. Surprisingly,
no one within the camp had a clear memory of seeing him after
the conference in Caesar's tent. Perforce, I had to go outside
the camp.

The unfortified camp of the ill-starred First Century stood
neat and orderly, almost a miniature of the main camp. The
men looked a bit weary after their watchful night, but otherwise
perfectly fit. The tents were arranged century-fashion, forming
three sides of a square with the fourth side open. The sentries
stood a long javelin cast from the tents, leaning on their shields.
I gave the watchword even though they could see perfectly well
who I was and they allowed me to pass with surly expressions.

I found the *optio*, Aulus Vehilius, conferring with his decurions next to their fire, where a slave tended a pot of *posca*. I could smell the vinegar reek fifty feet away. The *optio* watched me with the by now customary look of annoyed disgust as I dismounted.

"How did the night go?" I inquired politely.

"We're alive, aren't we?" he said.

"Yes, please accept my congratulations. I need to ask some questions about the last hours of Titus Vinius."

"Still trying to save your precious client and his messmates?" said a decurion. "They're safe in the camp and we're out here. Why are they so favored?"

"They are the ones facing a dreadful execution," I pointed out.

"If the Gauls attack in any force," interjected another, "we'll die before they will."

"Listen to me, you ungrateful peasant wretches," I said affably. "Nobody is going to die if I have anything to say about it. I do not believe Vinius was murdered by the men of that *contubernium*, nor do I believe that his century was responsible in any way. I feel sure that Vinius brought about his own death and that it was richly merited. But I have to prove it first. I have been given a special commission by Caesar himself to investigate and I am empowered to interrogate anyone within his *imperium*. If you object, you may argue with the Proconsul when he gets back. Do not expect a sympathetic hearing."

This seemed to sober them a bit and I reflected that these were terrified men. Roman soldiers are the best in the world and brave as lions, but much of that has to do with the way they identify with their legions and the eagles. A soldier separated from his legion becomes diminished. I was just the most convenient target for their anger. In a perverse but understandable way, they held it against Burrus and his companions that they were not being executed for the good of the rest.

The crusty *optio* actually managed a barely detectable smile. "All right, Captain, we'll back off. What do you need to know?"

"The last account I have of Vinius's whereabouts that night says that he attended a conference in Caesar's tent with some locals who wanted judgments on land disputes. That was just after the evening parade. Did any of you see him after that?"

"You know that we had the north wall that night," said Vehilius. "We marched straight from parade to guard mount."

"The whole century?"

"Yes. This doubling of the guard means there's two centuries to each relief and the First is in my charge."

"And Vinius never made an inspection of the guard posts?"

"He seldom did that," the *optio* said, confirming what I had already heard. "When he inspected, it was always toward the end of the watch, to catch anyone sleeping."

"And he knew that wasn't going to happen," a decurion commented, "not with all the noise the barbarians were making."

There was something wrong with this, but I could not decide what it might be. Perhaps, I thought, I was just too unmilitary to detect the inconsistency.

"There was the odd way he was dressed," I pointed out. "Did anyone ever see him in a rough, dark-colored tunic?"

"Centurions in the Tenth wear white tunics, as you've probably noticed," the *optio* said.

"On regular duty, certainly. But did Vinius ever undertake reconnaissance at night? I used to do that in Spain and I always

165

wore dark clothes and no armor, for obvious reasons."

"Then you must have been an officer of auxilia," Vehilius said, quite accurately. "Every legion I've ever heard of uses cavalry and scouts for that sort of thing. It stands to reason—a man who spends years clumping around under a full load of legionary gear is going to be no good for quiet work at night. Titus Vinius would never have done such a thing."

Another dead end. I did not dare ask these men about Vinius's sudden wealth. Isolated though they were, the news would be all over the camp within hours.

"If you want to know what he was doing that night," said a decurion, "ask that ugly slave of his, Molon. He's a lying little sneak like all slaves, but if you lash him for a while, or put a hot iron to his feet, he just might tell you what you need to know."

This advice was in keeping with the common belief of Romans that slaves are inveterate liars. Even our courts will not allow the testimony of slaves unless they are tortured first, on the assumption that only torture will make a slave tell the truth. I have never understood the reasoning behind this widespread prejudice, because it has been my experience that *nobody*, slave or free, ever tells the truth if they see the slightest advantage in lying.

"You might try the German girl," hazarded another, "although I'd hate to mark that one up." They all took on a look of collective lust.

"Don't bother," said the one who had recommended tormenting Molon. "That one'll spit in your eye if you threaten her with thumbscrews or a hot iron. Germans are like that."

"How do you know so much about Germans?" I asked him.

"It's what we've heard," he answered, as if that explained everything. Soldiers place enormous confidence in rumor. I do not think this is confined to Roman legionaries. Things were probably the same at the siege of Troy. Our whole system of taking auguries is an attempt at rumor control. Before taking any military action we first observe for omens to see if the gods are favorable. If the omens are good ones, everybody feels better. If they are unfavorable, we usually go ahead and fight anyway. Then, if we lose, we can blame the general for ignoring the bad omens. It works out.

"In recent months," I said, "did Vinius display any major change of behavior or character?" I watched the faces of men struggling with an unfamiliar concept.

"He did say something strange a few weeks ago," the *optio* said at last. "I said to him that next year, if he didn't transfer to another legion, he'd be able to step in as Prefect of the Camp when Paterculus retires. You know what he said?"

"What did he say?" I prodded gently.

"He just shrugged and said, 'Let someone else have it.' "

"He said that?" a decurion gasped, disbelieving.

"Doesn't make sense," said another. "I mean, First Spear's a fine slot, but Prefect of the Camp's where you get a chance to clean up and provide for your retirement. What's the point of soldiering for twenty-four years if you're going to pass up the best rating in the legion?"

"At the time I just thought he meant he was thinking of transferring," said the *optio*. "Crassus is offering big bonuses for centurions to help raise and train the legions he wants for his war with Parthia. But now I think of it, he probably couldn't. Caesar is serious about a big, long war with the Gauls, and he has this five-year *imperium*. The only way anyone's going to transfer out of his legions is by hopping a ride with the ferryman."

"Crassus's agents have been nosing around?" I said. "He doesn't even have Senate approval for a war with Parthia."

"I guess he figures he can buy it," said Vehilius. "People say that Crassus can buy anything, including his own legions."

This last was quite true. Crassus always did things in a big way. But he was supposed to be raising legions for Caesar, not building his own. This would bear thinking about.

Think about it was what I did as I made my way back to the camp. Crassus had for years been jealous of Pompey's military glory, and glory counted for much in Roman politics. During the years that Pompey had been subduing one enemy after another, Crassus' only military distinction had been in defeating Spartacus, a victory now more than twelve years past: an eternity in Roman politics. Granted, Spartacus had been an enemy more dangerous than all the others combined, but there was precious little glory to be had from defeating slaves. Even then, Pompey had followed his usual pattern of stepping in at the last minute, wiping out a remnant of the already defeated slave army, and then taking credit for the whole war.

It was no wonder that Crassus drooled at the prospect of a war with Parthia. It was the only really credible enemy we had on our frontiers at the time. They were a relatively civilized people, militarily powerful and, best of all, they controlled the silk route, a source of inestimable wealth.

Crassus was getting old, and was all too aware of the fact. Lately, he had been running on to any who would listen about his upcoming Parthian war, even though the Parthians had done little to provoke our wrath. Certainly, the war in Gaul would absorb our energies for some time to come. Were these just the senile ramblings of a frustrated politician? Little matter. His wealth made him a power to fear no matter how crazy he might have become.

Even so, Gaul was a long way from Rome and I had difficulty crediting even the wealth of Crassus with such a reach. Vinius had somehow achieved wealth far beyond the most lavish bribes a centurion could hope for.

I knew that, as always in a case like this one, I lacked all the evidence. In truth, one almost never gets all the evidence, but you need a certain minimum to approach any conclusions at all. It didn't help that I was working in barbarian territory among soldiers who were only marginally less hostile than the barbarians themselves.

I found Paterculus in his tent, which was situated in the praetorium not far from Caesar's. The Prefect of the Camp was going over some paperwork with a clerk. When I entered, he looked up with all the warmth and interest of a rock. "What can I do for you, Senator?" Leave it to a man like that to turn a civilian title of respect into a disgusting epithet.

"A little information about the last night of the late Titus Vinius, if you please," I said, putting as much upper-class disdain into my tone as I could, which was considerable. Time to put this ill-bred sod in his place.

"Last saw him at evening parade. Will that do?" So much for intimidation.

"Hardly. Did you not attend the meeting Caesar held afterward? The one with the Provincials bringing land disputes for judgment?"

"Why should I have? I had duties to attend to; inspecting

the guard, posting the officers of the gates, that sort of thing. I'm responsible for the security of this camp, you know. Do you think I get to laze around like a tribune?"

I allowed his insolence to pass. "Then I take it that the location, movement, and disposition of civilians to, within, and from the camp also lie within your purview?"

"They do. You talk just like a lawyer."

"A qualification I share with our commander and Proconsul," I reminded him. "At what time must foreigners leave the camp?"

"When the sunset trumpet sounds, unless they have an extended pass from me or from the Proconsul or the *legatus*, and those permissions have to be submitted to me first."

"Were there any such special passes granted that evening?"

"Yes, to the party with the land disputes. Caesar thought the business might extend well after sunset, so he had me make out passes for them."

"Did the pass list them all by name?"

"No, of course not. It was for the party as a whole. There were forty or fifty of them."

"So many? Nobody mentioned that many at the meeting."

"These are substantial men, by local standards; big landowners. They arrived with personal guards, grooms, slaves to handle their animals, the lot. Most of them stayed in the forum or the livestock compound while the meeting was going on."

"Who had charge of the pass?"

He looked honestly puzzled. "What on earth could that mean to you?"

"It has considerable bearing on the matter," I said, looking serious and wise to cover my confusion.

"The Druids held it. It's their custom. Gauls think writing is some sort of magic. For all they know, you hand them a papyrus with writing on it, you might be putting a curse on them. They think their Druids are proof against evil magic."

"Do you know which Druid took charge of the pass?"

"It was the youngest one brought it to me for validation, but any of them might have presented it at the gate."

"Are departing civilians allowed to use any of the gates?"

He shook his head. "Only the Porta Praetoria."

"Who was the officer in charge of the Praetoria that night?"

He turned to the clerk. "Get the roster."

The clerk wore armor, so he was another soldier pulling special duty. He didn't bother to look for the roster. "It was the ninth night after the full moon, so it was the tribune of the Ninth Cohort."

"That's Publius Aurelius Cotta," Paterculus informed me. "Another snot-nosed shavetail sent to plague my days."

"Was he on the gate all night?"

Paterculus looked at me as if I had handed him a mortal insult. "No officer of the guard leaves his post unless properly relieved. If he does, by every god of the State I'll see him beheaded in front of the whole army, no matter how ancient and illustrious his name is!" Obviously, I had trod on the sensitive corns of his authority.

"Very good, Prefect. Carry on." I turned neatly and walked out of the tent. Behind me I fancied I could hear him fuming.

I pondered upon the minutiae of military practice as I went in search of Aurelius Cotta. Soldiers could blithely ignore the grossest acts of cruelty and depravity, yet grow infuriated over minuscule breaches of procedure and precedence. To an inspecting centurion, a speck of rust on a sword blade or a dangling bootlace was exactly the same thing as a military defeat: It was something that shouldn't happen and must be punished. He could work up precisely the same amount and degree of rage over each.

That same centurion could watch his soldiers sacking an enemy village, slaughtering and raping and destroying everything in sight, and it was "just the boys acting up a bit." The fundamental difference between the military and the civilian mentality, I believe, is a totally divergent sense of proportion.

I found a gaggle of tribunes dicing their time away beneath a lean-to erected near the stables. As officers elected by the centuriate assembly, they had the privilege of bringing their own horses along on campaign, so they regarded the stables as part of their territory. Their current occupation was typical of tribunes, who usually lack for meaningful duties. Of soldiers generally, for that matter. I firmly believe that an army's load could be lightened considerably just by getting rid of all the dice.

I walked up behind my cousin Lumpy and nudged him with my toe. "Where is that hundred you owe me?" It had become my invariable greeting.

"Do you think I'd be trying to win some drinking money if I was rich?" he grumbled. "Besides, no man who's been given that German piece has any cause for complaint."

"Tell you what," I proposed. "Give me that hundred and you can have Molon."

"I'll trade you my horse and my personal slave for that German girl."

"Your keen business acumen will bring credit to our family

yet. I'm looking for Aurelius Cotta. Has anybody seen him?"

One of the tribunes looked up from the bone cubes. "I saw him over by the armory a while ago."

"Thanks." I turned to go. Lumpy got up and began to walk along beside me.

"Listen, Decius," he began, hesitantly, "I know Caesar appointed you investigator, but that was just a matter of form, don't you think? Like when a praetor appoints an *iudex* for a case that's really not important, but constitutional forms have to be followed?"

"Lumpy, I know that, in your tiresome way, you're trying to say something. Why not just say it?"

"Decius, you're building up a lot of bad feeling here, the way you've been interrogating officers and centurions like common felons. I think you had better back off and let those men take their punishment."

I stopped and turned on him. "What is this to you?" I demanded.

"I am a Caecilius Metellus, too. Everything you do rubs off on me!"

"You'll smell none the worse for it," I said. "You can't really care about this—you aren't involved in any way. Did someone put you up to this? Someone involved in the activities of the night in question?"

"Nobody!" he said, but his eyes kept sliding away from mine as if he found my ears to be of some interest. "I'm just catching a lot of grief from the others because of the way you're acting."

I stepped close and stared him down. When his eyes dropped, I addressed him. "Lumpy, I had better not learn that you are holding out on me. If the son of my old retainer is flogged to death with sticks because you withheld information from me, you'll wish you'd gone with him."

He laughed nervously. "Don't get in such a state, Decius! We are family, after all. I'd never interfere with your duties, and if the boy is a client of the Caecilii, he deserves our help. I'm just asking you not to tread so heavily. You have a way of questioning people that infuriates these soldiers. They don't care about birth and officeholding and education. They respect only a better soldier, and you aren't that."

"Just remember what I've told you." I whirled and stalked off. There was some truth in what he said. This was not a good place to sling my arrogant weight around, but it is not easy to suppress fifty generations of breeding. And I knew perfectly well that he was not telling me the whole truth. Was anybody?

I found Cotta having an edge put on his sword. This was a sure sign of nerves. The armorer was doing a great business sharpening the weapons of the tribunes, as if they had much chance of using them. Youngsters going into their first campaign always do two things: they spend all day fussing over their weapons and all night making out their wills.

"A word with you, Publius Aurelius, if you don't mind," I said.

"Certainly," he said, his eyes on the armorer's hands. The man was working the edge of the sword in tiny circles on a very large whetstone set in a long, wooden box full of oil. His movements were slow and precise. The edge on a Roman sword is not so much ground as polished into the steel. With such an edge it takes amazingly little effort to inflict a horrendous wound.

"I think you can leave the man to his work," I said. "He won't fail you."

"Oh, yes, of course." He came away reluctantly. "How may I help you?"

"Paterculus tells me that you were officer in charge of the Porta Praetoria the night Titus Vinius was killed."

"I had that duty." His eyes slid back toward his sword.

"Publius, pay attention. The Gauls are a long way off and Caesar will be back with reinforcements long before they can attack."

He looked shamefaced. "Sorry."

"After the sundown trumpet sounded, did anyone pass through the Porta Praetoria?"

"About two hours after the trumpet sounded a party of locals presented a pass from the Proconsul, validated by the Prefect of the Camp, and I let them through."

"Describe this party."

He thought about it. "Well, the men were important, you could see that by the amount of gold jewelry they wore, and their horses were good ones. There were seven or eight of them, plus those three Druids who've been around the camp the last few days. It was one of the elder Druids who handed me the pass." So Badraig hadn't been designated as the writing handler.

"Describe the rest of the party."

"There were a dozen or so guards. They were all armed in the Gallic style: longswords, narrow shields, no armor except a helmet or two. They were from the Province, though, you could tell that. They weren't all painted up and spike-haired like the wild men."

175

"Who else?" I asked.

He frowned, puzzled. "Well, there was nobody else. Just some slaves."

"Describe the slaves."

Now he looked at me as if I must be demented. "They just looked like slaves: dark clothes, some carrying loads, some leading pack animals or remounts. I didn't pay much attention." Reasonable enough: Who ever notices slaves?

"And did no one else leave through the Porta Praetoria after that party?"

"Not while I was on duty."

I clapped him on the shoulder. "Thank you, Publius, you've been a great help. You can go back to your sword now."

"Well—certainly. Any way I can be of assistance." He obviously considered me a prize loon, but I was well satisfied. Another little piece of the puzzle had just been handed me and I walked away from him with a little more cheer in my heart.

Who ever pays attention to slaves? We live our lives surrounded by them and we act as if they are not there at all. Men will speak indiscreetly in their presence as if they did not have ears. Noble ladies who would never appear in public without shawls and veils, in their own homes will parade around naked in front of male slaves as if they were not men.

The high-born citizenry wear mostly finely woven white clothes with a touch of color here and there. The lower born wear the most colorful garments they can afford. Slaves wear dark, rough clothes.

Now I knew how Vinius had left the camp unnoticed. He had gone out with that pack of slaves. Dressed in that dark, coarse tunic, probably with a burden over his shoulders to further hide his face, he had simply walked through, knowing nobody would notice.

So what had happened, out there on the heath? Not what he was expecting, that much was certain. Whatever game he had been playing for a year or more had backlashed him.

I wanted a few words with those Druids.

But it was late and I was hungry and I had no idea where the Druids might be. The Provincials with their land dispute were doubtless halfway back to Massilia by now. First things first.

Back at my tent, I dropped into my folding chair beneath the awning and pounded on the little table. "Hermes! Molon! Where is dinner?"

Hermes came out of the tent. "Aren't you having dinner with the other officers anymore?"

"Labienus doesn't keep as liberal a table as Caesar, and anyway, I've become the prize leper here."

"Just like home, eh? I'll find something."

"Where is Molon? I have some questions for him."

"You'll find him behind the tent," Hermes sneered. "Good luck with the questions."

"What now?" I got up and walked around the tent. On the ground in back Molon lay, blissfully snoring away. He reeked of wine, and when I kicked him he just muttered and smacked his lips and made other, equally disgusting sounds. I went back in front and plopped back down.

"Did you know he was getting into the wine supply?" I demanded of Hermes.

"Of course I did. I told him to stop and he told me to mind my own business."

177

"And you didn't protect my wine? Where is your sense of duty?"

"Why should I? You can always buy more wine."

"Remind me to flog him in the morning. I may flog you, too. Where is Freda? Has she failed me as well?"

"I am here," she said, pushing past the tent flap. She carried a basket full of bread with pots of oil and honey.

"Well, at least you haven't been into my wine supply."

"I don't drink wine," she said, sliding the basket onto the table in front of me. She spoke as if this conferred upon her some sort of superiority.

"Are you Germans beer drinkers then?" I asked. I had tried the stuff in Egypt and found it to be perfectly horrible.

"Sometimes. But true warrior people don't render themselves senseless."

For some reason I was stung by this. "Drunk or sober, Romans are better than anyone else." As if to prove this, I took a deep swallow from the cup Hermes had filled for me.

"You have never fought any real men," she said. "Just Greeks and Spaniards and Gauls, worthless trash, the lot of them. When you meet German warriors in battle, it will be different."

"For a slave woman you've gotten belligerent all of a sudden," I protested. "Why this devotion to people who gave you to a Roman as a present?" I held out my cup for Hermes to refill.

"That was not my tribe," she said, as if that made a difference.

"Better eat something before you soak up too much of this," Hermes muttered as he poured.

"What is this, Saturnalia? That's the only time slaves

get to lecture the master and if I have my dates straight it is still some months away!" Actually, I couldn't even be sure of this. As *pontifex maximus*, Caesar had allowed our calendar to get so bolloxed up that any festival might drop in just about any time. "You two both shut up and let me eat in peace." They kept a smug silence, for which I was only half grateful. It was getting so that they were about the only people in the camp willing to talk to me. I probably did drink too much.

Eventually, as some late trumpet calls sounded through the camp, I rose and Hermes helped me off with my gear. As I lurched into the tent, I called back over my shoulder. "Freda, come here. I want to talk with you."

This time she was smiling as she came in. "Are you sure you are up to this?"

I sat and tugged off my boots. "I said talk, nothing else."

"Naturally," she said mockingly.

"I need information," I began, determined to show her what a monument of self-control and rectitude I was. I fell back on the cot, my head landing with greater force than I had anticipated.

"Information. I see."

"Yes. Information. To begin: What is your tribe?"

"The Batavi. We live far to the north, on the cold sea. You would think it cold, anyway. Romans are oversensitive to cold."

"You are determined to provoke me. What brought you here, to become the property of Titus Vinius? I have heard Molon's account but I want to hear your version."

She sat on the cot beside me, unbidden. I let the minor insolence pass. She smelled unbelievably enticing.

"My tribe fought a great battle with the Suebi and I was captured. Cimberius, co-king of the Suebi, chose me from among the spoils. He had first pick and I was by far the most desirable item there." She certainly did not lack for self-regard. Casually, she rested a hand on my knee.

"Yet Molon says that it was his brother, Nasua, who gave you to Vinius." I felt heat radiating from the place where her hand rested.

"Nasua won me in a game."

"What sort of game?" I thought I could detect a tiny stroking motion from her hand.

"Wrestling."

"Kings wrestle among the Germans? That's undignified behavior, even for barbarians."

"My people prize manly things," she said, definitely stroking now. "The brothers knew they would never stop contending over me, so they agreed to give me away to someone important."

"Then why to Vinius? Why not to the Proconsul?"

"They know who really runs your legions."

"Oh." So much for the lofty office of Proconsul.

She stood and began to tug down her furry tunic. "You didn't call me here to talk, did you? Romans don't care about the lives of slaves." Her magnificent breasts sprang free, looking more like globes of solid muscle than the usual soft, wobbly milk-providers commonly adorning the female torso. Next, she bared a ridged belly that looked as if it could absorb a boxer's punch without winding her. The next push cleared her full but sinewy hips and she stood there like a statue of Venus, only far more accessible, warmer and more fragrant.

She leaned over me and began to pull at my tunic. "Are all Romans as lazy as you?" I fumbled at my clothes but my fingers had grown clumsy. She went at her task with great deliberation, though, and in moments she mounted me like a cavalry horse, sinking down with a guttural growl.

"Now," she said, "let's see what Romans are made of."

10

IN WHAT HAD BECOME A MONOT-
onously regular custom, somebody was trying to wake me in
the middle of the night. At first I thought it was Freda, wanting
me for another session. The woman reminded me of the arms
masters who had been drilling me so mercilessly.

"Captain, darling! Wake up, beloved!" It was Indiumix.

"What now?" I said, shaking my head. "Are the barbarians
here?" Another of my Gauls stood just outside the tent, holding
a torch.

"The *legatus* wants you, Captain, Labienus himself. He's
with Captain Carbo over by our quarters."

I sat up and tugged on my boots. "What's this all about?"

"I do not know. A runner came to us from the Prefect of
the Camp and said to saddle up and be ready to ride. He also
said you were to be summoned."

I looked around for Freda but she wasn't in the tent. Hermes came stumbling sleepily in and he helped me into my armor by the light of the flaring torch.

"Where are Freda and Molon?" I asked him.

"No idea. What do you need them for, anyway?" He fastened my sword belt.

"Nothing, but they shouldn't be wandering around in the middle of the night." My mind was on other things, though. What new emergency had come up? One thing was certain: Caesar was gone, and if Labienus wanted me, it had to be something bad. Hermes handed me my helmet and I ducked out through the tent doorway, clapping the metal pot on my head and fastening the cheekplates beneath my chin as we walked toward the cavalry quarters.

The camp was sound asleep—by army standards, anyway. At least one quarter of the men were up and standing sentry duty at all hours. Watchfires glimmered here and there, and a smell of smoke drifted over everything. An overcast sky rendered the stars invisible, but I judged it to be somewhat past midnight. With the torchbearer walking ahead of me, I managed to make it the whole way without tripping over a tent rope.

Labienus, Paterculus, and Spurius Mutius, the acting First Spear, stood by the watchfire with Carbo and Lovernius. They all wore the expressions of combined anger, fear, exasperation, and puzzlement that, in this army, had become as much an item of official issue as the *scutum* and the gladius.

"What's up?" I said cheerily, not feeling cheery at all.

"Carbo's men have found something," Labienus said. "I think you ought to have a look at it."

"Damned barbarians," Mutius grumbled. "Why can't they act like civilized people?"

The answer seemed incredibly obvious to me, but sometimes you have to point things out to soldiers. "Because they aren't civilized people," I told him. "What have they done this time?"

"I am going to show you," Carbo said. "The less said here in camp the better. Our Provincial allies are going to be spooked enough as it is."

"Metellus," Labienus said, "I want a full report from you at morning officer's call. Speak to no one else about this before you have reported to me."

"You aren't going out this time?" I said.

"The Prefect can't leave the camp and Caesar ordered me not to venture beyond the rampart before his return."

"Beyond the rampart?" I said, my stomach sinking.

"I'll tell you about it as we ride," Carbo said impatiently. "Come on. I want to be back before daylight."

As we were conferring, my *ala* had been assembling. Each man held a flaming torch and had a bundle of spares tied to his saddle. Indiumix led my own horse up and boosted me into the saddle.

"You're probably safe enough tonight," Labienus said. "But if you should be captured, keep your mouths shut and die like Romans."

With these touching words of encouragement we rode off through the Porta Decumana. Out in the open, I could just make out the watch fires of the lonely First Century in their exposed camp to the northeast. I almost envied them. At least they had the security of the great rampart to the north.

"What in the name of all the gods is going on, Cnaeus?" I demanded.

"Something so strange that my first thought was to get hold

of you," Carbo answered. "Tonight we completed our sweep early. Not a single Helvetian to be found. But the guards on the rampart reported unusual activity in the hills to the northwest. It's heavy woods up there, but they could see lights flickering, like a lot of men running around with torches, and one big glow like a bonfire in the woods. They could hear sounds, too—drumming and singing.

"I figured the barbarians might be massing up there under cover of the woods for a morning assault. It's not very far, and the Gauls like to fight at a run. If they were to come out of the woods at first light, when there's a heavy ground fog, they could be at the rampart before anyone would even know they were there."

"Clear so far," I assured him.

"So I sent a runner to inform the *legatus* that I was undertaking a mission beyond the rampart to see if there was a Gallic army up there." He said this as if he had taken out a work party to improve the ditch. This is why the whole world pays tribute to Rome instead of the other way around.

"What did you find?" I asked. "I don't suppose you just want to show me a million painted savages dancing around and working themselves up for a morning attack."

"Nothing that simple," he said. "You'll see."

We rode to a sally port in the rampart. This was a narrow slot, just wide enough for horsemen to pass single-file. It was blocked at entrance and exit by heavy logs studded with long spikes. The auxilia manning that port dragged the logs aside and we rode through. On the other side waited a wild-looking little detachment of Carbo's scouts, more like hunting hounds than human beings. Among them I recognized Ionus, the man who had discovered Vinius's body.

"Let's go," Carbo said. The Scouts set off at a lope. On the uneven ground their progress was more a series of leaps than the long strides of a civilized runner. Bent over almost double, their arms held a little away from their bodies for balance, they looked as if they were following a scent trail. They kept ahead of us easily, even though we were riding at a swift trot.

As we drew away from the rampart, I felt the chilling dread experienced by most soldiers when they are separated from their legions. Precarious as military life can be, there is tremendous comfort to be had from six thousand shields with six thousand resolute Roman swordsmen standing behind them. Even the primitive fortification of an earthen wall topped by wooden stakes takes on the permanence and solidity of a fortified city when you are out on your own in enemy territory.

A short ride across the grassy plain brought us to the foot of the densely wooded hills. The Helvetii, whose agriculture was primitive, never bothered to clear this hill country to till the slopes. They dwelled in the valleys and plains, where the land was hospitable and yielded easily to their wooden plowshares. The great labor required to clear and plant vineyards on steep slopes was repellant to the Gauls, who thought such work fit only for slaves. True, most Gallic peasants were little more than slaves themselves, but they had no liking for hard toil either.

A small detachment of Carbo's skirmishers awaited us at the base of the first hill. "Any sign of the enemy?" Carbo asked them.

"Not a hair of them," a decurion said.

"We continue on foot from here," Carbo said, dismounting. "You skirmishers get some torches from the horsemen. Lover-

187

nius, you come with us. The rest wait here. Be ready to run for it, but don't run before we get back."

"Are you sure this is a good idea?" I asked nervously. I didn't like the idea of being separated from my horse. When I have to flee, I prefer not to waste time at it. Armored and in hobnailed boots, I would have no chance of outfooting a horde of near-naked Gauls. It wouldn't even take a horde of them. Two or three would do the job. Mabe even one. I'd had an exhausting night.

"The woods are too thick for horsemen," Carbo said phlegmatically. "Come on."

We went up onto the slopes with the Scouts in the lead. I wondered what the watching Helvetians were making of all this activity. Our little torchlit cavalry procession must have been visible for miles, and the torchbearing skirmishers probably presented a twinkling display as we ascended.

Our climb was all but silent, the only sounds the faint rustle of mail links against sword sheaths and the hiss and crackle of the torches. The massive, ancient trees pressed close in upon us, the undersides of their limbs luridly illuminated by the torches. Night-roaming animals scurried away from us as we climbed. It was all monstrously oppressive and frightening.

We Romans do not like wild places. We like open, cultivated land that has been tamed by the hand of man. Deserts repel us; mountains are just obstacles; and we dislike forests with their wild animals and their swarms of spiteful spirits. Only pastoral poets pretend to like nature, and their sylvan dales occupied by nymphs and handsome shepherd lads are as unreal as a wall painting. The real thing is vicious, messy, and unforgiving.

Soon I detected a faint glow ahead of us. "Almost there

now," Carbo said. Iron man though he was, he was breathing heavily. This was his second such climb of the night.

Abruptly, we were at the edge of a clearing. The Scouts halted, then the skirmishers, and finally Carbo, Lovernius, and me. The trees ended at a roughly circular patch of mossy ground perhaps thirty paces in diameter. Big, rough rocks protruded from the ground, strangely shaped, although they were apparently nature's work, showing no marks of hammer or chisel. Tremendous oaks marked the periphery, their branches interlacing overhead to form a ceiling.

These details were made faintly visible by the low-burning remains of what must earlier have been a huge bonfire. It was nothing but embers now, crackling and sending up smoke to the heavens. It was an uncanny place, and I had the uneasy but certain feeling that I was looking at what the Greeks call a *temenos*: a sacred place consecrated to the gods.

Carbo stepped into the clearing and walked toward the fire. I took a deep breath and followed. Lovernius and the others hung back until Carbo turned and beckoned impatiently.

"Come on, bring those torches. What was done here is done."

I went to the remains of the fire, dreading what I might see there. To my relief it seemed to be ordinary wood, not wicker. I detected none of the charred bones I half expected to see. I scanned all around the clearing but could see nothing but the ominously surrounding trees.

"I don't see anything," I said, relieved but disappointed.

"That's because you're looking in the wrong direction," Carbo said. I looked to see his head tilted back, gazing straight up.

Beneath my helmet, my scalp prickled and icy fingers

danced up and down my spine. In the gloom above, my eyes were at first confused by the interlacing of the branches and the uncertain light of the torches. Then I saw three shapes dangling from three stout limbs, slowly turning as if there was a breeze up there that I could not feel down below. They were dressed in long, white robes and upon the breast of each was a richly worked golden pectoral. Their faces were distorted, but I recognized them, two old, one young.

"The Druids!" I cried, my voice far louder than I had intended.

Lovernius grasped an amulet that hung around his neck and began yammering some sort of prayer or spell, a look of superstitious terror on his face. The skirmishers were equally upset. I grasped his arm.

"Lovernius," I said sternly, "you are a civilized man with a Roman education, not a superstitious savage. Possess yourself!" Gradually he calmed.

"What can this mean?" I demanded. "Who sacrifices Druids? I thought they did the sacrificing!" For I had no doubt that this was a ritual killing. Ordinary executions do not take place at such remote sites or under such bizarre circumstances; the grove, the stones, the fire—all were redolent of barbaric religious practice.

"I don't know!" Lovernius said, his voice shaky. "I have never seen anything like this, nor heard of any such. Sometimes—sometimes a Druid is sacrificed when the people face a terrible calamity; famine, plague perhaps. But then the Druid is chosen by lot and there is a great festival. Only one dies, and the body is sunk into a sacred marsh."

"Any ideas, Decius?" Carbo asked.

"Absolutely none. I won't admit it to Labienus, but I'm as

devoid of answers as a Bruttian is of table manners. You might as well ask an Egyptian to exhibit bravery in battle."

"No, you'd better not tell Labienus that," he concurred. "Just smile your superior smile and pretend you know more than you're letting on." Carbo knew me all too well.

"I'll figure it out sooner or later," I assured him. "It's just that we're dealing with barbarians here."

"That's why I brought you to see this."

"So what do we do now?" I asked. "It doesn't seem quite right to just leave them hanging there." It wasn't that I really thought their spirits would harm us if they weren't properly buried, but I was in no mood to take any chances.

"No, we get away from this place. It will be light soon. If the Helvetii didn't do this, they'll be along to investigate soon. This hill has looked like the first evening of Saturnalia all night. The Druids were Gauls, let the Gauls take care of them."

This was eminently sensible advice and we followed it forthwith. Our little party did not exactly run back down the hill but we did move out smartly. We found our horses where we had left them and remounted. We rode back at an easy pace, because Carbo refused to leave his skirmishers behind. This was an estimable display of loyalty, but not one close to my own heart.

"Was there anybody else there when you found the place?" I asked him as we rode. I kept looking over my shoulder for an advancing army.

"Not a soul. Whoever did it was not long gone, though. The fire was still burning high, so I didn't need any torches to see them hanging there."

"I wish I could go back to investigate after daylight," I said. "But I'm only going to do it if Labienus agrees to give me the whole legion for security first. With the hill surrounded I might be able to keep my mind on my work."

"Don't count on that," Carbo said. "What do you think you might find?"

I shrugged. "I don't know, but somebody always drops something. I might find an indication of who did it or why it happened."

"Do barbarians always need reasons for doing things?" he asked.

"Always," I assured him. "It may not be something that we would understand but there has to be a reason." The Gauls and the Druids and Titus Vinius. Somehow they were tied together by the gold in that chest and in some way it had led to these bizarre killings.

We rode back into the camp as gray light was staining the eastern horizon. As always, the legion was wide awake by this hour. The clatter and bustle was reassuring after the strange events of the night.

"Any activity from the barbarians last night?" I called up to a sentry on the gate.

"Not a sound from them," he answered. "Doesn't seem right, somehow." Any break in routine seems ominous to soldiers, even a reduction in danger and harassment.

"I know it's useless to tell your men to keep their mouths shut about this," Carbo said as we dismounted. "Mine certainly won't."

"We are all loyal to Rome!" Lovernius insisted.

"Of course. But things are chancy enough now without all our Gallic auxilia getting agitated. They're not all educated men like you, and the Twins know our own soldiers are as superstitious as a bunch of old peasant women." The trumpets sounded officer's call. "Let's go report to the *legatus*." He turned and walked toward the praetorium. I gave my reins to Indiumix and started to follow, when Lovernius touched my arm. I stopped and faced him.

"Decius Caecilius, when you return from the praetorium, ride with us on our morning patrol."

I was about to ask him what this was about, but I could see from his expression that he was turning over some painful thoughts. Clearly, he wanted to speak with me. It was quite as clear that he did not want to do it just here or just now. More than anything else, I wanted to get some answers from someone, anyone, who might hold another piece of the puzzle. I turned back to Indiumix.

"See that my horse is ready to ride out." He nodded solemnly.

When we arrived at the meeting, Labienus had Carbo give a quick summary of the night's events. The expressions of the other officers were incredulous. It was all just too far outside their experience.

"Any conclusions, Decius Caecilius?" Labienus asked.

I ruthlessly suppressed the urge to make a facetious request for a six thousand–man escort to go back and examine the site. "Just that I feel certain that this event and the murder of Titus Vinius are somehow connected."

"You are grasping at anything to save your client," Paterculus said. "Commander, in my twenty-five years of soldiering I have never seen so many strange things happen at once, but what has any of it to do with fighting a war? They can hang a Druid from every tree between here and the Northern Sea for all I care. It's all just native doings and none of our concern. Let's stick to matters that make sense and have a bearing on our situation." A murmur among the assembled officers indicated a good deal of agreement.

"I'd say the same thing if we weren't stuck out here all alone and dependent on our Gallic allies," the *legatus* told him. "They may proclaim allegiance to Rome and execrate the Helvetii, but they're as religion-besotted as so many Egyptians. They've been jumpy for days and something like this could trigger mass desertions. I hate to contemplate exemplary executions, but I won't hesitate to order them. See that everyone knows this. Now, officer of the night watch, your report."

After the meeting broke up, Labienus kept me for a private talk. "So you learned nothing, eh?" he said.

"I gathered a good deal of information from which to draw conclusions," I said evasively. "And I expect to have some answers from a trusted informant by midday." I thought this sounded impressive.

"You'd better. I am very tired of these matters and I want to see an end to them almost as much as I want to see Caesar arrive with those legions."

From the praetorium I went to my tent to grab some breakfast before setting out on the morning patrol. Hermes was gone to his arms drill. Molon and Freda were likewise absent. Just when you want them, slaves always manage to duck out. Grumbling, I located the provisions and found some bread and cheese. This I choked down with plain water.

I was in a bad mood as I clumped toward the cavalry quarters. It seemed to me that the sleeplessness and poor diet of army life was probably calculated. The Gauls had better watch out when this lot was turned loose on them. Just a few days of it had put me in a murderous temper and these men lived this way for years at a time.

I found my little squadron of the *ala* mounted and ready for their patrol. The praetorian area was subdued and apprehensive, with men who were usually cheerful and boisterous speaking in low tones and frowning. Word of the Druid killings had spread. I could only imagine what the atmosphere must be like in the auxilia camp.

We rode out through the Porta Principalis Sinistra in the eastern wall of the camp. We rode until we were out of sight of both camp and rampart, then Lovernius called a halt near a small clump of trees.

"There will be no Helvetii to chase this morning," he said, dismounting. "Let's make ourselves comfortable."

"That sounds good to me," I said, feeling the accumulated soreness of the night's activities as I heaved myself from the saddle. One of the men took our horses to picket them among the trees. We all sat in the shade. Lovernius had thoughtfully brought along a fat skin of native wine and we began passing it around our circle.

When it came to me, I leaned back against the bole of a tree and directed the pale stream into my mouth. For native stuff it was excellent, or else my tastes were coarsening. I didn't try to rush things. The turf was springy and comfortable beneath me. Lovernius would tell me what he had to say when he was ready and I had run out of people to badger in the camp.

"I do not want you to think," Lovernius said at last, "that we who are loyal to Rome are in any way in sympathy with these Helvetii."

"I would never think it," I assured him, not insincerely. In truth, while we Romans tended to lump all Gauls together, they had only the sketchiest sense of national kinship. In no way did they feel that they were taking sides with foreigners against their brothers. A member of another Gallic tribe was as foreign to them as a Syrian is to a Roman.

"We do not allow the Druids to dominate us," he asserted. "Not as they do the Helvetii and others. But we still regard them with respect."

"Quite understandable." I took another pull at the wine. Not bad at all, really. I passed it to Lovernius, feeling that he needed a little more lubrication. He had almost worked himself up to saying what he had to say. He took a couple of sizable swallows and passed it on. Then he sat in silence for a while. Then, with an effort, he spoke.

"Titus Vinius was triple-slain."

I knew, at last, I was onto something. "What does that mean?"

"You recall that you told me Vinius had been strangled, stabbed, and axed on the head?"

"More like clubbed on the head, but I recall telling you." I also remembered the distressed reaction of his men. At the time he had said that they were upset at the defiling of a sacred pond.

"Well, that is a Druid thing. For some sacrifices, the victim is triple-slain; he or she may be hanged or throttled. In either case the noose is left around the neck. Then the victim may be stabbed or the throat cut, then smashed on the head, then thrown into a pond or sunk in a marsh. Sometimes only hanged and stabbed or axed, the drowning being the third death."

I remembered now the triple-headed god on Badraig's staff and the Gallic habit of doing things by threes. "You think the Druids killed Vinius as a sacrifice?"

"They must have! Who else could have done it, and why?"

"The why of it is a major question," I said, my mind speeding for a change. "But I know that Vinius had some sort of dealings on the side. He was amassing wealth from somewhere, and it certainly wasn't from the army. Might he have been dealing with the Druids? If he somehow betrayed them—and this would certainly be in character—they might have done away with him in revenge."

"But to do this without a festival of the people?" he objected. "That is terribly irregular."

"In time of war," I said, "we often simplify our religious rituals. Perhaps that is what they did. Am I correct in believing that the Druids never use arms?"

"Except for the instruments of sacrifice, they never even touch them. It would be polluting."

"There," I said, spreading my hands, "what could be more sensible? They can't use swords or spears, so they used what they had." It didn't answer everything, but I liked the sound of it.

"Well, perhaps," he said, still very uneasy.

"But there is more, isn't there?" I prodded.

"Yes. What we saw last night."

"That had the look of a sacrifice as well," I said. "But you said that is never the way a Druid is sacrificed."

"It is not," he said, taking another pull at the skin.

"Then tell me, Lovernius: Who sacrifices their victims by hanging alone?"

"The Germans!" he said, vehemently. "In their sacred groves, they hang their victims in oak trees. At one great festival held every twelve years, they sacrifice twelve of every living thing: men, beasts, even birds and fish. Hundreds of corpses hanging in a huge oak grove near the Northern Sea."

"The smell must be appalling," I said. "You have seen these things with your own eyes?"

"No, of course not. The only Gauls who see their rites are the ones who get sacrificed. But I have heard of this. Everyone has."

"I see." More reliance on rumor. But this probably had a greater core of truth than the hearsay of soldiers in a strange country. "Have you any idea what these strange events might portend?"

He shook his head dejectedly. "None, save that things like this should not happen. Is this a war of men or of gods?"

"The two do seem to be getting confused," I told him. "But I feel that all this mystical confusion is nothing but concealment for depressingly human evils."

"What do you mean?" he asked earnestly.

How to explain the way my mind worked to a group of Gauls, half-civilized though they were. It was hard enough to explain myself to my fellow Romans, steeped as they were in traditions of Greek logic and native commonsense. I had a try at it. The Gauls paid my words close attention, with serious expressions on their faces. They wanted answers as badly as I did.

"Lovernius, men explain their actions with a great many words, imputing all sorts of noble motives to themselves. They may say they are driven by patriotism, or by devotion to the gods, or by the interests of the people, or loyalty to a king, or any number of other great things. Usually, they are lying. Far more often, their motives are base. They are after power, or wealth, or some other man's woman."

"This I understand," Lovernius said, "but these are religious matters."

I held up a pedantic finger, the wine lending eloquence to my teeming mind. "Always, Lovernius, when men perform ignoble deeds and seek to justify themselves with high-flown words and portentous actions, I look for the shoddy, base element that ties everything together. A few days ago I discovered that Titus Vinius had amassed a great deal of gold from no obvious source. Forget about gods and priests and dreadful sacrifices. The gold is the thing. When I find out where it came from and where it was destined, I feel sure that I will have all parties involved in this matter tied together as with a chain. A chain of gold." I was absurdly pleased with the conceit, then reminded myself to go easy on the wine so early in the day.

The Gauls, with their love of flowery rhetoric, did not consider my speech excessive, and Lovernius seemed relieved to have the matter out in the open. He was loyal to Rome, but superstitious dread had caused him to hold his silence about the triple slaying. The triple hanging, on the other hand, had been too much. He now felt that I would be able to set these matters to rest with dispatch. I hoped that his faith in me was not entirely without justification.

11

W E RODE BACK INTO THE CAMP AT
midday, when the trumpets were sounding cheerily and the men
were assembling by messes for their noon meal. It says much
for our soldiers that they can anticipate even such Spartan fare
with pleasure. I left my horse with the *ala* and went to my tent,
where I found Hermes laying out my lunch. He had managed
to scrounge a pot of fruit preserved in honey and a roast duck.
I was not about to ask him how he had accomplished this minor
miracle.

"Keep this up and I might just manumit you when you're
too old to be useful," I told him as I sat down and launched
into the food. He poured me a cup of watered wine, which I
hardly needed. "Where are Molon and Freda?"

"I haven't seen them all day," he said. "I thought maybe
you'd sent them off on some errand."

The news stole some of the pleasure from my lunch. Slaves are not supposed to roam around at will, even such eccentric specimens as those two. More and more, they were behaving like free persons and would have to be disabused of that notion.

"When did you last see them?"

"Molon was drunk behind the tent last night and I didn't look in on him. I didn't see either of them when your Gauls came for you last night, and when I got up this morning I didn't see them, either, not that I was looking for them. They have to be around here somewhere. They wouldn't dare set foot outside the camp."

"That would be foolish," I agreed, but I was not happy about this. One more concern when I already had far too many.

With lunch finished, I was temporarily at loose ends. I rose to go look for my errant slaves with Hermes dogging my steps. I badly wanted some sleep, but I knew that it would not come if I lay down in my tent. I had too much to think about. As we traversed the camp, I told Hermes the latest developments. He was far from a brilliant conversationalist, but I had long ago learned that talking to someone helped to sort out confusing matters.

"If Germans hanged the Druids, then there are Germans nearby, right?" Hermes said.

"Your grasp of logic is phenomenal," I commended.

"No, I mean there are a *lot* of them, right? More than just those two you saw a few nights ago?"

"Not necessarily." In fact, I had been brooding over that very question. The boy wasn't really foolish. "Those were two huge, powerful warriors, and two of the Druids were elderly, and no Druid is trained to arms. Two such brutes as Eintzius and Eramanzius could easily have overpowered these sacerdotal Gauls."

"Still," he said dubiously, "getting them all the way up that mountain, and building a bonfire and hauling them up into the trees: that sounds like a big job for two men."

"Well, they proclaimed themselves to be of royal lineage. Doubtless they came here with companions. But a few dozen Germans are nothing to worry about."

"Just as long as it's not an army of them." Hermes was getting to be like everybody else; jumping at every shadow, worried about our tiny numbers and exposed condition. Like everybody else, he had ample justification for his fears.

A thorough search of the forum and other more or less public areas failed to turn up Molon or Freda. The centuries were no more helpful. Even an encampment of six thousand men is a small community and Freda was the most noticeable creature for a hundred miles in all directions. An elephant could not have drawn more attention.

"Maybe they went to the camp of the auxilia," Hermes said. "Slaves and foreigners go in and out through the gates pretty freely during daylight."

"I don't know what they'd be doing there but it's worth a look," I grumbled. So it was back out through the Sinistra gate I had ridden through that morning. Nobody on the gate remembered seeing them, but that watch had only been on duty for a short time.

The other camp was only two bowshots away, so that there was no dead ground between them where an enemy could be safe. Its defenses were much less elaborate, for in real danger the auxilia would simply move into the legionary camp, doubling its manpower. Because a high proportion of the auxilia were cavalry, the camp sprawled over a greater area than that of the legionaries, and foraging parties went out every day with sickles to cut fodder for the animals.

I found Carbo drilling his spearmen just outside the camp while his scouts lounged around, trying to look too important for such drudgery.

"They don't look too bad, for barbarians," I commended.

"Gauls don't take well to close-order drill," he said, "but they'll learn. Once they've seen how easily disciplined troops deal with howling, sword-brandishing savages, they'll get the spirit."

"If they don't get massacred first," I said.

He shrugged. "Not much you can do about overwhelming numbers. A single legion can deal with double the number of savages. Three legions together can handle ten times as many. Ten legions can defeat any number at all. The trick seems to be getting the legions here."

"It is a problem. By the way, Cnaeus, have you happened to see my German girl today?"

He cocked an eyebrow toward me. "Don't tell me you've misplaced her?"

"Haven't seen her since, well, fairly late last night, before all the excitement. I've been so busy that I haven't had a chance to look for her. Molon is gone, too."

"That one's no loss. The girl, though—a prize like that doesn't fall to every soldier's lot. No, I haven't seen her." He questioned his men and they talked for a while among themselves, making lascivious faces and many hand gestures indicating the feminine form. Apparently Freda was as well known among the auxilia as among the legionaries.

"No, they haven't seen her either," Carbo said. "And believe me, they'd have noticed. You might try in the camp."

"I intend to. By the way, I've come across some more information, but keep this to yourself for a while." I gave him a brief summation of what Lovernius had told me.

"So now the Germans are in it, eh? Do you think the girl sprinted for the hills to join her kinsmen?"

"I can't see why," I told him. "She was just a slave among them to begin with, so why go back? No slave in the world has as easy a life as a Roman house slave. Why trade that for some filthy village where a flea-bitten chieftain's wife will treat her worse than a dog?"

"That makes sense to me, but who knows how a barbarian's mind works? She may prefer bad treatment in familiar surroundings."

"Anyway, that doesn't explain Molon. That rogue certainly knows whose boots taste better, since he's licked such a variety of them. He'd never trade the soft billet he has with me for one on the other side of the Rhine. Besides, if he was going to run, why didn't he run from Vinius? The vicious bastard beat him like a practice post."

"Good question. I hope you locate her, Decius. If you've lost the one item in Gaul that everyone was panting after, you are going to be an even bigger figure of fun than you already are."

"How true. The gods do not love me, Carbo. I leave you to your drill. Come along, Hermes."

We went into the camp and began combing it. "I can tell you want to say something, Hermes," I said as we walked along a street where I could hear at least three languages being spoken.

"You and your friend talk like you know all about slaves, considering you've never been slaves yourselves," he said sullenly.

"Then I shall consult an expert. What are your thoughts on the matter?"

"That maybe they didn't run over to the Germans and the Gauls. Maybe they went the other way, down the river."

"Toward Massilia? Whatever for?"

He looked exasperated. "What for? Doesn't it occur to you that every slave in this army knows that any day the Gauls may pour in and annihilate us? Those that aren't killed in the slaughter will probably get sacrificed afterwards."

"You're making too much of the situation," I chided him. "Roman armies are rarely exterminated by savages. At worst, we'll make a fighting retreat downriver and hold Massilia until our reinforcements arrive."

"Oh, that's reassuring! I don't have a lot of experience with armies, but I'll bet when they're on the run they don't take along things like pack mules and baggage and slaves."

"I can see that it would be a distressing prospect," I admitted.

"I can guarantee that a lot of slaves here are getting ready to bolt."

"I don't suppose that you would be among that fainthearted crew," I said.

"My loyalty to you is unshakable," he said, in that straight-faced, sincere fashion that is the mark of a truly gifted liar.

"Excellent," I commended. "What you say makes a certain amount of sense, but how could they escape?"

"Massilia is a pretty big place, and Molon can pass for a

native. Besides, it's a port city. They could buy a passage to anywhere. Molon could steal passage money in a morning."

"If that's what they are thinking, they're out of luck," I told him. "The place is filling up with slavers. They always flock to wherever Roman armies are fighting. After a successful battle they can buy up all the prisoners dirt cheap. Those scavengers can spot a runaway on a moonless night."

"Hadn't thought of that," he said. "But they might not have, either."

"Molon would know."

The truth was, I did not want to believe that they had run. I would not mourn the loss of Molon, and he would certainly seize any chance to better his lot. I was not about to deceive myself on that score. But Freda—I had thought we had reached some sort of understanding the night before, that in her brutish, untutored way she had conceived an affection for me.

Had it all been a cold-blooded ruse? Had Molon feigned drunkenness while Freda had taken it upon herself to exhaust me so that I would not wake when they made their stealthy escape? I did not want to believe it, but I recognized this as a purely visceral reaction. The rigorously logical part of my mind told me that this was exactly what they had done. The objections I had raised with Hermes were still valid, though. How did the two of them expect to better their condition with this act?

Our search of the auxilia camp failed to turn them up, as I had expected. I tried to look cheerful as we returned to the legionary camp, but I was more downcast than I had been since arriving in Gaul. It was the crowning catastrophe in an experience rife with disaster. If my luck kept holding like this, I would be executed along with Burrus and his friends.

"Are you going to post a notice that they've run?" Hermes asked when we returned to my tent.

"No, I've had enough humiliation to last me for a while. And don't you say anything, either. It wouldn't look right, making a fuss over a couple of runaways when the whole country is about to plunge into war."

"If you say so," he said doubtfully.

"That doesn't mean I won't turn out the guard if you should run, though. That would be different."

"You don't trust me!" he said indignantly.

"It's just that I know you all too well." I pushed the tent flap aside and went in, suddenly bone-tired. "I'm going to get some sleep. Wake me only for an emergency or if those two return."

I got out of my armor and boots and lay back on the cot I had abandoned when the summons came to ride into the hills. Even through the haze of fatigue my mind kept turning over the latest bewildering developments. I could not put it out of my mind that Molon and Freda were still two of my suspects in Vinius's murder. If they thought they were about to be found out, running was the most sensible course they could take. But if they had done it, why the Druidic mumbo-jumbo? And how did it tie in with the three hanged men? If, indeed, the two were tied together at all.

It was the most maddening situation of my by no means uneventful career. Whatever happened to politicians who murdered one another for perfectly sensible, understandable motives? Why did armies and barbarians of several sorts and priests with their disgusting sacrifices have to get involved?

I tossed restlessly, weary to my bones but unable to sleep. I knew that I would have to do something or I would know no rest. In my long experience I knew that, when things reached this awful pass, there was only one action to take. I would have to do something colossally stupid.

I got up, rummaged around until I found a wax tablet, and opened the wooden leaves. With a stylus I scratched my message and called Hermes in.

"Run this over to Lovernius. Tell him to have one of his men deliver it to Captain Carbo at once." He must have seen something in my face.

"What are you planning?"

"I'm going to go out tonight and maybe get killed. When you get back from your chore you'd better try to get some sleep, too. You're going with me."

I dropped back on my cot, suicidally at peace with myself. My mind made up at last, I was asleep as quickly as a lamp is extinguished.

When my eyes opened again, it was dark outside. I felt rested and invigorated, things I rarely feel upon first waking. Then I remembered what it was that I planned to do. It was simple fear that made me so lively. Hermes was on his pallet snoring gently and I prodded him awake. He went out to fetch a basin of water for me.

While he did this, I found my short sword and muffled its sheath with strips of cloth so that the suspension rings wouldn't rattle. I added my dagger to the harness and belted it all on. I located a pair of civilian sandals and put them on. Not only do hobnails make a lot of noise, but they can strike sparks from stone, visible for great distances on a dark night. I rolled up a hooded cloak and slung it over my shoulder. The night would probably turn very cool and rains were frequent.

When Hermes got back with the basin, I instructed him

to fetch his cloak and give his sword the same treatment as mine. "We're going out on a little reconnaissance," I told him. He followed my instructions with the sort of excitement that only the young and foolish feel when danger is near. I was just finishing my ablutions when Carbo arrived, accompanied by Ionus to guide us.

"Here he is. Now what sort of lunacy are you planning, Decius?"

"I'm going back to that grove, Gnaeus. I want to look it over in daylight tomorrow."

"I thought it had to be something that stupid. If you're going to do it, why not go out with your cavalrymen?"

"What would be the use? It would only make us more visible. I wasn't joking when I said I would feel safe only with the full legion along for security. Either we'll remain unseen and be safe, or we'll be detected and killed. Come on, Hermes."

We walked toward the Porta Decumana and Hermes tried not to strut, his fingers flexing repeatedly on his sword hilt. He had had several lessons and now accounted himself a master swordsman. At the gate I informed the officer in charge that I was going out on a night mission. His jaw dropped at so outlandish an idea, but he had no authority to stop me.

While we went through this rigmarole I gazed along the top of the wall, noting how the sentries were spaced, wondering how difficult it would be for a pair of determined slaves to get away by scaling the parapet and jumping the palisade. Not difficult at all, I decided. The guards were widely spaced, the nights were dark, and everyone's attention was on danger from outside, not what was going on behind them. Choose a late hour when the men were groggy, be very quiet, and escape would present very few problems. They were gone. I could no longer fool myself about that. But where?

"When will you return?" Carbo asked.

"We'll have to stay in the hills while it's daylight. As soon as it's dark, we'll head back. I can't cover ground like your scouts but we should be back well before sunup the day after tomorrow."

"If you aren't, I'll have a cavalry sweep out looking for you at dawn."

"If I'm not back by then I probably won't be back at all, but go ahead. It won't do any harm."

"Good hunting, then." He clapped a hand on my shoulder in soldierly fashion, believing that I was a brave man instead of a suicidal fool.

We went out through the gate and walked toward the great rampart. This night we heard no overeager Gallic warriors taunting the men atop the walls. In fact, it was rather pleasant, with a sliver of moon and a multitude of stars in the sky. I could even make out the reflection of moonlight from the white crests of the nearby mountains. Night insects made their chirping sounds and a wind rustled the grass and the rushes in the ponds.

At the sally port in the rampart I repeated my story to the officer of auxilia who was in charge there. This one showed no particular astonishment, just writing down my name and the size of my party. We went on through. A few paces past the wall I called a halt.

"Do you have any paint?" I asked Ionus. He took a small pot from his belt purse and handed it to me. I dipped my fingers into the foul-smelling paste and smeared it on my face, then streaked my bare arms and legs. Then I tossed the pot to Hermes.

"Put this on. The only way we're going to live through this is by not being seen. Ionus, what's this paint made with?"

"Just soot and bear fat."

"Good. Woad or walnut juice leave stains that last weeks. Now, Hermes, once we are one bowshot from the rampart we are truly on our own in enemy territory. Anyone who sees us out there will want to kill us on sight. Stay close to me, but not so close that you'll bump into me. We have to maintain enough distance so that we can use our weapons if we have to. If you start falling behind us, say something, but don't shout. Is that understood?" He nodded dumbly, his face a little frightened. Suddenly, this wasn't such an adventure.

"Ionus, set us a good pace, but we aren't accomplished cattle thieves who can see in the dark like you. Now let's be off."

Ionus set off and I let him go ten paces, then followed. We moved across the dark plain at a pace that was somewhere between a walk and a run; not the steady, plodding military pace but a sort of lope accomplished with the feet widespread to maintain balance on the uneven ground. The turf was springy beneath my feet and now I was grateful for the hard training Caesar had made me perform, for I found the experience exhilarating rather than the exhausting ordeal it might have been.

After about an hour of this we stopped by a little stream, dropped to our knees, and lapped up the cool water like thirsty dogs.

"How much farther?" I asked.

"As much more as we have come," Ionus answered.

"I was afraid of that," Hermes said. He was breathing heavily, but seemed to be in better shape than I was. He was no longer the soft city boy who had left Rome with me.

"This is good for you," I assured him. "My father has always told me that suffering is the best thing for a man, and that young people these days don't suffer enough and that's why we're such a degenerate lot."

"If it's all the same to you," Hermes said, "I'll let your father do the suffering, if he likes it so much."

Ionus listened to us with a look of great puzzlement. He lived his whole life like this. Hardship for him had an entirely different meaning. He was barefoot, wearing trousers and a brief cloak that covered only his shoulders and upper back. He seemed perfectly comfortable thus attired.

After a short rest, we went on. The night grew chilly, but our exertions kept us warm. I strained my ears to hear approaching Gauls, or a cough or rustle from warriors lying in ambush, but we seemed to be protected by a spell of invisibility. Or perhaps the Gauls had turned sensible of a sudden and decided that nights were better spent sleeping instead of skulking about with weapons.

When we reached the foot of the mountain, I called another halt. "This is a hard climb and I don't want to be out of strength when we get where we're going," I said. "If there's anyone up there, we could have a fight on our hands when we arrive."

Hermes and I sat down, gasping. Ionus just squatted, one hand resting idly on the hilt of his short, leaf-shaped sword. With his paint and his bushy hair sticking out in all directions, he looked like some forest goblin come calling.

The night chill struck our cooling, sweaty bodies and I donned my cloak. Hermes did the same. "Why do people live in a place like this?" he asked. He couldn't understand why

anyone would live anyplace except Italy, and Rome in particular. I was not far behind him in this.

"I'm sure it must be better in summer."

I surveyed the moonlit plain and pointed to the southeast,
where a series of silvery crests reared against the starry sky.
They were the high Alps.

"One of those mountains over there is said to be the highest in the world."

"I thought Olympus was the highest," Hermes said.

"Olympus is just the highest mountain in Greece. If the
Greeks had lived here, they would have thought their gods lived
up on that one. Ionus, what do your people call that mountain?"

He shrugged. "I am not from here. My people dwell in the
lowlands. If it is the tallest, maybe it is where Taranis lives.
He makes the thunder."

"Must be their name for Jupiter," Hermes said, muffling
himself in his cloak.

"That could be," I said, but I doubted it. The Gallic gods
seemed to me quite different from our familiar Italian and
Olympian deities. "Does Taranis bear the thunderbolt? Is he
accompanied by eagles?"

"The thunderbolt, yes. No eagles," was the reply. "His is
the wheel with which the sacred fire is kindled. We always start
the fire of Beltain with a wheel."

I remembered the little wheels that I had seen adorning
so many of the helmets worn by Gauls. It seemed like an awk-
ward instrument for starting a fire though.

"He's not Jupiter, then," Hermes said with the certainty
of a *pontifex*. "Vesta's in charge of starting fires."

"Where would the gods be without us mortals to apportion
their duties?" I said, standing. "Come on, enough of this phil-

214

osophical chitchat. We have work to do. Hermes, from now on we move slower and stay closer together. If you need to say something, touch my shoulder and then whisper. We are going into the woods and enemies can lurk very close without our seeing them. There is no hurry, dawn is still an hour away. It is utterly important that we move quietly. Ionus, lead off."

So we began our climb. As before, the trees were oppressively close and accumulated dew dripped on us. Ionus swept ahead of us, his footsteps as silent as a ghost's. He did not ascend in a straight line. Instead, he zigzagged from one side to another, sniffing for ambushes like a hound searching out game scent. I felt that my own ascent was commendably quiet, although I had nothing like the Gaul's level of skill. Behind me, Hermes seemed to be making an unconscionable racket. I was probably overcritical, but my nerves were taut with suspense, and every rustle he made was to me as the sounding of trumpets.

We carried no torches this time, and we lacked the unjustified confidence that comes with having a number of companions. A slow step at a time we climbed, our eyes, our ears, even our noses quivering in search of impending doom. Even at this pace, it was not long before we reached the clearing. This time, without torches or the glowing embers of the bonfire, I could see almost nothing.

Ionus squatted at the edge of the trees, peering grimly inward. I looked long enough to determine that I would see nothing of use for some time, then we backed a little way downhill. I gestured for the others to sit and we hunkered down to wait. With the hood of my cloak drawn over my head, the sounds of the night were muffled except for the patter of dewdrops striking the wool. Hermes looked miserable, his adventure turned into a boring tedium, waiting in the cold and dark.

Gradually, I grew aware that I could see tiny details of my surroundings that had been invisible. Then I heard a single bird call melodiously. Dawn had arrived. Slowly, almost imperceptibly, visibility expanded until I could see trees a hundred feet away and the sky overhead was a leaden gray. My two companions had dozed off and I nudged them awake. Hermes yawned and stretched, then he started to say something. I clamped a hand over his mouth and shook my head vehemently.

I leaned close to Ionus and whispered: "Scout the clearing for us." He bobbed his head and set off in his crouching lope, making a sweep of the treeline surrounding the grove. A few minutes later he returned.

"All clear."

I got up. "Come along, Hermes. We can talk now, but don't raise your voice and don't let your guard down. Ionus will provide security while we see what we can see."

We went into the clearing. The bonfire was now just a heap of cold ashes. I looked up and saw that, as I had expected, the bodies had been taken down, along with the ropes from which they had dangled. It was no surprise, but still I felt a rush of relief when I saw that they were gone. It would have been too ghastly to have them there, silently watching. At the very least, it would have been an unbearable distraction.

"What are we looking for?" Hermes asked.

"Anything that looks like it didn't grow here naturally," I told him, having no idea myself what I expected to find. We began combing over the turf in the growing light of morning. The surface was springy, covered with moss and overlaid with rotting oak leaves. The ground was much trampled, which came as no surprise. In the last day or two it must have seen an inordinate amount of traffic for so small and remote a spot.

"Found something!" Hermes said eagerly.

"Keep your voice down," I told him. "What have you got?" He held out a small, curved object of brownish color. It appeared to be the tip of an antler, pierced in its center for a thong, either a part of a necklace or a toggle of some sort.

Ionus looked it over. "German," he said. "For fastening one of their fur tunics here." He clapped a palm over his shoulder.

"Lovernius was on the right track, then," I said, inordinately pleased. "Let's see what else we can find."

A minute later Ionus, prodding at the ashes of the fire, called us over. Protruding from the cinders was a charred bit of wood that still bore a recognizable carving: three faces turned in three directions.

"That's adding sacrilege to murder," I said, "burning the Druids' staffs in the bonfire." For it had to be the staff of Badraig or possibly one belonging to one of the others.

Further search turned up more than I would have expected, but nothing terribly helpful. There were some wisps of dyed wool, probably from the garments of the Gauls who came and took down the bodies. There were some bits of fur that might have come from the clothes of the Germans. Hermes even found a couple of tiny arrowheads beautifully fashioned from flint, but these might have lain there for centuries.

Ionus turned out to be something of a disappointment. It seems that among the Gauls, hunting is pretty much restricted to the upper aristocracy, so common warriors like Ionus did not develop great facility with things like tracks and other signs.

Their skills were those of cattle raiding and warfare. Hermes and I, sons of the City that we were, displayed even less acumen.

At midday, we halted our desultory search and dug into our provisions. I had brought along some bread and dried figs. Hermes had prudently dropped a hunk of cheese into the front of his tunic before leaving the camp and Ionus had some salted fish in his pouch, along with a few early onions bought from one of the peasants who hawked their produce in the fora of the camps.

"Have we learned much?" Hermes asked, munching away.

"Not yet," I told him. "But we have plenty of daylight yet. There's still the ground under the trees all around here to look at, and it might be worthwhile climbing into the trees."

"Climbing?" Hermes said. "What for?"

"Somebody had to go up there to arrange the ropes," I told him. Actually, I was not certain of this. I had never dealt with a hanging before.

The food was so dry that I barely choked down the last few bites. I asked Ionus where we could find some water.

He pointed to the eastern edge of the clearing. "There's a spring a little way over there." We got up, brushing crumbs from our tunics, and followed his lead. A few minutes of walking brought us to a little gorge carved into the side of the hill where water tumbled noisily over jagged rocks. We found a relatively calm spot and knelt by the stream, thrusting our faces into the water and drinking deep. It was delightful stuff, far better than anything you can get from a well.

I can't really say how we were caught so easily. It may have been that concentrating on the ground sapped our alertness to our surroundings. Possibly the noise of the stream deafened us to other sounds. Most likely, it was simply that Romans ought to stay in Rome. I never would have left, given a choice.

We had our faces out of the water, taking a breath, when Ionus' head jerked up abruptly. "We are not alone," he said quietly.

Hermes and I scrambled to our feet as the Gaul straightened from his crouch effortlessly, pivoting to scan this way and that. Then I saw them; shadowy shapes coming closer, weaving between the trees. They were hulking figures, more like beasts than men, for they wore the hides of animals.

With a single bound, Ionus dived headfirst into a clump of brush. Wriggling like a snake, he was gone from sight in an instant and no sound betrayed his passage.

"I wish I knew how to do that," I said.

"He's deserted us!" Hermes cried, panic in his voice.

"Wouldn't you?" I demanded.

One of the men barked something to the others. Some of them continued to approach us, not bothering any longer with stealth. Others combed through the brush, poking it with their spears, trying to find Ionus. There were at least a dozen closing in on us with their weapons leveled. I heard a rasping sound next to me and saw out of the corner of my eye that Hermes had drawn his sword. With the edge of my hand I chopped at his wrist and he dropped the weapon with a yelp.

"What did you do that for?" he demanded. "They've come to kill us! We have to fight!"

"Settle down, you idiot," I told him. "We're not going to fight our way out of this."

"Well, we're certainly not going to talk our way out! Do you know some magic that will get us away from here?"

"No." I struck my haughtiest pose and addressed the approaching men. "Gentlemen, you seem to think that some sort of hostility lies between us. I am Senator Decius Caecilius Metellus of Rome, and Rome desires only the friendliest relations with the great German people." Dressed and painted as I was, the effect must have been ludicrous, but when there is no substance, sheer style must suffice.

One of them said something in their fighting-wolves language and the others laughed heartily.

"You've made a good impression," Hermes said shakily. One of them stepped up to him and clouted him alongside the head with a spear butt. Another did the same for me, staggering me sideways. Someone grabbed me from behind and I was quickly divested of my weapons.

"Yes, it seems we're not to be killed instantly," I said. "So far, so good." My hands were bound behind me and Hermes was hoisted to his feet and likewise bound.

Our captors were big men, even bigger than Gauls, and twice as savage-looking. Gauls painted themselves and bleached their hair with lime and made it stand up in spikes for a frightening effect. These men exuded wildness and menace just by standing around breathing. Their hair and beards were every shade of yellow and their eyes were frighteningly blue.

Their heavy furs made them seem even bulkier, but they were not massively built, like the big-shield gladiators so familiar to Romans. Although they were immensely strong, they were built like wolves or racehorses, with lean muscles stretched over long bones. They had absurdly small waists and moved gracefully despite their size.

"Oh, we've had it now," Hermes said, blood trickling from a lump rapidly swelling on the side of his head. "Why didn't we break and run for it when we had the chance?"

"We never had the chance," I told him. "Look at these beasts. Do you think you could have made it all the way back to the camp with them at your heels?"

He looked them over, cringing at their outlandish fearsomeness. "Well, no."

"So be calm and we may get out of this alive. As yet, there's no war between Rome and the Germans. They just aren't pleased with the way Caesar has handled the Helvetian migration. Maybe they'll hold us for ransom."

"Would anybody pay to get you back?" he demanded.

"No, but there's a special fund for just that purpose," I assured him, hoping it was true. I knew that the eastern legions maintained a ransom fund, because ransom was a major source of income for the Oriental kings.

A German yapped something and swatted me in the ribs with his spear butt. "I think we've been told to shut up," I wheezed. Hermes just nodded. He learned fast.

A man fastened a noose around my neck and then did the same for Hermes. I thought: They hang their sacrifices.

12

I F THEY HAD LED US BACK TO-
ward the grove I probably would have dropped dead from terror,
but instead they began leading us to the northwest, up over a
shoulder of the hill. As we trudged along at the end of our
leashes, I made a closer examination of our captors. Besides
the usual fur tunics, most of them wore fur leggings that came
to just below their knees.

There was no uniformity to their armament. Most possessed belt-knives with crude handles of wood, antler, or bone.
A few had bows cased across their backs. Each had a long
spear and most carried a couple of short javelins as well. What
surprised me most was their poverty when it came to metal.
Among the Gauls, most warriors had an iron-tipped spear, an
iron-bossed shield, and most men owned a long- or short sword.
To this basic armament the better-off warriors added a bronze

or iron helmet and the chiefs usually had a shirt of mail. Not these Germans. Except for the knives, many had no other metal save a copper bracelet and a few studs on their wide leather belts. Only the leader of this band had an iron speartip, the others contenting themselves with points of bone or of fire-hardened wood. Their long, narrow shields were made wholly of wooden planks, bossed with oak and bound around the edges with rawhide.

Primitive though they were, they looked nonetheless deadly for it. You just have to shove harder to thrust a wooden spear through an enemy. These men looked eminently strong enough to accomplish the task. A Roman soldier was a veritable ironmonger's shop by comparison, but these men seemed fit to make up the difference with sheer ferocity.

We had not been walking long when we were joined by another dozen men. These had sour looks on their faces and the words they spoke to their leader in their growling language were clearly not expressions of joy.

"No blood on any of them," Hermes muttered. "Maybe Ionus got away." A warrior backhanded him across the mouth. Considering the blow that arm could have delivered, it was a mere love pat, but it bloodied his mouth and his lips began to swell.

We went over the shoulder of the hill, through a small pass, and descended into a dark valley set among densely wooded slopes. I tried to remember in which direction the river lay, but I was disoriented. I knew I could find my way back to the camp if I could make my escape, but in exactly what re-lationship we lay to the rest of the world, I had no idea.

Once in a while the man in the lead whistled quietly, a sort of bird-call sound. When he did this, he was answered from somewhere overhead. The second or third time he did so, I looked up and could just make out the form of a warrior crouching high in a tree, still as a hiding fawn.

It was late afternoon when we reached a large clearing in the middle of the hills. Around the periphery of the clearing crude huts had been erected, no more than saplings bent into bows and covered with peeled bark or brush. There was one hut that was three or four times the size of the others, but still a rather modest structure. From all the signs that I could see, the little village was newly established. The smell of fresh-cut wood was everywhere. I saw no women. This was a warrior band, not a tribe on the move.

On several racks, deer and other game hung ready for butchering. I wondered if our captors were hunters who had stumbled upon us or men specially detailed to keep an eye on the grove. I suspected the latter.

In the very center of the clearing stood a tall post crudely carved into manlike form. The staring eyes were made from lumps of hammered tin and its grimacing mouth was studded with real teeth taken from a variety of beasts; a cloak of wolf-skin hung from its rudely defined neck. Arms were sketchily carved in low relief, one hand holding what appeared to be a noose of braided hide, the other an ax or hammer. The extreme stylization made details difficult to interpret and my mood was not one conducive to art appreciation.

The leader of our party called out something and men came running with a pair of heavy stakes and a wooden maul. They pounded the stakes into the ground a few paces in front of the wooden god or whatever it was. When they were finished, I watched with great interest to see what their next move would be. If they had proceeded to sharpen the stakes, I planned to

225

find the largest, meanest-looking German in the camp and spit in his eye. If I did that, he might strike me dead immediately. I did not like the idea of impalement, the one death that may be even more horrible than crucifixion.

To my relief, they merely whittled deep grooves around the stakes a few inches below the hammered tops. Hermes and I were then thrust down into a sitting posture and our tethers tied securely to the grooves in the stakes. After testing our bonds to make sure they were secure, the Germans wandered off in search of dinner or perhaps a quick pot of mead or ale or whatever awful stuff they drank.

"Wonderful," Hermes muttered. Then, seeing that nobody was going to hit him for speaking, he went on in a firmer voice, "Now we're going to be sacrificed. Maybe eaten. We should have run. At least it would have been quicker."

"Not necessarily," I said. "They might simply have crushed the bones of our feet to prevent us escaping and then marched us back here. Altogether, we made the more comfortable choice."

"If Ionus makes it back and reports us captured," he said hopefully, "someone will come out to rescue us, won't they?"

"Undoubtedly," I said, knowing that nobody would bother. One expendable, supernumerary officer and a slave were hardly worth exposing a large number of men to unknown dangers.

For the remainder of the evening I tried to assess the number of the Germans, but I was able to gather little intelligence. Men were always coming and going, singly or in parties. The great simplicity of their dress and belongings made it equally difficult to judge things like purpose or permanence. They probably lived much like this at home, and I could not guess whether this was a raiding party or a part of an army gathered for a genuine campaign. Although most were warriors in their prime, some were boys too young to shave even if Germans shaved, while a number were gray-bearded men of astonishingly advanced years for such a life. These elders seemed just as active as the rest, though.

Sometimes I saw men bearing swords and perhaps a few ornaments of hammered silver, but whether these were just leading warriors or princes I could not guess. Nobody saluted or showed particular signs of deference to anyone and I began to wonder whether this society resembled one of those Golden Age legends when everyone was supposed to be equal. Well, I suppose equality makes sense when every man is an unwashed, bloodthirsty savage.

As the dark drew on, hunting parties and patrols converged upon the camp. I saw a number of men, most of them beardless youths, leaving at this time. I guessed that they would take up their posts in the trees, relieving the sentries I had seen that afternoon.

Fires were built up and the now-butchered game animals began to roast on spits. The smell that drifted over the clearing made my stomach rumble and my mouth water.

"You'd think they'd bring us something to eat," Hermes complained as the warriors tore into the rations with their wolfish teeth.

"It does seem somewhat lacking in courtesy," I said. "However, this beats being on the menu ourselves." The Germans ate like characters out of Homer, whose heroes never seem to eat anything but meat. These men from beyond the Rhine were capable of wolfing down several pounds at a sitting, with never a morsel of bread or bite of fruit by way of variety. They tossed the bones into the fires and wiped their greasy hands on the ground, dusting off the dirt fastidiously. A few of them began a sort of communal growling which may have been a form of song.

Nobody paid us the slightest attention, for which I was cautiously grateful. At this point, a swift death seemed an impossibly optimistic prospect. The less notice I received from these terrible predators, the better. Exhausted by the long, sleepless night and the day's events, I began to nod off into a stupor when a change in the pervasive mutter made me jerk awake. The band had fallen silent.

"Somebody's coming out of that big hut," Hermes almost moaned. "What now?"

I could see shapes moving within the larger hut's doorway. Then someone ducked through and strode toward where the two of us were tethered. There was something familiar in that walk. Then I was looking up those long, shapely legs, past that lush, fur-clad body to that incomparable face.

"Well, Freda! Fancy meeting you here! This is just a misunderstanding, isn't it? Why don't you just release us and we'll all make ourselves comfortable and . . ." If I hadn't jerked my tongue back quickly I would have bitten it clean off when she kicked me in the jaw. The warriors all laughed uproariously at this display of sterling wit.

"Good thing she's barefoot, eh?" Hermes said. I detected satisfaction in the little wretch's voice. He had been catching all the punishment so far.

I managed to regain a sitting position and blinked stars from my eyes. When I could see clearly again, the fires were flaring high. Freda still stood over me, but her customary sullen expression was gone. She was smiling merrily, delighted at having me at her mercy.

Her facial expression was not all that had changed. She still wore a fur tunic, but this one was a bit more modest, and instead of common fox skin it was made of magnificent pelts, probably sable. Over her shoulders was a short mantle of ermine, the black-tipped tails dangling. She wore a heavy Gallic necklace of gold, and bands of gold around her wrists and upper arms.

"You seem to have come up in the world," I said. "Congratulations."

She covered her lips with her fingers and giggled girlishly, then she called something and a warrior handed her a thick, four-foot rope of braided hide. With this she proceeded to flog me into a state very little short of unconsciousness.

"That was uncalled for, Freda," I said as I lurched dizzily back to a sitting posture. "I always treated you with unfailing kindness."

"You treated me as a slave, Roman," she said, finally able to restrain her mirth sufficiently to force out a few words.

"You were a slave," I pointed out, bracing myself for another flogging. Fortunately, this particular sort of fun seemed to have lost its charm for her.

"I have never been any man's slave," she told me.

"If that is so," I said, "then you are not the only person to have lied to me recently."

Somebody approached from behind her and her shapely, bare foot came up again. I braced myself for another kick, but her foot only settled gently, almost caressingly, into the jointure between neck and shoulder. She began to press downward.

"On your face, Roman." I went over on my side, then sprawled on my belly and turned my face to one side lest I be smothered. Freda pressed my face into the dirt, and it was no symbolic gesture. The woman leaned her whole weight upon that foot until I was sure my neck would snap. I could barely drag air into my lungs. All I could see before my painfully bulging eyes was a pair of enormous feet, shod in soft leather sewn with gold wire.

A voice almost too deep to be human said something and the foot was lifted. Another voice, male and familiar, translated: "Your obeisance is accepted. You may sit up now."

From my facedown sprawl I struggled back into a sitting posture. This is a difficult feat with one's hands tied behind. I fear that what little dignity I had left suffered. This being the case, I was careful to keep my face immobile, a perfect mask of Roman *dignitas* and *gravitas*. It was well that I did so, for when I was upright with my eyes uncrossed, I was looking up at the most terrifying human being I had ever beheld.

Well above seven feet tall, he stood on widespread legs heavy as treetrunks, two fists each as large as my head braced against his hips. Unlike the Germans I had seen so far, he was broad in proportion to his height, his body like a barrel, his neck so thick that his head seemed to sit directly upon his yardwide shoulders.

His hair was so blond that it was almost white and it was carefully combed out almost to his elbows. His full beard was curly and unusually fine in texture, neatly trimmed in contrast to the unkempt hirsuteness of the others. His features were craggy and dominated by a pair of pale gray eyes that would have looked more at home staring out from beneath the shaggy brows of a wolf. And yet, in that savage and intensely masculine face, I detected some vaguely familiar features. With a start, I realized that he bore a distinct resemblance to Freda.

His brief, sleeveless tunic was of a heavy, feltlike cloth, elaborately embroidered with stylized animal and twining plant designs. It was neither Gallic nor German, but looked vaguely Sarmatian to me. He had a good deal of heavy gold jewelry on him, and from his coral-studded belt hung a sword as oversized as himself, of Spanish workmanship.

I assumed my most formal and official tone. "Senator Decius Caecilius Metellus the Younger of the Republic of Rome greets Ariovistus, King of Germania." It could be nobody else. My words were translated by the same, familiar male voice. So overwhelming was the German king that only now did I see Molon, standing to one side and a little behind him. He too was transformed. He wore a tunic of fine Gallic wool, dyed scarlet; expensive, imported sandals; and a massive silver chain around his neck. Silver bracelets banded both wrists. His lopsided, sardonic grin was unchanged. He translated as the words rumbled forth.

"You talk like an ambassador, Roman, yet you came here with no embassy. You came as a spy in my territory."

"The Senate of Rome does not recognize this land as German. In the consulship of Caesar and Bibulus you were proclaimed 'King and Friend' by the Senate, but this was in recognition of your dominion in the lands east of the Rhine. Rome is at war with the Helvetii, and I was scouting in Helvetian territory."

He rumbled a while. "Titles bestowed by a council in a foreign land mean little. Occupation of land means everything. I hold land west of the Rhine by right of conquest and I now have one hundred and fifty thousand men on this side of the river, all of them warriors, men who have not slept beneath a

231

permanent roof in many years. Do not confuse us with Gauls, who are mostly just slaves and tillers of the soil. Among us, all men are warriors."

"The manly valor of the Germans is famous over the whole world," I said, thinking it a good moment for a bit of flattery. "But so is the martial spirit of Rome. There is no quarrel between our nations, King Ariovistus."

"What are your words to me?" he said through Molon. "You are not empowered to treat with me."

"It is you who came over here to speak with me, not I with you," I answered. Freda slashed me across the face with her rope, but Ariovistus just laughed. He turned and said something. A warrior freed my tether from its post and two others took me beneath the arms and lifted me as if I weighed no more than a dead hare. I felt about as lively as one, too.

"What are they doing?" Hermes cried as they dragged me toward the large hut.

"I'll know soon," I told him. "Don't go anywhere."

The interior of the hut was dim and smoky. A small fire burned on a flat rock in its center, the smoke making its way out through a round hole in the roof. The only furnishings were some crude pallets, a couple of jugs, and a few ox horns. It seemed that King Ariovistus did not keep elaborate state when he traveled.

The warriors set me on the turf floor near the hearthstone and left me there to contemplate my probably limited future for some little while. Then Molon walked through the doorway. He did not need to duck to do this. He grinned and winked at me.

"Keep it up," he said in Greek. "You're doing fine." Freda barked something at him as she came in, having to stoop low. "She says to talk so she can understand us," Molon said.

Then Ariovistus came in. He had to bend almost double and when he was inside, he seemed to fill the whole hut. The three of them sat cross-legged by the fire so that we formed a little circle. The king said something to Molon and the little man (I could scarcely think of him as my slave) went around behind me and efficiently untied my bonds. To my surprise, a warrior came in and placed several strips of seared venison on the ground before me, some broad oak leaves serving as a platter. Molon poured a pale liquid from one of the jugs into an ox horn and handed it to me. I managed to take it between my numbed hands without spilling it and raised it to my lips. It was honey mead, but I was so thirsty that I scarcely noticed the vile taste. As soon as my fingers would work, I picked up a strip of the flesh, gnawed a mouthful loose, and swallowed it. Most people have strict laws regarding the sacred bonds of hospitality. I desperately hoped it was so among the Germans.

They watched me with a sort of grim amusement; then, when I was finished, Ariovistus spoke.

"There, you have sat beneath my roof, eaten my food, and drunk my mead. Do you feel safe now?"

"Was I in danger?" I said. This sent them into transports of laughter. I certainly couldn't fault their sense of jollity.

"I like you Romans," Ariovistus proclaimed. "You are not all bluster, like the Gauls. You have real nerve. Listen to me, Metellus. I want you to deliver my words to Caesar. The land of the Helvetians is mine. You may let them migrate as they wish or kill them all, I do not care. If you feel like fighting a war, be sure that after you finish you go back to Italy. If you keep expanding into Gaul, sooner or later you must fight me and I will beat you. I have never been defeated in battle and to this my enemies will attest."

"That is certainly blunt enough," I said. "No one will ever claim that you couch your thoughts in a lot of confusing rhetoric. But you err if you think that Rome is easily swayed by threats from a foreign king."

At this, Ariovistus chuckled. "Rome? I am not facing war with Rome." He pointed a thick finger in the general direction of the lake. "Over there I face *Caesar!* Do all Romans love Caesar? I do not think so. Many great and noble Romans have contacted me through their agents. They have praised me as a great king and assured me that, when I defeat Caesar's armies and kill Caesar himself, Rome will seek no revenge against me. In truth, they have promised me great rewards. I will be paid a heavy tribute, and the Senate will recognize me not only as King of Germania but of as much of Gaul as I can seize save for your little Province."

With a sinking feeling I knew that he was telling the truth. The soldiers had spoken of Crassus's agents operating in the area. I myself had told Caesar how many of his enemies were counting on his meeting with disaster in Gaul. How deep had this rot gone? Were Crassus and his allies in the Senate (and Caesar had many enemies who were not allies of Crassus) actually aiding the ambitions of Ariovistus materially? Crassus was so rich that this was possible.

"You still must deal with the Roman soldiers," I told him, "and they rarely ever see Rome. Their loyalty is to their general."

"Roman loyalty is to be bought by anyone who has gold," he sneered.

Now I knew that the answers were almost within my grasp. "Not all, but some. Only a few. Was it with the gold Crassus and Pompey and the others gave you that you suborned the First Spear of the Tenth Legion, Titus Vinius?"

For a moment he looked nonplussed. "It was with my own gold that I bought Titus Vinius."

Now I was taken aback. "But Germania is not rich in iron, much less in gold."

"That does not mean we are poor," Ariovistus maintained. "Wealth lies in land and in fighting men. All else is to be taken when you have those. A few years ago I crossed the river as ally of the Sequani in their war against the Aedui. First I smashed the Aedui, then I took a third of the land of the Sequani." He chuckled and rocked back and forth. "They owed me something for defeating their enemies, didn't they? In the conquered land, my hunters found a great heap of treasure in a marsh. It was a dedication from the Gauls to their gods after a battle long ago."

"I have heard of the custom," I said.

"Most of the iron was too rusted to salvage, after so many years. The bronze was corroded away as well. But silver and gold last forever." He gestured at the gold he and Freda wore. "I have plenty of gold now. I will be paid even more when I kill Caesar, unless he is wise and goes back home. It is all the same to me."

"What was it you bought from Vinius?" I asked him.

"When the time came, when my army clashed with Caesar's, he was to betray the camp to me. He assured me that it would be easy to do. He could weaken the guard on the wall on a night of my choosing. You Romans do not like night fighting. We do. With an enemy in your camp in the middle of the night, when you cannot form your battle lines and every man is on his own, you can be slaughtered like sheep. Tell Caesar that. Let him know that his soldiers are not as loyal to him as he thinks."

I wanted to call him a liar, but I could not. Almost fifty years before, in the war with Jugurtha, corrupt Roman officer-politicians had sold out our legions and let the Numidians in at night, all for gold. The results had been as Ariovistus said. Even in the middle of these depressing thoughts, the light of revelation dawned over me.

"You violated a Druid sanctuary," I said.

"What of that? I despise the Druids. They only make trouble, trying to unite the Gauls against me. When Gaul is mine, I will hang them all in the groves." A sentiment he seemed to share with Caesar.

"But they somehow got wind of your arrangement with Vinius and decided to do you a bad turn, is that it? They killed him. Druids can't bear arms, but they can kill men in sacrifice."

"They will pay for killing the dog I paid for," he vowed.

"Three have already paid," I pointed out.

"It was not enough. I made of those three a gift to my gods, and a warning to the others that I respect their lives no more than I respect their treasure." He seemed to be in an explaining mood, and I was in a mood to exploit that.

"How did they learn about Vinius?" I asked.

His face twisted. "I cannot be sure. I suspected that he might be double-dealing. The man's treachery was boundless, and the Druids had plenty of gold with which to bribe him. As a pledge of the bond between us, I gave him first my counselor Molon to use as interpreter and go-between, then I gave him my sister, Freda. In truth, they were to keep an eye on him and see if he stole off privily to confer with the Druids or any other high-placed Gauls. I bade Molon be a good slave and submit to his beatings and he would be richly rewarded. Freda, of course, he had to treat well, although he was to pretend she was a captive slave." The woman favored me with a chilling smile and I wondered how much she had told her brother.

There was something otherworldly, almost dreamlike, about this. Here I was, sitting on the dirt in a crude hut among hairy savages, hearing from their chieftain a tale of intrigue and espionage worthy of the Great King of Persia and his subtle ministers. Well, I already knew from my experience with Freda that just because you wear fur and can't quote from the odes of Pindar, it doesn't mean that the possibility for sophistication isn't there.

"You misjudge your position of strength," I told him, "and you misjudge the determination of Rome. We are at war with the Helvetii, but many other Gallic tribes lie under our protection or are bound to us by ties of alliance. And you overestimate the degree of treachery and corruption in our army from the example of a single man. Granted, it was a particularly egregious example."

"My course was determined long ago and I am not here to discuss diplomatic affairs with you. I want you to take my words to Caesar. In return, you should be grateful to have your life. Your title sounds impressive, and Molon tells me that your name is that of one of the great families, but I know that there are many of you Senators, and more Senators are made every year, and few of you are of any importance." For a barbarian, he had a certain clear-eyed regard for the realities.

"Then I shall deliver your words," I said. "You have my pledge as a Roman." I chose to ignore his snort of contempt. "And now, King Ariovistus, if I have your leave, I must return to the camp. Certain pressing matters call me there."

"You will go when I say so," he said, glaring like an angry bear.

"But we have no further business," I pointed out, "and I must return at once. Caesar has charged me to investigate the murder of Titus Vinius."

"So Molon has informed me. What of it?"

"A whole *contubernium* lies under suspicion and imprisoned under guard at this minute. If I do not denounce the Druids as the guilty parties, eight innocent men will die a most lingering, excruciating death."

He and Molon muttered back and forth for a while. I suspected that the interpreter was having a hard time explaining the word "innocent" to Ariovistus. Then the king addressed me once more, through Molon.

"There are no innocent Romans."

13

ARIOVISTUS KEPT US IN HIS CAMP
for five more days. There were no more beatings, and we were
fed regularly. Our bonds were not too tight. But we were under
constant guard by men for whom the word "unsympathetic"
must first have been coined. In the absence of physical abuse,
mental anxiety fully occupied us. This was a barbarian king,
who might change his mind at the slightest whim. Nobody spoke
to us. A few times Freda walked by and I tried to engage her
in conversation, but she had lost interest even in beating me.
Oddly, I almost felt slighted in this. Perhaps there was a little
Titus Vinius in me after all. Molon, likewise, merely shook his
head when I addressed him.

So Hermes and I talked to each other for lack of better
company, as men will when they are confined together. I told
him that, when we got back to Rome, I would enroll him with

a schoolmaster, for I would be needing a secretary in my future career. He said that maybe staying with the army and fighting Gauls and Germans wouldn't be such a bad idea after all.

He tried to wheedle out of me exactly when I expected to manumit him, but I knew better than to answer that. Keep them in suspense is the best policy. After a while we stopped talking about the future. Too much talk of the future makes the present seem all that much more precarious.

On the morning of the sixth day, we woke in a deserted camp. I jerked up and looked around wildly. "Hermes! They're gone!"

"Huh?" he said brightly, blinking and staring owlishly. "Where did they go?"

"Back to Germania, I hope! Come on, let's get loose from these bonds." So we sat back to back and made a ridiculous attempt to untie one another's ropes. Then we gave that up and tried to tug up our stakes. No luck there, either.

"This is going to take some thought," I said finally. "Maybe we can rub the cords through against a rock."

"No rocks around here," Hermes said, looking about him. "Hey, where did the god go?"

I looked behind us and saw a hole in the ground where the ugly thing had stood. "They dug it up and broke camp without waking us," I observed. "These Germans know how to handle themselves in the dark."

"Here comes somebody," Hermes said apprehensively. We watched the treeline and a moment later an ugly, gnomish, but familiar figure came through.

"Thought I'd sneak back and make life a little easier for you two." From within his tunic he produced a knife with a short blade and cut our bonds. "Get along now, before the Germans notice I'm gone."

"Tell me something, Molon," I said.

"What?"

I grabbed his right arm and raised it. "Tell me about this." Around his wrist was the silver bracelet I had seen worn by Titus Vinius on the day of our first encounter. "How did you get it? From the Druids? What sort of private game have you been playing?" I twisted it off his arm.

"Ow!" he cried, rubbing his wrist. "If you must know, I took it when I heard Vinius was dead. It was with his dress gear in the tent."

"The others said he never took it off," I pointed out.

"Well, he couldn't very well be wearing it and pass for a slave, could he? Come on, give it back. I turned you loose, didn't I?"

"I need it," I explained. "I am going to show it to Caesar as evidence that this insane story is not just a lot of vaporing on my part."

"You are an ungrateful man," Molon said. "I gave you good service, even though I really wasn't your slave."

"Yes, and how you came to be an adviser to Ariovistus must make quite a story, but I haven't time to hear it. You'd probably just lie, anyway."

"Any chance of getting our swords back?" Hermes said.

"Are you serious?" Molon said. "That much iron?"

"Come along, Hermes, let's be away from here." I turned for a last time to Molon. "Tell Princess Freda, if that is her title, that I shall always remember her fondly."

"She'll be glad to hear it," he grinned. "I know she thinks

the world of you, Senator." Who knows when a man like that is telling the truth? He walked away, back into the forest.

We got lost a few times, but I had a general idea of where we were and how to get back. The hills were not unpleasant early in the day, and such was the menace from our two-legged enemies that we did not even bother to worry about wolves and bears and such. The air was fresh, we were free, and our bruises were fading. Best of all, I had found out the truth about the death of Titus Vinius and I would save Burrus and his friends. I explained this to Hermes, who was starting to complain.

"No, best of all, the Germans are going away. As for the rest, I'm tired, I'm sore, and I'm hungry."

"Don't be so joyful about the Germans," I chided him. "The Helvetii will kill us just as dead if they catch us."

"See? Things aren't so good after all."

The mountainside where the sacrifices had taken place seemed almost as familiar as home by the time we reached it, early in the evening. After that there was no great problem as to direction: just go downhill. The first stars were coming out as we reached the plain.

"Not far now," I said.

"Well, at least it's flat," Hermes commented.

I should have known by that time that no smallest aspect of my time in Gaul was going to be truly pleasant or easy. Shortly after midnight a heavy ground fog closed in. We strode on, but less confidently.

"Are you sure this is a good idea?" Hermes said. "Maybe we should wait for daylight."

"I don't want to be caught out here on the plain," I told him. "We'll just have to trust to my sense of direction." He looked dubious at this. "We have to reach the rampart pretty soon. It's nineteen miles long. That's pretty hard to miss."

"I have perfect confidence in you, master," he said, a remark open to more than one interpretation.

Daylight came, but not clarity of view. We were walking in white fog instead of dark fog. I thought I could determine the direction of the rising sun, but I may have been fooling myself in this. I betrayed no doubts to Hermes, though.

"Halt!" the command came out of the gloom with such authority that both of us were struck as by a thunderbolt. "Who's out there?"

"I am Captain of Praetorian Cavalry Decius Caecilius Metellus, accompanied by one slave. I must report to the *legatus* at once."

"What's the watchword, Captain?"

"Watchword? How would I know? I haven't attended a staff conference in seven days! Let us through—I have urgent business!"

"Sorry, Captain. I can't let you pass without the watchword. You'll have to wait until the officer of the watch gets here."

"I cannot believe this!" I shouted, all but tearing out my hair by the roots. "At least let me know where you are!"

"Oh, I guess that's all right. Just keep coming the way you were for a few steps." I did as he instructed and then I saw the great rampart in front of me. Just over its palisade I could make out the shapes of two helmets, close together. The fog was lifting rapidly now.

"Can't you see that I am a Roman officer?" I demanded.

"Well, you talk like one. What you look like is a beggar."

I could imagine how he would think so. My tunic was ragged and filthy, I was equally filthy as well as unshaven, with

243

my hair sticking out like a Gaul's. Then I heard somebody else clumping along the wooden walk and I saw a helmet with the transverse crest of a centurion.

"What's all this commotion, Galerius?"

"There's someone out there who says he's a Roman officer, though he doesn't look it. Got a slave with him."

"Somebody said something about a missing officer." The centurion peered over the palisade. "Let's hear your story."

"I was on a night reconnaissance and was captured by the Germans. We escaped yesterday and have been wandering in the fog all night." The shorter the better, I decided.

"Well, at least you sound all right." He pointed east, toward the lake. "There's a gate right down there about a quarter of a mile. Go on and I'll see they let you in."

We hurried down to the narrow sally port and a group of extremely puzzled men let me through at the centurion's orders. I was so agitated and frustrated that only now did I notice that I was looking at legionaries, not auxilia.

"When did legionaries take over guarding the rampart?" I said. They just stared and then I noticed the stars painted on their shields. "What legion are you?"

"The Seventh!" said one, proudly.

I whooped and hugged Hermes, much to his embarrassment. "Our reinforcements! When did you get here?"

"Late yesterday evening," said a decurion. "Caesar came riding in when we were camped just the other side of the Alps. He didn't march us here; he made us *run* here!"

"Six men dropped dead from exhaustion in the mountains," another said, nodding and grinning, as if this was a great distinction. "Caesar had his lictors marching in the rear, with orders to behead any that fell out."

"Caesar truly believes in having his orders obeyed," the decurion said with considerable awe. It was as if they were talking about a god, except that they spoke with affection. I could not believe it. Lucullus had tried to enforce stiff discipline in his army and the soldiers had rebelled. Caesar demanded inhuman discipline and they worshipped him for it. I will never understand soldiers.

As Hermes and I walked toward the camp of the Tenth, the rest of the fog cleared off and we saw the most heartening sight in the world: Where there had been only the solitary camp of the legion and its auxilia, there were now three full legionary camps and three auxilia camps, and since these had been newly raised for this campaign they were at full strength; something in excess of thirty-six thousand men.

"There's enough soldiers here to conquer the world!" Hermes said.

"I'm sure Caesar would like to do just that," I told him, "but we've marched ten legions at a time against an enemy and still had a hard fight of it. Still, this army should be able to take on the Helvetii handily."

"And the Germans?"

"Caesar won't take on both at once. Ariovistus may have been exaggerating his numbers, but he may have three times as many men as Caesar."

"That sounds bad."

"It isn't good, but Marius overcame odds that great, fighting Germans. Sheer ferocity and courage can only accomplish so much. Discipline counts for more than that, and you saw how they were armed. Those flimsy shields won't even slow a *pilum*. Wooden spears won't penetrate a *scutum* or a mail shirt. As long as the legions hold their formations, they can deal with greater odds than that."

"But they're huge!"

"Just big targets," I assured him. "Without helmets or armor, they are just meat for a sharp gladius." I hoped that I was not just reciting a lot of propaganda. Roman armies had been destroyed before, and Hannibal had even done it with inferior numbers. But Hannibal was the best general who ever lived. Alexander's reputation is greatly exaggerated, in my opinion. Romans are rarely outfought, but we have been outgeneraled from time to time.

But I knew that those wild men had none of the discipline of Hannibal's veterans. Caesar's legions would deal with the Germans right after a victory over the Helvetii, when their morale was soaring, and that would make a tremendous difference.

Or am I just indulging in hindsight here? Perhaps I was really far less confident and far more frightened back then. I may have just been putting on an act for Hermes.

"Speaking of swords," he said, "are you going to get me another one?"

"Not until I replace my own. I still have my cavalry sword, but I need a gladius, too. We'll see how my luck at dice runs. Maybe I'll ask Burrus and his *contubernium* to take up a collection to replace the swords we lost on their behalf. They ought to be grateful for . . ." Then, with rising horror, I remembered.

"Run!" I shouted, breaking into a sprint.

"Why?" Hermes cried from somewhere behind me. I didn't waste any breath on answering him.

The camp of the Tenth was the easternmost. I ran past the others through a heavy smell of new-dug earth. They were still digging their ditches and raising their ramparts. Under the watchful eyes of their decurions the men paused to stare at the crazy, ragged man running by as if all the Furies were clawing

246

at his buttocks, until the decurions barked at them to stop being lazy sods and get back to work.

As I got to the north wall, I saw that all the sentries were facing inward and I prayed to Mercury to lend wings to my heels. I dashed through the Porta Decumana and behind me someone shouted: "Hey! Stop, there! What's the watchword?" The muscles in my back tensed in anticipation of the untimely arrival of a *pilum*, but I knew the likelihood was remote, for it can be extremely bad luck to kill a madman.

Through the deserted quarters of the praetorian guards I ran, noticed only by horses and other livestock. As I neared the forum, I saw Caesar and his officers atop the speaking platform, watching something below them. What it was I could not see, for the legion was drawn up by cohorts around three sides of the forum. With a final, Olympic-quality surge of speed I ran between two cohorts and burst into the open amid surprised shouts.

Before the speaking platform stood Caesar's twelve lictors. In the middle of them, incongruously, stood a painted stone pillar. Before this odd grouping stood the men of the First Century of the First Cohort, dressed in their tunics and armed only with vinestaffs, looks of misery on their faces. But their expressions were as nothing to the woeful countenances of the eight naked men who stood at one end of the double line. First among them was Burrus, who was about to walk between the lines. The vinestaffs were already raised to strike.

"Stop!" I bellowed. "Stop at once! These men are innocent!" A babble of astonishment erupted around the forum and the commands of the centurions did little to quiet it. I ran up to the platform, panting and gasping, and stopped before the odd stone pillar. I saw that it was the grave monument of Titus

Vinius. He was to witness the execution, if only in effigy.

"I see you retain your flair for the dramatic, Decius Caecilius," Caesar said. "You had better explain yourself quickly
if you do not wish to join your friends about to go under the
vinestaffs."

I was panting too hard to speak, so I reached into my tunic
and took out the silver bracelet. I tossed it up to Caesar and
he caught and examined it.

"This gets you a hearing. Come up here, Decius."

I managed to stagger up the praetorium wall and thence
to the platform. Someone shoved a skin into my hands and I
choked down a mouthful of heavily watered wine. The next
mouthful went down easier and the third easier yet.

"You had better talk before you drain that thing," Caesar
said. Then, to the others, "Gentlemen, give us leave." The officers filed off the platform, eyeing me like a visitation from the
underworld. When we were alone, I talked very swiftly, in a
low voice. Caesar's expression changed little during my reci-
tation. He paled a little when I told him of Vinius's treachery,
but the terrible danger I had undergone seemed to cause him
little distress. When I was finished, he stared at me for a while.

"Well done, Decius," he said at last. "I want full particulars of your experience in the German camp later." He called
for his officers to rejoin us and he gave them, very succinctly,
the basic facts of my discoveries. Their expressions were a mar-
vel to behold.

"Well, I always said Titus Vinius was a bastard," Paterculus remarked, an observation applicable to most centurions.
"But, Proconsul, we've got the legion formed up here to witness
an execution. If we don't kill *somebody*, they're going to feel
that things aren't quite right."

Caesar smiled. "Oh, I think I can give them a pleasing show." He leaned over the parapet and spoke to one of his lictors. "Go to the blacksmith's and fetch me a hammer and chisel." The man dashed off and Caesar raised his hands for silence, which descended instantly.

"Soldiers! The gods of Rome love the Tenth Legion and will not allow dishonor or injustice to befall it! They have furnished me with proof that the Druids murdered Titus Vinius as a barbaric human sacrifice, and that this fate befell him as a result of his own treachery. The First Cohort, and its First Century, are restored to full honors and their disgrace canceled!" The legion erupted in a tremendous roar and the morning sun flashed from the tips of waving spears. The other legions probably thought we were under barbarian attack. The soldiers began to shout Caesar's name over and over again, as if he had just won a great victory.

"Wait here," Caesar said. "I shall be back presently." He left the platform and walked toward his tent.

Burrus and his friends were so numb with relief that the men who had been about to kill them had to help them on with their tunics. A few minutes later the First Cohort was intact again, standing in armor, crests fluttering in the breeze, shield covers off to flaunt their bright colors. Caesar was giving the gods all the credit, but I took a great personal satisfaction in the sight. It is not often that one gets to see the good results of one's actions in so dramatic a fashion.

When Caesar came back, he was out of military uniform. Instead, he wore full pontifical regalia: a striped robe bordered with gold, a silver diadem around his balding brows, the crook-topped staff of an augur in his hand. The jubilant legion fell silent at this unusual spectacle.

He descended into the forum and stood before the grave marker of Titus Vinius. The stonecutters of Massilia, in anticipation of legionary casualties, kept a stock of these three-quarters finished, needing only to add the inscription and details when one was commissioned. For Vinius, the relief of a standing male figure had been furnished with the insignia of his rank: the transverse crest on his helmet, the greaves on his shins, the *phalerae* atop his scale shirt, the vinestaff in his hand, all painted in bright colors. The face bore only the vaguest resemblance to the man. Below the figure were inscribed his name, the posts he had held, and his battle honors.

Caesar stood before this monument with hands raised and pronounced a solemn execration, using the archaic language of ritual that nobody can really understand now. When he had finished the resounding curse, he turned to face the soldiers.

"Let the name of Titus Vinius be stricken from the rolls of the Tenth Legion! Let his name be forgotten, his honors stripped from him, his estate forfeit to the Rome he would have betrayed!"

He turned around and faced the gravestone. The lictor placed the hammer and chisel in his hand and he shouted: "Thus do I, Caius Julius Caesar, *pontifex maximus* of Rome, strike from the memory of mankind the accursed name of Titus Vinius!" With deft blows of the hammer, he chiseled away the face of the figure. Then he obliterated the inscription in the same fashion. Then he dropped the tools and remounted the platform.

"It is done! Let no man speak that accursed name! Soldiers, you have witnessed justice. Return to your duties." Instantly, the *tubas* and *cornicens* roared and the cohorts marched from the forum, smiling broadly. It was a happy army once more. Gauls and Germans out there by the horde, and they were happy.

"Decius Caecilius," Caesar said as we walked back toward the big tent, "you have one hour to bathe, shave, and get back in uniform. Then I want to hear your detailed report." I suppose I should have been grateful that he allowed me even that long.

An hour later, shaved, barbered, dressed in my battle gear but still feeling somewhat ragged, I reported to the praetorium and went over the events since Caesar's departure several times. Caesar asked frequent, pointed questions, his lawyer's acuity ferreting out facts even I had overlooked. When he was satisfied with my report, we got out the infamous chest and, to my great sadness, Caesar made note of every deed and every bar of gold, and double-checked it all against my inventory. He was not a trusting man.

"Well," he said finally, "that concludes this sorry business. My congratulations, Decius. Your performance exceeds even my best expectations."

"What will you do with all this treasure?" I asked.

"I have condemned him as a traitor. Everything he owned is forfeit to the State." He closed the chest and locked it. I made a mental vow to check the treasury records some day to see how much of it got turned in.

"This calls for a celebration," Caesar said. "I shall hold a banquet this evening in your honor. Now go catch up on your sleep. Tonight, we banquet; tomorrow, it's back to the war."

I needed no encouragement. As I walked back to my tent, everyone I passed saluted me. There were smiles all around. I found Hermes already asleep, waiting in the tent door for me. I spread a cloak over him, stripped off my armor, and collapsed like a dead man.

That evening, we feasted on wild boar brought in by Gallic hunters and washed it down with excellent wine from Caesar's personal store. Smiles and backslaps and congratulations were heaped upon me. Everyone was my friend. From being the most detested man in the legion, I was now its hero. I enjoyed it enormously, all the more so because I knew that it wasn't going to last. Caesar even gave me a fine new sword to replace the one the Germans had taken from me.

Gradually the other officers wandered off to their beds or their night duties and I bade the Proconsul good night and went off in search of my own tent. Hermes, long experienced at this work, waited outside to make sure that I did not get lost. I handed him the napkin full of delicacies I had collected for him and we ambled slowly down the line of officers' tents.

"It's been a frantic few days, Hermes," I told him, "but the worst is over now. Once the war gets going it will seem easy after all this."

"If you say so."

I thought about all that had happened since young Cotta had awakened me in the middle of the night, summoning me to the praetorium. The memory was like a blow to the head and I stumbled, almost falling.

"Did you trip on a tent rope?" Hermes asked.

"No, a revelation."

He scanned the ground. "What's it look like?"

"It looks like I'm a fool," I said. "Druids, Germans! Nothing but distractions!"

"I think you'd better get to bed and sleep it off," he said with a look of concern.

"Sleep is the last thing I need. You go on back to the tent. I'll be along soon."

"Are you sure about this?" he said.

"I am sober, if only from shock. Leave me now."

He obeyed me and I was alone with my thoughts. Publius Aurelius Cotta had been the officer in charge of the Porta Praetoria the night Titus Vinius had died. What had Paterculus said? *No officer of the guard leaves his post unless properly relieved.* But Cotta had come to my tent to fetch me, and it was still dark at that hour.

He was preparing for bed when I stopped by his tent. "Decius Caecilius," he said, surprised, "my congratulations once again. What brings you to my tent?"

"Just a small question concerning the night Vin . . . that man died."

"Is it still bothering you?" He grinned. "You are the most single-minded man I ever met. What is your question?"

"You were officer in charge of the Porta Praetoria that night. You let the Provincial party through when they displayed their pass. But you came to summon me to the praetorium later that night. How did that happen?"

"A little past midnight I was relieved and told to report to the praetorium as officer on call. Some of Caesar's lictors were there and they told me he'd turned in. There's a spare cot in the lictor's tent where the duty officer can sleep when there's no excitement. He's got a runner who has to stay awake at all times. Mine was a Gaul who barely knew ten words of Latin."

"Were you told why you were relieved and your duty changed?"

"Do they need to give you a reason?" he asked.

"Usually they don't bother," I agreed. "Who took your place at the gate?"

"It was your cousin, Lucius Caecilius Metellus."

"Thank you, Publius. You've cleared something up for me."

"Happy to be of service," he said, looking utterly mystified.

I didn't bother to announce myself when I barged into Lumpy's tent. He sat up in his cot, consternation on his face, then disgust.

"Decius! Look, if it's about that hundred . . ."

"Nothing that easy, Lumpy," I said jovially. I sat on his cot and clapped a hand on his shoulder. "Dear cousin, I want to know who you passed through the Porta Praetoria and then readmitted on the night the centurion whose name must not be mentioned was murdered."

"Decius," he hissed. "Let it go! It's over. You proved your client and his friends didn't do it. Everyone is pleased with you. You're Caesar's favorite. Don't ruin it, I warn you."

I pushed him back on the cot, drew my pretty new sword, and placed its point just beneath his chin. "Who went out, Lumpy?"

"Easy, there! Put that thing away, you lunatic!"

"Talk, Lumpy."

He sighed and it was as if all the stuffing went out of him. "I was on night officer duty at the praetorium. Paterculus told me to go relieve Cotta on the gate. He said later on there'd be a party leaving and they'd have a pass from him. I was to let them out and back in and say nothing to anybody about it."

"And did he tell you why he was doing this?" I asked, knowing the futility of it.

"Why would he do that? It was some business of his own or Caesar's and I wasn't about to ask." No, Lumpy wouldn't ask. That was why they had sent him. They wanted an experienced political bootlicker on that gate, not an inexperienced boy who didn't know enough to watch out for his own future. I got up and resheathed my sword.

"Lumpy, I am ashamed to share the same name with you."

He rubbed his neck, which was bleeding from a tiny nick. "That won't be the case much longer if you keep this up." But I was already out through the tent flap.

The guards at the praetorium entrance saluted me and smiled. Everyone was smiling at me lately, except for Lumpy.

"Good evening, sir," said one of them.

"I forgot something earlier this evening," I said. "I'll just go in and fetch it."

They turned and looked at the tent. Light poured from its entrance. "Looks like the Proconsul's still up. Go on in, sir. He says all his officers are to have access during his waking hours."

Caesar was sitting at a table with a line of lamps burning behind him. Before him on the table was the silver bracelet. He looked up as I came in.

"Yes, Decius?"

"The Druids didn't kill Titus Vinius," I said. "You did."

He glared at me for a few moments, then he smiled and nodded.

"Very, *very* good, Decius. Really, you are the most amazing man! Most men, having settled a problem to their satisfaction, will never reconsider it to see if they overlooked something."

"You'd have gotten away with it if you hadn't sent Cotta to fetch me. I knew he'd been assigned to the gate that evening, not to the praetorium."

"Ah, I see. Upon such minutiae do great matters balance. By the way, I did not 'get away' with anything. I am Proconsul of this Province, with complete *imperium*. I am empowered to carry out executions without trial where I see need, and no one may hinder me in this or call me to account, even if his name is Caecilius Metellus."

"How did you do it?" I asked. "Did Paterculus throttle him while you stabbed him?" I suppose I sounded truly bitter. I never liked being someone's dupe, and I had been feeling particularly good that evening.

"Don't be impertinent! The *pontifex maximus* of Rome does not befoul his hands with the blood of traitors. The execution was carried out in accordance with my instructions by my lictors, in constitutional fashion."

"Except for the Druidic embellishments."

He looked at me sourly. "Oh, sit down, Decius. You're spoiling my digestion with your righteousness. If you ever hold high office you'll have to perform some disagreeable tasks. Be grateful if they involve nothing more unpleasant than exterminating a treacherous scoundrel like Vinius."

I sat. "But why? If you found out what he was up to, why not just denounce him, whack his head off, and confiscate his property?"

Caesar pinched the bridge of his nose, looking suddenly very tired. "Decius, I have here the largest task ever handed to a Roman proconsul. I must use every tool that comes to my hands if I am to accomplish it. Out there"—he released his nose and pointed northeast—"are the Helvetii. You've had some experience of the Germans and you know they're pouring across the Rhine. I cannot afford an alliance between them. I must fight them one at a time. I saw an opportunity to drive a wedge between the Germans and the Gauls and I acted upon it."

"You interviewed the Druid Badraig concerning their religious practices. That was how you learned of the triple slaying."

"Exactly. Since I intend to break the power of that priesthood, blaming them for the murder seemed an elegant way to accomplish several of my aims at once. I was sure that Ariovistus would revenge himself upon them and that the Gauls would never ally themselves with someone who killed Druids."

"But why not just denounce the Druids at once? Why blame the soldiers and leave me to puzzle things out while you went off to find your legions? That is labyrinthine even for you."

"It certainly made me look innocent of conspiracy, didn't it?"

"Ariovistus said there are no innocent Romans. Maybe he was right." I felt as tired as Caesar looked. "How did you learn of Vinius' treachery? Was it Molon?"

"It was. That ugly little schemer is playing more games at once than I am. He came with information for sale, told me that Vinius was storing away big bribes from somewhere. I find it is often a good idea to retain a slave to spy on his master."

"I'll remember that."

"I told him to find out when Vinius was next to meet with his paymaster. This time it was that German, Eramanzius. He went out with the Provincials, who were too lofty to notice that they had an extra slave following them. I suppose he would have returned at first light and mingled with the peasants coming in to sell their produce. It would have been easy enough. He met with the German out by the lake. Molon knew he would have to pass close by the pond and we were waiting for him there." He poked at the bracelet on the table before him. "Treasonous bastard though he was, Vinius retained a bit of his soldier's sentimentality. He would never take this bracelet off. He covered it with a bandage when he went out."

I remembered the scrap of dirty white cloth I had found at the murder site. Another little anomaly explained. "And the bracelet was Molon's pay for betraying his master?"

"Part of it. And I thought it fitting. It offended me to see a traitor wearing a Roman award for valor, even dead. Why not give it to a wretched slave? Of course, I never dreamed that he was working for Ariovistus as well."

"Do you think he'll tell Ariovistus?"

"He cost Ariovistus his spy in my camp. It would be death for him to speak of it now. I think he will want to stay in my good graces. He did what he could for you while you were captive."

Most matters were answered now. "How could you condemn eight innocent men?"

He looked almost ashamed, if that were possible. "I was sure you'd have it pinned on the Druids before I got back. I never dreamed that you would do something as insane as go beyond the rampart on your own and get captured by the Germans."

"But when I ran in this morning, you were about to have their friends flog them to death."

"Decius, here in Gaul we are playing the highest-stakes game in the world. When you set a game in motion, you must see it through, however the dice fall."

I rose. "I will take my leave now, Proconsul. Thank you for answering my questions. I realize that, with your *imperium*, you owe no answers to anybody."

He stood and put a hand on my shoulder. "I respect your

scruples, Decius. Such are rare in Rome these days. I owe you no less. And, Decius?"

"Yes?"

"I am very pleased that you did not touch the contents of that chest. I inventoried it myself before I had that boy summon you. I would have been most upset if any of it had been missing. Go on and get some sleep."

So I walked out of the praetorium, satisfied if not happy. I had rather liked Badraig, but a lot of Gauls were going to die soon, and a lot of Romans as well. Oddly enough, I was going to miss Freda. I would even miss Molon, but I suspected I hadn't seen the last of him.

I went through the darkened camp, asleep now except for the doubled guard. It was a legion fully ready for war. I was determined to get a full night's sleep at last. A soldier needs his sleep when there's a war on. The Gauls might arrive to-morrow, and then I might not get a decent night's sleep for ages.

These things happened in Gaul, in the year 696 of the City of Rome, the consulship of Lucius Calpurnius Piso Caesoninus and Aulus Gabinius.

GLOSSARY

(Definitions apply to the last century of the Republic.)

Acta Streets wide enough for one-way wheeled traffic.

Aedile Elected officials in charge of upkeep of the city and the grain dole, regulation of public morals, management of the markets, and the public Games. There were two types: the plebeian aediles, who had no insignia of office, and the curule aediles, who wore the toga praetexta and sat in the sella curulis. The curule aediles could sit in judgment on civil cases involving markets and currency, while the plebeian aediles could only levy fines. Otherwise, their duties were the same. Since the magnificence of the Games one exhibited as aedile often determined election to higher office, it was an important stepping stone in a political career. The office of aedile did not carry the *imperium.*

Ala Literally, "wing." A squadron of cavalry.

Ancile (pl. ancilia) A small, oval sacred shield which fell from heaven in the reign of King Numa. Since there was a prophecy that it was tied to the stability of Rome, Numa had eleven exact copies made so nobody would know which one to steal. Their care was entrusted to a college of priests, the *Salii* (q.v.), and figured in a number of ceremonies each year.

Aquilifer The chief standard-bearer of a legion, the "eagle-bearer" The eagle was semidivine, the embodiment of the legion's *genius*.

Atrium Once a word for house, in Republican times it was the entry hall of a house, opening off the street and used as a general reception area.

Atrium Vestae The Palace of the Vestals and one of the most splendid buildings in Rome.

Augur An official who observed omens for state purposes. He could forbid business and assemblies if he saw unfavorable omens.

Auxilia Non-citizen units supporting the legions. A full term of service, usually twenty years, conferred citizenship upon the soldier at discharge. Citizenship was permanent and would be inherited by his descendants.

Basilica A building where courts met in inclement weather.

Caestus The classical boxing glove, made of leather straps and reinforced by bands, plates, or spikes of bronze.

Caliga The Roman military boot. Actually, a heavy sandal with hobnailed sole.

Campus Martius A field outside the old city wall, formerly the assembly area and drill field for the army. It was where the popular assemblies met. By late Republican times, buildings were encroaching on the field.

Censor Magistrates elected usually every fifth year to oversee the census of the citizens and purge the roll of Senators of unworthy members. They could forbid certain religious practices or luxuries deemed bad for public morals or generally "un-Roman." There were two Censors, and each could overrule the other. They wore the toga praetexta and sat in the sella curulis, but since they had no executive powers they were not accompanied by lictors. The office did not carry the *imperium*. Censors were usually elected from among the ex-Consuls, and the censorship was regarded as the capstone of a political career.

Centuriate Assembly (comitia centuriata): Originally, the annual military assembly of the citizens where they joined their army units ("centuries"). There were 193 centuries divided into five classes by property qualification. They elected the highest magistrates: Censors, Consuls, and Praetors. By the middle Republic, the centuriate assembly was strictly a voting body, having lost all military character.

Centurion "Commander of 100" (i.e., a century) which, in practice, numbered around sixty men. Centurions were promoted from the ranks and were the backbone of the professional army.

Circus The Roman racecourse and the stadium which enclosed it. The original, and always the largest, was the Circus Maximus, which lay between the Palatine and Aventine hills. A later, smaller circus, the Circus Flaminius, lay outside the walls on the Campus Martius.

Client One attached in a subordinate relationship to a patron, whom he was bound to support in war and in the courts. Freedmen became clients of their former masters. The relationship was hereditary.

Coemptio Marriage by symbolic sale. Before five witnesses and a *libripens* who held a balance, the bridegroom struck the balance with a bronze coin and handed it to the father or guardian of the bride. Unlike *conferreatio* (q.v.), coemptic was easily dissolved by divorce.

Cognomen The family name, denoting any of the stirpes of a *gens*; i.e., Caius Julius *Caesar*. Caius of the stirps Caesar of *gens* Julia. Some plebeian families never adopted a cognomen, notably the Marii and the Antonii.

Coitio A political alliance between two men, uniting their voting blocs. Usually it was an agreement between politicians who were otherwise antagonists, in order to edge out mutual rivals.

Colonia Towns which had been conquered by Rome, where Roman citizens were settled. Later, settlements founded by discharged veterans of the legions. After 89 B.C. all Italian coloniae had full rights of citizenship. Those in the provinces had limited citizenship.

Compluvium An opening in a roof to admit light.

Conferreatio The most sacred and binding of Roman forms of marriage. The bride and groom offered a cake of spelt to Jupiter in the presence of a *pontifex* and the Flamen Dialis. It was the ancient patrician form of marriage. By the late Republic it was obsolete except for some priesthoods in which the priest was required to be married by conferreatio.

Consul Supreme magistrate of the Republic. Two were elected each year. Insignia were the toga praetexta and the sella curulis. Each Consul was attended by twelve lictors. The office carried full *imperium*. On the expiration of his year in office, the ex-Consul was usually assigned a district outside Rome to rule as proconsul. As proconsul, he had the same insignia and the same number of lictors. His power was absolute within his province.

Contubernium An eight-man section or squad. There were usually eight *contubernia* (pl.) to each century, although the number varied. Each *contubernium* shared a tent made of cowhide, and rations were usually broken down and distributed by *contubernia*, making them "messmates" in the army sense.

Cornicen A large, circular trumpet with a crossbar that rested on the trumpeter's shoulder. Unlike the *tuba*, the *cornicen* remained with the standards and was used primarily to summon the soldiers to their eagles.

Curia The meetinghouse of the Senate, located in the Forum.

Cursus Honorum The chain of offices held by men in public life: Quaestor, Praetor, and Consul. The aedileship was not required by constitution for higher office but was a necessity by the first century B.C. The office of Tribune of the People or Plebs could not be held by patricians and Censor was a special office. Therefore these three offices, although prestigious, were not a part of the *cursus honorum*.

Dictator An absolute ruler chosen by the Senate and the Consuls to deal with a specific emergency. For a limited period, never more than six months, he was given unlimited *imperium*, which he was to lay down upon resolution of the emergency. Unlike the Consuls, he had no colleague to overrule him and he was not accountable for his actions performed during office when he stepped down. His insignia were the toga praetexta and the sella curulis and he was accompanied by twenty-four lictors, the number of both Consuls. Dictatorships were extremely rare and the last was held in 202 B.C. The dictatorships of Sulla and Caesar were unconstitutional.

Dioscuri Castor and Pollux, the twin sons of Zeus and Leda. The Romans revered them as protectors of the city.

Eques (pl. equites) Formerly, citizens wealthy enough to supply their own horses and fight in the cavalry, they came to hold their status by meeting a property qualification. They formed the moneyed upper-middle class. In the centuriate assembly they formed eighteen centuries and once had the right of voting first, but they lost this as their military function disappeared. The publicans, financiers, bankers, moneylenders, and tax-farmers came from the equestrian class.

Faction In the Circus, the supporters of the four racing companies: Red, White, Blue, and Green. Most Romans were fanatically loyal to one of these.

Fasces A bundle of rods bound around an ax with a red strap, symbolizing a Roman magistrate's power of corporal and capital punishment. They were carried by the lictors who accompanied the curule magistrates, the Flamen Dialis, and the proconsuls and propraetors who governed provinces. When a lower magistrate met a higher, his lictors lowered their *fasces* in salute.

Flamen A high priest of a specific god of the state. The college of flamines had fifteen members: three patrician and twelve plebeian. The three highest were the Flamen Dialis, the Flamen Martialis, and the Flamen Quirinalis. They had charge of the daily sacrifices, wore distinctive headgear, and were surrounded by many ritual taboos. The Flamen Dialis, high priest of Jupiter, was entitled to the toga praetexta, which had to be woven by his wife, the sella curulis, and a single lictor, and he could sit in the Senate. It became difficult to fill the college of flamines because they had to be prominent men, the appointment was for life, and they could take no part in politics.

Forum An open meeting and market area. The premier forum was the Forum Romanum, located on the low ground surrounded by the Capitoline, Palatine, and Caelian hills. It was surrounded by the most important temples and public buildings. Roman citizens spent much of their day there. The courts met outdoors in the Forum when the weather was good. When it was paved and devoted solely to public business, the Forum Romanum's market functions were transferred to the Forum Boarium, the cattle market, near the Circus Maximus. Small shops and stalls remained along the northern and southern peripheries, however.

Freedman A manumitted slave. Formal emancipation conferred full rights of citizenship except for the right to hold office. Informal emancipation conferred freedom without voting rights. In the second or at latest third generation, a freedman's descendants became full citizens.

Gaul Roughly, modern France, Alsace-Lorraine, Belgium, and the Netherlands; the land between the Rhine and the Pyrenees. Most of the inhabitants were of Celtic descent and spoke Celtic dialects, although there were Germanics and others. The Romans tended to call them all Gauls, whatever their ethnic and linguistic origins.

Genius The guiding and guardian spirit of a person or place. The *genius* of a place was called *genius loci*.

Gens A clan, all of whose members were descended from a single ancestor. The nomen of a patrician *gens* always ended with -ius. Thus, Caius *Julius* Caesar was Caius, of the Caesarian stirps of *gens* Julia.

Gladiator Literally, "swordsman." A slave, prisoner of war, condemned criminal, or free volunteer who fought, often to the death, in the munera. All were called swordsmen, even if they fought with other weapons.

Gladius The short, broad, double-edged sword borne by Roman soldiers. It was designed primarily for stabbing. A smaller, more antiquated design was used by gladiators.

Gravitas The quality of seriousness.

Haruspex A member of a college of Etruscan professionals who examined the entrails of sacrificial animals for omens.

Hospitium An arrangement of reciprocal hospitality. When visiting the other's city, each hospes (pl. hospites) was entitled to food and shelter, protection in court, care when ill or injured, and honorable burial should he die during the visit. The obligation was binding on both families and was passed on to descendants.

Ides The 15th of March, May, July, and October. The 13th of other months.

Imperium The ancient power of kings to summon and lead armies, to order and forbid, and to inflict corporal and capital punishment. Under the Republic, the *imperium* was divided among the Consuls and Praetors, but they were subject to appeal and intervention by the tribunes in their civil decisions and were answerable for their acts after leaving office. Only a dictator had unlimited *imperium*.

Insula Literally, "island." A large, multistory tenement block.

Itinera Streets wide enough for only foot traffic. The majority of Roman streets were itinera.

Janitor A slave doorkeeper, so called for Janus, god of gateways.

Kalends The 1st of any month.

Latifundium A large landed estate or plantation worked by slaves. During the late Republic these expanded tremendously, all but destroying the Italian peasant class.

Legates Subordinate commanders chosen by the Senate to accompany generals and governors. Also, ambassadors appointed by the Senate.

Legion Basic unit of the Roman army. Paper strength was six thousand, but usually closer to four thousand. All were armed as heavy infantry with a large shield, cuirass, helmet, gladius, and light and heavy javelins. Each legion had attached to it an equal number of non-citizen auxiliaries consisting of light and heavy infantry, cavalry, archers, slingers, and others. Auxilia were never organized as legions, only as cohorts.

Lictor Attendants, usually freedmen, who accompanied magistrates and the Flamen Dialis, bearing the *fasces*. They summoned assemblies, attended public sacrifices, and carried out sentences of punishment. Twenty-four lictors accompanied a dictator, twelve for a Consul, six for a propraetor, two for a Praetor, and one for the Flamen Dialis.

Liquamen Also called *garum*, it was the ubiquitous fermented fish sauce used in Roman cooking.

Lituus The crook-topped staff carried by an augur. Also, a cavalry trumpet of similar shape.

Ludus (pl. ludi) The official public Games, races, theatricals, and so on. Also, a training school for gladiators, although the gladiatorial exhibitions were not *ludi*.

Munera Special Games, not part of the official calendar, at which gladiators were exhibited. They were originally Funeral Games and were always dedicated to the dead. In *munera sine missione*, all the defeated were killed and sometimes were made to fight sequentially or all at once until only one was left standing. *Munera sine missione* were periodically forbidden by law.

Municipia Towns originally with varying degrees of Roman citizenship, but by the late Republic with full citizenship. A citizen from a municipium was qualified to hold any public office. An example is Cicero, who was not from Rome but from the municipium of Arpinum.

Nobiles Those families, both patrician and plebeian, in which members had held the Consulate.

Nomen The name of the clan or *gens* (e.g., Caius *Julius* Caesar).

Nones The 7th of March, May, July, and October. The 5th of other months.

Novus Homo Literally, "new man." A man who is the first of his family to hold the Consulate, giving his family the status of nobiles.

Optimates The party of the "best men" (i.e., aristocrats and their supporters).

Optio A centurion's assistant, second in command of the century.

Patria Potestas The absolute authority of the paterfamilias over the children of his household, who could neither legally own property while their father was alive nor marry without his permission. Technically, he had the right to sell or put to death any of his children, but by Republican times this was a legal fiction.

Patrician A descendant of one of the founding fathers of Rome. Once, only patricians could hold offices and priesthoods and sit in the Senate, but these privileges were gradually eroded until only certain priesthoods were strictly patrician. By the late Republic, only about fourteen *gens* remained.

Patron A man with one or more clients whom he was bound to protect, advise, and otherwise aid. The relationship was hereditary.

Peculium Roman slaves could not own property, but they could earn money outside the household, which was held for them by their masters. This fund was called a *peculium*, and could be used, eventually, to purchase the slave's freedom.

Peristylium An open courtyard surrounded by a colonnade.

Pietas The quality of dutifulness toward the gods and, especially, toward one's parents.

Pilum An extremely heavy javelin peculiar to the Roman legions. It was employed primarily to deprive the enemy of his shield and was designed in various ways to be disabled upon impact so that it could not be thrown back.

Plebeian All citizens not of patrician status.

Pomerium The line of the ancient city wall, attributed to Romulus. Actually, the space of vacant ground just within and without the wall, regarded as holy. Within the *pomerium* it was forbidden to bear arms or bury the dead.

Pontifex A member of the highest priestly college of Rome. They had superintendence over all sacred observances, state and private, and over the calendar. There were fifteen in the late Republic: seven patrician and eight plebeian. Their chief was the *pontifex maximus*, a title now held by the pope.

Popular Assemblies There were three: the centuriate assembly (comitia centuriata) and the two tribal assemblies: comitia tributa and consilium plebis, q.v.

Populares The party of the common people.

Posca A mixture of sour wine vinegar and water, often heated, drunk by Roman soldiers and the poor.

Praenomen The given name of a freeman, as Marcus, Sextus. Caius, etc. (e.g., *Caius* Julius Caesar); Caius of the stirps Caesar of *gens* Julia. Women used a feminine form of their father's nomen (e.g., the daughter of Caius Julius Caesar would be named Julia).

Praetor Judge and magistrate elected yearly along with the Consuls. In the late Republic there were eight Praetors. Senior was the Praetor Urbanus, who heard civil cases between citizens. The Praetor Peregrinus heard cases involving foreigners. The others presided over criminal courts. Insignia were the toga praetexta and the sella curulis, and Praetors were accompanied by two lictors. The office carried the *imperium*. After leaving office, the ex-Praetors became propraetors and went to govern propraetorian provinces with full *imperium*.

Praetorian Guard Prior to the reign of Tiberius Caesar (A.D. 14–37), a guard or reserve force of varying size and makeup organized at the pleasure of a general. During the Republican and Augustan periods, it was not the permanent, "kingmaking" unit it became under the Principate.

Praetorium A general's headquarters, usually a tent in camp. In the provinces, the official residence of the governor.

Princeps "First Citizen." An especially distinguished Senator chosen by the Censors. His name was the first called on the roll of the Senate and he was first to speak on any issue. Later the title was usurped by Augustus and is the origin of the word "prince."

Proscription List of names of public enemies published by Sulla. Anyone could kill a proscribed person and claim a reward, usually a part of the dead man's estate.

Publicans Those who bid on public contracts, most notably builders and tax-farmers. The contracts were usually let by the Censors and therefore had a period of five years.

Pugio The straight, double-edged dagger of the Roman soldiers.

Quaestor Lowest of the elected officials, they had charge of the treasury and financial matters such as payments for public works. They also acted as assistants and paymasters to higher magistrates, generals, and provincial governors. They were elected yearly by the *comitia tributa*.

Quirinus The deified Romulus, patron deity of the city.

Rostra A monument in the Forum commemorating the sea battle of Antium in 338 B.C., decorated with the rams, "rostra" of enemy ships (sing. rostrum). Its base was used as an orator's platform.

Sagum The Roman military cloak, made of wool and always dyed red. To put on the *sagum* signified the changeover to wartime status, as the toga was the garment of peace. When the citizens met in the *comitia centuriata*, they wore the *sagum* in token of its ancient function as the military muster.

Salii "Dancers." Two colleges of priests dedicated to Mars and Quirinus, who held their rites in March and October, respectively. Each college consisted of twelve young patricians whose parents were still living. On their festivals, they dressed in embroidered tunics, a crested bronze helmet, and breastplate, and each bore one of the twelve sacred shields ("ancilia") and a staff. They processed to the most important altars of Rome and before each performed a war dance. The ritual was so ancient that, by the first century B.C., their songs and prayers were unintelligible.

Saturnalia Feast of Saturn, December 17–23, a raucous and jubilant occasion when gifts were exchanged, debts were settled, and masters waited on their slaves.

Sella Curulis A folding camp chair. It was part of the insignia of the curule magistrates and the Flamen Dialis.

Senate Rome's chief deliberative body. It consisted of three hundred to six hundred men, all of whom had won elective office at least once. Once the supreme ruling body, by the late Republic the Senate's former legislative and judicial functions had devolved upon the courts and the Popular Assemblies and its chief authority lay in foreign policy and the nomination of generals. Senators were privileged to wear the tunica laticlava.

Servile War The slave rebellion led by the Thracian gladiator Spartacus in 73–71 B.C. The rebellion was crushed by Crassus and Pompey.

Sica A single-edged dagger or short sword of varying size. It was favored by thugs and used by the Thracian gladiators in the arena. Classified as an infamous rather than an honorable weapon.

Signifer A legionary standard-bearer.

Solarium A rooftop garden and patio.

Spatha The Roman cavalry sword, longer and narrower than the gladius.

SPQR "Senatus populusque Romanus." The Senate and People of Rome. The formula embodying the sovereignty of Rome, used on official correspondence, documents, and public works.

Stirps A subfamily of a *gens*. The cognomen gave the name of the stirps (e.g., Caius Julius *Caesar*). Caius of the stirps Caesar of *gens* Julia.

Strigil A bronze implement, roughly S-curved, used to scrape sand and oil from the body after bathing. Soap was unknown to the Roman Republic.

Strophium A cloth band worn by women beneath or over the clothing to support the breasts.

Subligaculum A loincloth, worn by men and women.

Subura A neighborhood on the lower slopes of the Viminal and Esquiline, famed for its slums, noisy shops, and raucous inhabitants.

Tarpeian Rock A cliff beneath the Capitol from which traitors were hurled. It was named for the Roman maiden Tarpeia who, according to legend, betrayed the Capitol to the Sabines.

Temple of Jupiter Capitolinus The most important temple of the state religion. Triumphal processions ended with a sacrifice at this temple.

Temple of Saturn The state treasury was located in a crypt beneath this temple. It was also the repository for military standards.

Temple of Vesta Site of the sacred fire tended by the vestal virgins and dedicated to the goddess of the hearth. Documents, especially wills, were deposited there for safekeeping.

Toga The outer robe of the Roman citizen. It was white for the upper class, darker for the poor and for people in mourning. The *toga praetexta*, bordered with a purple stripe, was worn by curule magistrates, by state priests when performing their functions, and by boys prior to manhood. The *toga picta*, purple and embroidered with golden stars, was worn by a general when celebrating a triumph, also by a magistrate when giving public Games.

Tonsores A slave trained as a barber and hairdresser.

Trans-Tiber A newer district on the right or western bank of the Tiber. It lay beyond the old city walls.

Tribal Assemblies There were two: the *comitia tributa*, an assembly of all citizens by tribes, elected the lower magistrates—*curule aediles*, and *quaestors*, also the military tribunes; and the *concilium plebis*, consisting only of plebeians, elected the tribunes of the plebs and the plebeian aediles.

Tribe Originally, the three classes of patricians. Under the Republic, all citizens belonged to tribes of which there were four city tribes and thirty-one country tribes. New citizens were enrolled in an existing tribe.

Tribune Representative of the plebeians with power to introduce laws and to veto actions of the Senate. Only plebeians could hold the office, which carried no *imperium*. Military tribunes were elected from among the young men of senatorial or equestrian rank to be assistants to generals. Usually it was the first step of a man's political career.

Triumph A magnificent ceremony celebrating military victory. The honor could be granted only by the Senate, and until he received permission, the victorious general had to remain outside the city walls, as his command ceased the instant he crossed the *pomerium*. The general, called the triumphator, received royal, near-divine honors and became a virtual god for a day. A slave was appointed to stand behind him and remind him periodically of his mortality lest the gods become jealous.

Triumvir A member of a triumvirate—a board or college of three men. Most famously, the three-man rule of Caesar, Pompey, and Crassus. Later, the triumvirate of Antonius, Octavian, and Lepidus.

Tuba A straight trumpet used for most signaling.

Tunica A long, loose shirt, sleeveless or short-sleeved, worn by citizens beneath the toga when outdoors and by itself indoors. The tunica laticlava had a broad purple stripe from neck to hem and was worn by Senators and patricians. The tunica angusticlava had a narrow stripe and was worn by the equities. The tunica picta, purple and embroidered with golden palm branches, was worn by a general when he celebrated a triumph.

Usus The most common form of marriage, in which a man and woman lived together for a year without being separated for three consecutive nights.

Via A highway. Within the city, viae were streets wide enough for two wagons to pass one another. There were only two viae during the Republic: the Via Sacra, which ran through the Forum and was used for religious processions and triumphs; and the Via Nova, which ran along one side of the Forum.

Vigile A night watchman. The vigiles had the duty of apprehending felons caught committing crimes, but their main duty was as a fire watch. They were unarmed except for staves and carried fire buckets.